RAGE AND RUIN

THE AZAR TRILOGY BOOK THREE

GRACE MCGINTY

For my Alpha and Beta Readers. For my spit ballers and i dotters. Thank you for your hard work. I appreciate it more than I can express.

G x

RAGE AND RUIN

*S*trangers surrounded her. Some were her kin, half-siblings she'd only just met, and some were just nameless faces that blurred together. Every person in attendance was an Ifrit; a malevolent form of Djinn with the ability to transform into a beast of fire, able to bend the flames to their will. But instead of flaming, cloven-hooved devils, today everyone was in their human forms. The crowd circled around a single point. An urn that contained the ashes of her father, Saraf.

Her eyes began to sting as tears pushed against the lids. Azar stood at the back of the crowd by herself. She'd given her condolences to the family, and his numerous ex-wives that seemed to have reappeared for the event. They had all known and loved her father for hundreds of years. She'd known the man less than six months and met him only a handful of times. But for reasons she couldn't comprehend, her heart was still breaking for the parent she'd barely known.

An official looking man strode in and stood over the urn. Without further ado, he started shouting something in the ancient tongue. No matter what the language, funeral rites sounded the same; mournful. He pinched some dust, sand maybe, and threw it to the four corners of the urn, wishing Saraf safe passage to the afterlife. Or maybe he was wishing upon a star that her father didn't come back as a fire ant. Azar didn't understand the old language. She shifted her focus to the people around the holy man.

The inner ring around the urn were all members of Saraf's family. Her family. Three of her brothers, Casper, Cy and Darius were protectively buffeting their mother, a small Ifrit woman who looked a hundred years older than she had less than three weeks ago. Her half-sister, Malee was huddled next to Casper's wife, sobbing gently into the other woman's shoulder.

There were the siblings she'd never met; Ashtoreth, who'd come to return her father's ashes to his seat of power in the Middle East. Yasmin and Roxx, who Azar had met in passing right before the funeral, who were pressed so tightly together it was hard to see where one ended and the other began. If meeting your long-lost siblings wasn't awkward enough, doing it at a funeral increased the bizarreness seven-fold.

Talia stood beside them, another sibling she had only met in passing. Even in the close confines of the circle, she managed to seem apart from the rest. Talia was the headmistress of a boarding school in Turkey. She'd flown in for the funeral, and was flying out again as soon as possible, unwilling to leave her vulnerable charges under the care of anyone else for an extended period of time. She was stern, her features sharper and more pinched than the others, but there was a sadness that dragged down her face and her eyes were red-rimmed with shed tears.

Finally, the twins, Keely and Killian stood side by side, stiff and regal. They both contained the aura of power, even though Killian was still recovering from the attack that killed hundreds of her kind, including her father. Guilt was etched all over Killian's face, and she felt his pain. She liked and respected Killian, even though she hadn't known him long. He had taken her into his life, and under his wing, without resentment or prejudice. To see him brought low with such heavy emotions hurt her heart. He was wracked with survivor's guilt, you could see it in the tenseness in his shoulders, the dullness of his eyes. So many had died, including every member of the Djinn Council, and Killian had laid the blame for their deaths at his own feet.

"Would the blood of Saraf come forward and pay their respects to the Leader of their House?" Her siblings took a step forward and held hands.

Cy looked from side to side, and then around at the crowd. Catching her eye, he leant over and whispered something to Darius, and then stepped out of the circle. She shrank back to the edges of the crowd, but it parted for him. Cy was the sibling she was closest with. A week of forced cohabitation in the Amazon would do that.

He looked at Azar sternly and put out his hand. Sighing, she took it and followed him back through the crowd. There was a general muttering in the room, and her face flushed hotly. It wasn't that she didn't want to pay her respects to her father. She was here, wasn't she? But she didn't belong up there, with people who had known and loved the man.

Cy placed her between himself and Darius. She

had only met Darius the once, and was surprised when his calloused hand curled around hers.

"He loved you. You deserve to be here," Darius whispered in her ear and just like that, the sadness she'd been trying to trap deep in her chest, poured out over her cheeks in waves of hot tears. The holy man started to speak in the old language again, and everyone began to chant along with him.

Cy leaned in to whisper in her other ear. "Just mime along. That's what I do." He gave her a reassuring smile. Pressed between the solid warmth of her kin, she could almost believe everything would be okay.

LATER, after the formalities were done and people stood around reminiscing about the greatness of her father, Azar realized that she'd had enough. Enough of the forced smiles, and politely ignoring the pointed conversations of people who were sharing every detail of her life as if she weren't in the room.

Feigning a headache, Azar left the wake early and ensconced herself in one of the guest bedrooms in Saraf's Central Park mansion. Or was it Killian's now?

The room was lavish, decorated like the interior

of *Aladdin's* lamp. Two walls were painted an emerald green, and the furniture was antique polished wood with heavy brass fixtures. Even the four-poster bed sported green curtains, shot through with gold thread.

She lay back on the large bed, wrapping herself in a goose down comforter, desperately tired but unable to sleep. She just kept going over and over the events of the past week, a chorus of what-ifs and endless questions that hurt her brain.

It all started with the goddamn Fae. The Djinn had always been a self-sufficient race, barely operating in the supernatural community. They paid no mind to the Fae, who they thought were safely tethered to the soil of the old country.

But revolution had been brewing within the Courts of the Fae. Two Fae heralds had popped into the Adel headquarters without an invitation, proclaiming that the Fae intended to subjugate the Djinn, peacefully if they could or by force if necessary. Then the Djinn had gotten upset. They'd been given a seven-day deadline to reconcile themselves with the inevitability before they were brought to heel by force.

The lying bastards had given them five days, thirteen hours and six minutes before they had attacked the New York headquarters. They'd razed the building to the ground, killing nearly everyone. Only Killian and Mira, who were both in the vaults at the lowest subterranean level of the building, survived. Mira, who was also rescued, was still in a coma that had to be magically induced. It seemed to be blocking her supernatural healing abilities.

The story of what happened exactly hadn't come out until Killian had recovered enough to speak.

Mira had called Killian from the vaults, with vague ill feelings. This had been the first sign that something was wrong. Mira was a senior member of the Adel, the Djinn equivalent to the army's Special Forces, and she wasn't prone to hysteria. Killian had left a strategy meeting with the Councilors to head to the vaults. 'The Vaults', which was a misnomer for the state-of-the-art floor with extremely high-tech biometric security, held the greatest treasures of the Djinn of this region. Centuries old texts and manuscripts, relics of a time long gone, artifacts so priceless that they made the Vatican look like a junk store. But the most important thing that was held within those magically fortified walls was the recently recovered Great Weapons. The Great Weapons were magically imbued weapons. A single cut from one of these weapons, even if it was no bigger than a papercut, could cause a painful and irreversible death.

Azar shook her head. She'd soon see about the irreversible part. When Killian had arrived at the seventh subterranean level, he'd found Mira in a puddle of blood and a Fae standing above her, a sword ready to swoop down on her head like a guillotine.

Then, from what Azar could piece together from the destruction that was left behind, everything happened at once.

A group of Fae soldiers flashed into the Council boardroom, killing most of the members before they could even rise from their chairs. Azar had seen the carnage; the Sila and Marid Councilors slumped forward on the desk, their heads lopped from their bodies. The Jann Councilor had swung around towards his attackers and his head had been cleaved through the middle. The Ghul Councilor had been sliced through the torso as he ran for the door, and then been executed as he lie dying on the floor.

Christos, the Councilor for the Shaitan, had also been run through from behind but he was next to a dead Fae soldier, who was haloed in a small pool of goop that had leaked from his ears. Christos wasn't the type to go down without a fight.

Her father Saraf, Councilor for the Ifrit, had done the most damage. Azar felt bile rise in her throat as she remembered the scene. She'd swept through the room looking for survivors with the rest of the Adel. There were three incinerated Fae scattered around, their mouths open in screams of anguish. Saraf's body had been shredded by a sword. A dozen or so large stab wounds ribboned his body, and his head hung from his shoulders at an unnatural angle. The memory of that room would never fade, locked away in her mind's eye like a photograph. In a building of horrifying scenes, that was the one that would haunt her forever.

She shook her head, trying to clear the image from her mind so she could sleep. She tried to close her eyes and count sheep, and then puppies, and then kittens. She hadn't slept in a week. She could feel the exhaustion right down to her toes. She wanted to go home, but she didn't really have one anymore. She'd given up her apartment when she'd joined the Adel, and her tiny dorm room had exploded during the Fae raids.

She was staying at Bast's apartment in Coney Island, but that settled a whole other set of worries onto her shoulders. What to do about Bast? She slapped her forehead to chase away the bad thoughts.

She needed to get out of here, preferably without meeting any well-meaning mourners who wanted to poke at her wounds for their own curiosity.

She straightened the bed, and then snuck out into the hallway. Poking her head around the doorjamb, she let out a relieved sigh to see it was empty. She crept toward the old cage elevator and cringed when the door screeched open, but no one came to investigate.

As it moved down slowly, she had a brief glimpse of the formal dining room, packed with mourners. People were dotted around like islands of grief, but there was a general tone of fear that made the knot in her stomach clench tighter.

Their fear was justified. They were a race with no leaders, and no plan. Killian had declared it a state of war, and he was currently in charge until a new Council could be elected, but he was still convalescing and the hysteria over the Fae attack was incendiary.

The cage shuddered to a stop in the entry foyer and she looked between the diamond shaped grate at the stern face of Cy. So much for sneaking out.

"I'll walk you to your car."

Azar shrugged but walked alongside him. He'd warned her earlier about going places alone, out of fear for her safety. Needless to say, she wasn't the Djinn's favorite person right now. Mainly because she'd adopted herself a Fae child in the Amazon Jungle. It was a long story.

"Where's the kid?" Cy asked. She trusted Cy with her life on more than one occasion, but she was wary about revealing Nevyn's whereabouts to anyone.

"He's with Oliver." She left it at that. While Oliver didn't initially understand how she'd ended up as Nevyn's guardian, he'd had her back from the very first moment. Now he liked the small Fae boy as much as she did, and willingly undertook his protection when Azar couldn't be there to do it herself.

Oliver was her best friend, a Werejaguar who was sexy, and sweet and as devoted to Azar, as Azar was to him. Her feelings about Oliver were all muddled up, but she knew without a doubt she loved him. Sometimes her feelings were the platonic kind that Oliver inspired by his loyalty. And sometimes that love wasn't platonic at all, it was burning hot and threatened to consume her. She pushed the thought away. She didn't have time to have feelings for anyone. She loved Bast, and look what happened. She doomed him to an eternity of incor-poreality.

"Azar…" Cy stopped her by placing a hand on her arm. "I just want you to know that if there is anything you need, I'm here for you." He sighed and toed at the ground. "Your life is difficult right now with Bast and the kid. And Father." He cleared his throat, but continued, "And I just wanted you to know that if you need anything, whatever it is, all you have to do is ask."

Her eyes began to water again at his kindness and she blinked rapidly, staring down at her boots. But it was futile to fight it, as emotion swelled in her gut and she couldn't hold them back. Big, fat tears dripped onto the marble tiles of the foyer and before she knew it, she was wrapped in Cy's arms. She felt like she was playing a game, where everyone was out to get her and she didn't understand the rules. She let herself be weak for a moment, sheltered in the strength of her brother's arms.

Embarrassed, she pulled away. Stepping through the ornate wood and brass door, she hurried to the curb and hailed down the cab that was turning onto the street. Cy was silent, giving her time to get herself under control and retain even a modicum of dignity. She gave him a thankful, tearstained smile.

"Thank you. You better go back up, they'll be missing you."

Cy opened the cab door for her, searching her face. "Take care, okay?"

Azar nodded, and he closed the door with a solid thump.

"Coney Island, please. The Boardwalk."

She let her head lean back on the leather seat. Then she closed her eyes and drifted off to sleep for the first time in days.

CHAPTER 2

The sound of children laughing halted Azar when she stepped through the door of Bast's warehouse in Coney Island. Not that the sound of laughing children on the boardwalk was an unusual thing, but to hear it from within the warehouse was strange.

Walking double-time towards the office, she recognized one of the childish voices as Nevyn.

As she got closer, she finally recognized the other voice too, and frowned. Opening the door to the office, she wasn't surprised to see Donovan standing there, Oliver close by. The whisper of Bast's presence wrapped around her like a soothing warmth.

She strode across the floor to join them. The sign of the Djinn was still burned into the polished concrete, a permanent reminder of how she'd ended up in this position. Azar veered around it. It was pure superstition, but she refused to set foot on that mark. "What's happened? Why isn't Freya with the pack?"

Freya, a sweet little girl who had the misfortune of being one quarter Shaitan, had been banished by the Council from Djinn society. Azar had arranged for the girl to live with the local Werewolf pack in Sterling Forest.

Djinn society had existed on the principle that one hundred years of servitude provided prosperity and security for the whole race; they basically auctioned off every Djinn on their twenty-fifth birthday for exorbitant amounts of money. It was enforced by the use of slave cuffs, which were activated from a brand that appeared at birth and disappeared once the servitude was completed. The problem with Freya, and others like her, was that they were so weak in Djinn blood that they were born without the slave mark, and thus were unable to be coerced into a hundred years of slavery.

Freya had the doubly bad luck of being born a Shaitan, possibly the most disagreeable of the six races of Djinn. Their powers were insidious; they could raise negative emotions in their victims, and those stronger in their powers could physically turn their opponent's brain to mush. Not the kind of people you'd want to invite to parties. Freya was nowhere near that strong, but there was a natural prejudice against the Shaitan, earned over years of violence and generally speaking, evilness.

Donovan, Freya's father, had changed Azar's views on the inherent evilness of the Shaitan. Donovan was still scary as crap, and if he focused his onyx eyes on her in anger, she had to resist the urge to wet her pants. And he was only a half blood. But they'd bonded awhile back chasing down a bad guy, and now she hesitantly called the man a friend. But still, sometimes she'd catch him looking at her with those intense black eyes, the look in them something completely inscrutable, like he was working out if he wanted to kiss her or tie her up and torture her in all the best ways. Another thing she was going to ignore. If she buried her head in the sand any further, she was going to pop out in Australia.

"The Weres have gone," Donovan said, his black eyes shining ominously under the fluorescent lights of Bast's office.

"Gone where?"

"Into hiding," Oliver finished. "They've taken the attack on the Djinn, and your warnings, very seriously. They've closed ranks and that means no outsiders allowed, including Freya. Including me."

They'd kicked Oliver out?

That shocked Azar more than anything. The Wolves loved Oliver like he was one of their own. For him to be asked to leave, they would really have to be in panic mode.

She could see the hurt of betrayal in her friend's eyes, and she went to him, wrapping him in a hug. Oliver was an affectionate man, and craved contact like he needed oxygen.

"I'm sorry," Azar whispered, and she was. The Sterling Forest Pack had been family to Oliver. He buried his face in her hair, breathing her scent in deeply. His arms tightened and then he pulled back and gave her a shadow of his normally bright smile.

"It's no big deal. I would have stayed with you anyway. You need me. But it sucks that they threw me out like yesterday's trash."

Donovan muttered obscenities under his breath. "They dropped Freya off at a roadside diner, like she was an unwanted pet."

"Tao stayed until you arrived," Oliver defended instinctively. Loyal to the core, that one.

Azar held up a hand, stopping them before they

both got ruffled. "What's done is done. The more pressing problem is what the hell do we do now?"

They were now in possession of two minors, one of which was the rightful heir to the Seelie Court, who was wanted dead by both sides of the conflict. The other was an "impure" Shaitan, who the naturally bloodthirsty members of her race would love to tear to pieces, just as a way to tie up loose ends and vent a little frustration.

The Djinn were in turmoil without any leaders, and although Killian was emergency commander-in-chief, and trying his hardest to maintain calm within the different races, they were starting to boil over into a mob mentality. Now, with the Weres gone into hiding, the chance of mounting a successful counter-attack were dwindling to zero.

Then there was Bast.

What the fuck am I going to do? She thought to him, and felt his presence wrap around her body, the closest thing they could get to an embrace these days. She missed Bast in his corporeal form. She longed to see him smile, to touch his face. But when he was stabbed with Posidagi, the Great Weapon that was lethal to Jann, he was stuck in his incorporeal form until they found a way to counter the magic-born necrosis that would spread through his body and kill him in minutes.

Don't worry, Jaanaman, we will figure it out. We always do.

Azar smiled. *I love you.*

She felt him laugh and press a ghostly kiss on her lips. *Until the end of forever.*

Oliver and Donovan were looking at her like she was wacky.

"Bast," she said by way of explanation. "Well, there is safety in numbers. I think we need to stick together."

She looked around at the room. There was a Shaitan, who had little to do with the other Djinn. A Werejaguar that was also solitary by nature, despite his previous chumminess with the Pack, and Azar, who had avoided the preternatural world for a hundred years until being dragged into it unwillingly half a year ago. A more antisocial group of people was yet to exist.

Donovan cocked his head at the sound of the childish giggling. Then he shrugged. "Whatever it takes."

"I know a place," Oliver said, and laid out a plan.

. . .

THE CABIN HAD SEEN BETTER days. The paint was peeling from the sagging eaves and the windows were dirty.

"I didn't realize you had a love shack," Azar teased. Oliver had said he used it when he needed some alone time, but who was he kidding? She'd seen him flirt with the women at The Onyx, where he worked as a bouncer. Though, she would definitely worry if some random guy brought her to a remote cabin in the woods. Serial killer, much?

"It's not a love shack. I got it for a steal, and sometimes it's just nice to get away from everyone."

"So, you've never brought a woman here?"

Oliver finally gave her the full beam, cheeky grin that she knew and loved. "Ok, so maybe it's a love shack."

The inside was much more loved than the outside. It was still worn, and most of the furniture was produced in the sixties, but it was comfortable enough. It had a little fireplace in the corner, and a fluffy shag pile rug in front of it.

A large refrigerator box stood out of place in the corner of the living area. Azar looked at the fridge in the kitchen across the room. An old Smeg. It definitely didn't come in the box.

"What's with that?" She nodded towards the box.

"I haven't gotten around to throwing it out yet," Oliver said, and blushed. Azar had never seen him blush before, didn't think it was even possible over the golden hues of his tan, but there it was, turning his face an unattractive beet-red.

Azar grinned, a giant shit-eating grin that made her cheeks hurt.

"Oliver, do you play fort in the giant box?"

If it were possible, he blushed even further. "My jaguar likes to play in a box, so what? It's still a cat you know." He crossed his arms over his chest and frowned.

She raised her hands defensively, and tried really hard not to laugh. "Hey, I'm not judging," she lied.

The kids decided it seemed like a good idea, and Nevyn and Freya were using the old box like a spaceship. She could see the large gouges in the cardboard where Oliver, in jaguar form, had stuck his claws over the top.

Donovan walked in, holding several boxes of groceries they'd picked up before leaving town. He looked at the box, and then at Oliver, and raised a single eyebrow. Oliver ignored him, and the laughter she'd been trying so hard to contain burst out of her mouth. Fuck, he was just so damn cute sometimes.

He stomped out of the room to grab the rest of their things. She'd make it up to him later.

Bast had stayed in the city to watch the powder keg that was Djinn society and give warning if it were about to explode. They were all suspended in a state of disbelief at the moment, but soon the water would boil, and rage would lead them all into doing something reckless in the name of revenge. It didn't matter that it was a suicide mission, as long as they had retribution.

The Fae outclassed them. They'd trained for hundreds of years to be elite warriors. Every offspring was trained in the art of war. They were stronger magically, physically and were a cohesive army.

The Djinn struggled to decide on what color to paint a room unless there were Councilors present to tell them what shade. Reason was now overruled by fear and anger. There had been fights about how to bury their dead leaders, some had wanted a ceremonial funeral for all of the Councilors together in a mass memorial. Killian had to work hard to convince them that having the rest of the Djinn in one place, at any time, was just asking to be finished off.

She felt a tug at her elbow.

"I would like to go outside and commune with the earth." Azar looked down at Nevyn and smiled. He was actually a cute kid. With his large eyes, devoid of white, he had the ability to be unnerving at times, but he'd adapted so well to what life had thrown at him and she had to respect that.

"Sure, Nevyn. Put on your jacket though, the wind is chilly."

Azar followed him out and watched him as he found a spot within a circle of trees. Being in the city had been physically painful for the boy, and she was glad that they'd ended up in the wilderness.

He sat cross-legged in the circle and was quiet. She knew from experience that he probably wouldn't rouse from his trance for a few hours, and she settled down to wait. She couldn't leave him exposed, but she found herself wishing she'd brought a good book.

Within moments however, Nevyn popped open an eye.

"He comes."

Azar shot up and a fireball formed in her hand almost instantly. Killian would be proud. She hovered protectively over Nevyn, her eyes whirling in every direction. "Oliver!"

Oliver was out through a window and in jaguar

form before she had a chance to draw another breath. He let out a snarl that reverberated through the air and made every hair on Azar's arms lift.

But it was Jack, Tuatha Dé Danann and Heart of the World, that stepped out of the woods surrounding Oliver's cabin. She let out a sigh of relief, and threw Nevyn an irate look. "You couldn't be more specific?"

The boy just shrugged, and Oliver let out a low, irritated grumble. She reached over and scratched behind his ear. "Thanks. Whoever said dogs were a man's best friend had never met a Werejaguar." Oliver chuffed and rolled his eyes, the effects of which were really disconcerting in the face of a jaguar. He turned his head and nipped at her ass with his big, jaguar teeth. "Hey, watch it," she scolded, but with his lips curled in a big cat grin, it was hard to be mad at him.

Jack was the start of this whole dilemma, though it wasn't his fault that everything had turned to shit. He'd just been the warning. He'd very directly, and concisely, told the Council that the Fae were hunting down Great Weapons for nefarious reasons. But the Council hadn't listened to him, too set in the old ways, self-assured that they were the apex predators in the preternatural food chain.

The smiling face of Jack made Azar's heart flutter a little in her chest, and she was glad Bast was back in the city. She had very mixed feelings for the handsome Fae man. Well, not technically Fae. He was Tuatha Dé Danann, literally translated to children of Danu, the goddess. She had met the goddess in question, and the adulation she felt when she was around Jack was a faint echo of the giddy joyfulness that she felt when she was in the presence of Danu herself. Nevyn was part Tuatha Dé Danann also, a watered down version anyway, and so was she. That was a concept that she was still trying to wrap her head around, and if she thought about it for a long period of time, it made her head hurt. Whenever she was in the presence of Lorcan, Black Prince of the Rebel Fae army, and his compatriots, they treated her as if she were an idol, a goddess to be worshipped. It wigged her out big time.

As if summoned by her thoughts, Lorcan and his soldiers melted out of the forest like a mirage. It was eerie how well they blended into the landscape, invisible unless they wanted to be seen. The army had doubled in size since the last time she had seen them fading into the Amazon jungle, and obviously they'd joined their two battalions together.

"We're going to have to get more food," she muttered to Oliver, and he chuffed in response.

"Azar, it gladdens me to see you alive and well."

Jack hugged her close. There was a definite connection between the two of them, but it was because the blood they shared rejoiced at the proximity of another Tuatha Dé Danann, rather than any actual physical attraction between the two of them. Yeah, sure, that was it. Apparently, she wasn't just sticking her head in the sand anymore, she was piling bullshit on top as well.

"It's good to see you too, Jack. How was the jungle?"

He grinned and revealed Abazhana from behind his back, like a grown up might reveal a present to a child. Abazhana was a spear, one of the Great Weapons, that targeted the Marid. She'd read that it turned their blood into liquid fire as it killed them. It wasn't a good way to go.

"It was a successful mission," he said somberly. "Lorcan has told me what happened with Bast. I am sorry. I feel partially responsible. And for your personal loss as well, your father was a good man."

Azar inclined her head, and pushed down the feelings that were bubbling below the surface.

"Thanks. What are you guys doing here? And, uh,

how did you know we were here? This spot is meant to be top secret." Azar raised an eyebrow at Oliver, and he growled back, then let out a grumpy huff as he stalked back to the cabin.

"I could sense the boy. Then we just sifted here."

Great, the kid was a paranormal LoJack.

"Is that a Fae thing, or a Tuatha thing?"

"I can sense my kindred blood in his veins, much the same way as I can sense yours now that you have communed with the Goddess and your blood sings with your heritage. Don't worry, your position is secure enough from the enemy."

Azar tried not to think too hard about the fact that Jack could find her anywhere.

"My Goddess, my Prince." Lorcan bowed deep to her and Nevyn. "My army is at your disposal. We have come to provide protection and arms."

"*My* disposal?" Azar looked to Jack desperately.

"I have informed the Black Prince that this fight is yours. I cannot interfere in matters such as this, it would upset the balance. His army is rightfully yours and Nevyn's."

Azar looked around at the men, in their odd khaki uniforms that looked somewhere between Steve Irwin and King Arthur. They all looked at her with adulation, ready to lay down their lives for hers.

All of a sudden, she felt ill. She needed three stiff scotches and a lie down. She did a rough count of them in her head. Forty soldiers. Forty more lives that could weigh down her conscience.

"I have nowhere to put you," she said lamely.

Lorcan waved away her objection. "We will camp in the forest. We are more at home there anyway." He did an odd whistle, and turned, striding back towards the woods.

She just nodded and watched them melt into the trees like ghosts.

THE DAYS PASSED SURPRISINGLY UNEVENTFULLY. Bast would appear periodically to update everyone on the news of the world. The Fae had randomly struck several other Adel compounds throughout Europe. Although the fatalities hadn't been nearly as high as they had been here in New York, the attacks had shown that even when they'd had time to prepare, the Djinn were horribly outnumbered and outclassed.

On the flip-side however, Azar had never felt so content. This tiny group of misfits felt like family.

Secure in the safety of a surrounding army, she could laugh and have fun with the kids, or watch Lorcan and his army train. The unconditional acceptance that she got from Jack, as well as the companionship from Oliver and Donovan, made her feel fuzzy on the inside. She felt more confident, stronger even, when she was surrounded by them. And Bast was always there with the constant blanket of his love. Azar thought it may have been the most idyllic week of her life.

She walked out onto the porch just as the sun was setting. Oliver's love shack might have been dilapidated, but she was starting to love the old place. The peace and quiet, the air that was so fresh it cleansed your lungs, the feeling of safety, it was a heady experience she'd never really felt before. Maybe is was the call of the wilderness that sung to her newly found Tuatha blood that made her feel so invigorated, so alive.

Donovan came out the front door, shutting it quietly even though it squealed like a cat with its tail caught on fire every time it opened. "The children are asleep. Apparently, their adventures in the woods today wore them out."

Nevyn and Freya had spent the day running through the woods behind the love shack, Lorcan's guards watching them closely from far enough away that they felt like they were on some big adventure into uncharted territory. She'd heard all about it from them over dinner.

She gave Donovan a small smile, which he returned. Those rare smiles made her stupidly proud.

The night was unseasonably hot and sticky, the humidity reminding her of the rainforest, and she doubted she'd be getting much sleep tonight. The love shack didn't have newfangled technology like air-conditioning or inside plumbing.

"It's nights like this that I think perhaps the Fae have the right idea, sleeping in the woods. Except for the spiders. And bugs. And coyotes."

"Hmm," Donovan grunted noncommittally.

Oliver stalked out of the woods, his spotted jaguar coat blending almost perfectly with the landscape. Oliver spent a lot of time in his jaguar form out here. It wasn't only Nevyn who felt the constraints of civilization.

He let out a weird chuffing snarl, and jerked his head. When no one moved, he did it again.

"What is it, Lassie? Did little Timmy fall down the well again?" Donovan said sardonically, and Azar laughed. Donovan had a dry sense of humor that was so sharp, it wouldn't surprise her if it could make someone bleed. But not Oliver. Shit like that just rolled right off his beautiful, soft coat.

And it was soft. She liked patting him in jaguar form, so what? It wasn't like she was cheating.

He let out another low snarl, and Donovan sighed. "We better follow him before he comes up here and chews off my arm."

She grinned and followed him down the porch steps. They reached Oliver, and he nudged her towards the woods with his head on her ass. Again.

Azar was beginning to think perhaps he just wanted to touch her butt. "Watch it, Fluffball," she mock-growled, which just made him let out a series of soft chuffs. He was laughing at her, the big jerk.

They walked a little further and came to a creek, which was quite full for the time of the year. Several big flat rocks sat on the banks. Oliver jumped up on the largest rock and changed from jaguar to sexy ass human. His tanned skin seemed to shine even in the fading light, and his California beach boy looks made heat pool in her belly. As always, he was naked. He spent more time naked than clothed, and she'd like to say that she was becoming immune to his nudity, but that would be a blatant lie. Every single time he bared any flesh in her presence, her eyes ate up his exposed skin like she was starving. Seeing him naked was a feast, from his broad, muscular shoulders to the lines and ridges that led downward to the dick he never even bothered to cover. And every single time he busted her, and gave her that devilish half-grin that told her he knew exactly the effect he had on her.

The waterhole was small, but from what she could see, it was quite deep. The water swirled lazily, enough to keep it fresh but not enough that you had to fight with any kind of current. As if to prove its depth, Oliver cannonballed from the rock into the water, splashing water over to where she and Donovan were standing on its banks.

Donovan growled, and Azar let out a squeak of protest. But the water was cool on her skin, and was just too enticing. She peeled off her shirt and her cutoffs, and stepped toward the water.

She could feel Oliver's eyes perusing her body with the same languid intensity he did everything else. It was only fair, she'd just done the exact same thing to him. What surprised her though was the feel of Donovan's heavy gaze at her back. She looked over her shoulder, and caught him staring at her ass. He pulled them upwards and met her eyes, and she sucked in a breath at the heat that made his lids heavy. She quickly jumped in the water, hoping it would cool the sudden rise in her temperature.

Oliver grinned as he swam closer. He looked less jaguar and more barracuda in that moment. His eyes were filled with lust, and she held her breath as he got close. He lifted his hand towards her face, and she held her breath.

Then he dropped it to the water and splashed her.

She sputtered as he laughed.

"Asshole," she laughed, winding back her arm and spearing it through the water.

Donovan slid into the water, and stood beside her, a small smile on his lips but his eyes still held a touch of the desire that had threatened to scorch her before. His body out of his normal black clothing was amazing, like an intricate artwork stretched over a seriously hot body. Swirling black tattoos dipped and moved over his abdominals, and she could probably spend hours just exploring all of his ink. If she could spend hours with him completely undressed. *Which you can't,* she scolded herself.

The sun was almost fully set now, and the insects made a deafening symphony as the three of them swam lazily around the small pool.

Oliver looked at Donovan. "D, I've been wondering."

Donovan rolled his eyes. "That's never a good thing."

Oliver splashed him, but was undeterred. "How do Shaitan get laid without, you know, scaring their potential mates to death?"

Azar swam over and punched him. "Seriously, Oliver? You can't ask that." But deep down, she was dying to know too.

Donovan raised an eyebrow. "I thought you would be the last person I'd have to give the birds and the bees talk to, Oliver. And don't call me D," he grumped.

"I definitely know the physical logistics," Oliver purred, and his voice when it was pitched all low and growly made goosebumps rise across her skin. "What I want to know is how. Until Freya, we had no idea that the Shaitan could even channel positive emotions. Did you have to do it with the BDSM bunnies?"

Donovan let out a long sigh. Azar could have told him Oliver wouldn't drop his train of thought. "We usually do it in pairs, with someone else. Or in a group. If the fear is dissipated between several people, it becomes less of a terror and more of a thrill, especially if we are keeping it reigned in." His jaw tensed. "That is, if you want your partner to enjoy it. There are others of my race who do not need such willing participants." Sometimes, the Shaitan deserved their reputation. Azar's stomach rolled in disgust. "Unwilling sexual partners has never been my preference, however."

He was closer to her now, and she reached out her hand to squeeze his fingers reassuringly. Donovan was proof there were exceptions to every rule.

Oliver lazily swam closer. "Did you know, the Were have multiple partners too?"

Azar narrowed her eyes at him. She had a feeling this had been the point of his line of questioning to begin with. "There have always been more males than females in the Were world, just a natural balance within nature, I guess. So, most females have several mates. You already know that we care for the pups as a society, so direct parentage has always been a non-issue."

He was so close now, she could see the droplets of water roll down his face. "What are you getting at, Oliver?"

He smirked at her. "What I've said all along, Az. This could be our life, and I'm willing to wait. I don't mind sharing, and I don't think D would either."

His body was pressed right along hers, and she could feel every groove in his body as his leg slid between hers.

She looked over at Donovan, whose face was completely impassive, until she got to his eyes. His eyes looked hungry. "I never said I wanted to be with Azar," he said quietly, although his fingers lifted to brush along her spine, sending tingles across her flesh.

Oliver just gave him a knowing look. "Not with your words, man. But I see you watching her."

She realized her breathing had become choppy, and Oliver leaned forward and kissed her. Well, kind of. His lips barely brushed hers, but she wanted nothing more than to leap forward and capture his mouth with hers. Donovan had shifted imperceptibly closer, so that he was a mere inch away from her back, wedging her between them.

She swallowed hard. "Bast."

She said his name like someone would say the Lord's name before being tempted into sin. Because despite how much she loved Bast, a part of her heart wanted what Oliver was offering.

He gave her a sad smile and floated away. "I'll wait, Az."

He grinned at her, that classic Oliver grin, and swam towards the shore. "Come on, we better go before Lorcan comes down to see if we've been attacked."

Azar turned, and Donovan was still there, staring down at her intently. She looked up at him under her lashes. "Is Oliver right?"

His jaw flexed. "The cat is rarely right about anything."

A non-answer. Azar shoved down all her insecurities to push for the truth. "Is he right about this?"

He was silent for a long time, and she was beginning to think he wasn't going to answer her. Finally, he ground his teeth. "Yes."

He climbed out of the water, grabbed his stuff and walked away, leaving Azar floating in a world of doubt.

CHAPTER 3

When the weather was unseasonably warm, Azar always wanted to barbecue. Actually, even when it was freezing, Azar like to barbecue. Partly because she liked her meat charred to a crisp, and partly because it was one of the few times she could use her abilities out in the open.

So, she'd persuaded the guys to build a fire pit so they could barbecue. And by barbecue, she meant Freya or Nevyn would hold a chunk of meat on a stick in front of her, and she would toast it like a marshmallow using her powers. The kids loved it.

Oliver's phone rang and he wiggled it out of the back pocket of his too tight jeans.

"'Lo?"

Azar watched as he turned ashen beneath his tan. Something was very wrong.

"Hold on!" he yelled, and was on his feet. Golden fur sprang up on his arm as he ran towards the car.

"Oliver! What's wrong?" Azar yelled as she ran after him.

"The Fae are attacking the Weres. I need to go!"

Azar's firefighter training set in, and she ran through a checklist in her mind of what needed to be done. "Oliver, wait! I'm coming with you. Lorcan!" The Fae man appeared in front of her almost instantly. "Guard the children. That's an order."

"Yes, Goddess. But with all due respect, we are coming with you. I will leave my most skilled warriors to guard the Prince and the young one. But it seems our skills will be better utilized wherever you are going."

She nodded once, no time to argue. "Where are we going?

"They've got an emergency den on Hamburg Mountain across State lines, with a couple of other packs. It's about five miles north of the end of Mud Pond Road." He was already in the front seat of the SUV.

Lorcan nodded to a soldier next to him. "Do you

have the ley lines for that position?" The soldier gave a curt nod. "May the Mother speed your journey and bring you home victorious." With that, he turned into the woods, barking orders in his rough form of Gaelic.

Azar looked at Donovan. "Are you coming or not?"

He had his arms crossed over his chest. "You would run to their aid, even though they abandoned you?" This was directed at Oliver.

"Yes. They took me in when I had no one. Much like they did Freya. They have earned my loyalty many times over." With that, he turned the ignition over and shifted into gear. Donovan looked back at Freya, clearly unwilling to leave her alone.

"Go Daddy, we'll be fine. The wolves were my friends too." Tears had welled in her own luminous black eyes, and they seemed to seal Donovan's decision. He slid into the backseat, and they tore down the road in a hail of gravel and fallen leaves.

Azar spent the thirty-minute trip to the Weres' emergency dens trying to prepare herself for what she might see. If the Fae could decimate the Djinn, then what chance to the Weres have? Would she see the faces of people she knew, dead at her feet? What about the pups, were they safe? The longer she was in the car, the more worked up she got.

Oliver was doing one-thirty on the freeway, swerving through traffic with preternatural precision. The waves of anger and fear pheromones pouring off Donovan in the back was starting to make her feel nauseous, like her skin was rippling.

They saw the smoke from ten miles out, and those last few minutes, jolting over every pothole at breakneck speed, were some of the longest of her life.

When they pulled into the clearing around the den mouth, Azar jumped from the car, fireballs flying.

It was carnage. Dead wolves lay fallen on the open field, more between the trees, some in human form, but most in wolf. It was just like the vision Danu had showed her.

She threw a fireball at a Fae soldier, stunningly attired in gold and white, like a sun god. Fortunately, he lit up like a supernova when her flame encompassed his body.

She fell naturally into a fighter's trance, where everything slowed to the person in front of her, yet her senses were attuned to the battle around her.

Oliver was cutting a path through the Fae with his powerful claws, shredding those in his way, heading for the mouth of the den. He was going to guard the front, a last line of defense between the attackers and the pups.

Azar could see Lorcan's troops fighting the other Fae. If people weren't trying to kill her, it would have been a beautiful dance to watch. More evenly matched than the Weres or the Djinn, they moved with choreographed grace, circling, slicing and stabbing with speed that was nearly invisible to the eye.

She saw a wolf bite the Achilles tendon of an attacking Fae, who was in hand to hand contact with one of the Black Prince's men. Azar breathed a sigh of relief that the wolves seemed to be able to differentiate the two, knowing friend from foe.

Not counting on the arrival of Lorcan's men, the Fae soon retreated, but not without leaving carnage in their wake. Dead wolves littered the ground like autumn leaves.

Azar stared around at the fallen bodies, looking but trying not to see. Donovan was kneeling over a body and she ran to him.

At his feet lay the body of Jerry, the head of security at Donovan's nightclub, The Onyx, until the place had been closed down for hiatus. Jerry had asked for permission to return to the pack, and

Donovan had easily agreed. Azar leaned down and checked for a pulse, out of habit, and felt sadness wash over her when she felt nothing but the rapid cooling of Jerry's flesh.

There was a soul-wrenching howl from somewhere behind them, and Azar turned toward the sound. Donovan just continued to stare down at Jerry.

She touched his arm, and he flinched away. "I'm sorry." It was inadequate, but it was all she had.

She wandered dazedly toward the plaintive howl, which had now been joined by many more voices. As Azar walked, she was joined by the Black Prince's army, who amassed at her back, guarding it with their own lives.

The remaining members of the pack were ragged. Bloody, and probably in shock, some had returned to human form, but most remained in their wolf form. They were all huddled around a single point, and Azar searched the faces for one in particular. Aaron. The boy she saved what felt like a lifetime ago. Her heart beat wildly, praying that he wasn't one of those wolves that lay motionless in the clearing.

She pushed gently through the crowd, indicating the Black Guard Fae should stay a good distance away. Lorcan ignored her request and moved through the crowd with her, protecting her back. When she made it to the center of the ring of wolves, shock made her feet still.

She saw the prone body of Anton, the Werewolf Alpha, and knew without checking for a pulse that the man was dead. He had a gut wound that Azar could smell from six feet away, and his eyes were glassy and lifeless. Another howl echoed around the group, and it was a lament so mournful that it raised the hairs on her arm.

She jumped as someone touched her arm. She whirled to see Aaron, dirty and bloody, but alive. Relief rushed through her body, and she flung her arms around the boy.

Her fate seemed to be inexplicably tied to that of the werewolf Aaron. She'd rescued him from a demented rogue Ifrit, and it was Aaron that had sent them to Canada to find the Great Weapon. While in Canada they'd found Jack, and the Fae, and the truth that they had a far more dire problem than the Great Weapons being in the hands of a human.

She pulled away. "I'm so glad you're safe! The pups?"

"They're okay. The Fae didn't manage to penetrate the den. It would have been a different story if those guys hadn't turned up though." He nodded toward Lorcan.

Azar let out a soft breath of relief. "Aaron, meet Lorcan, the Black Prince of the Fae. He's, err, lent me his army for the time being."

The two men, it was still hard for Azar to think of Aaron as a man and not the battered boy she had first met, nodded at each other.

Aaron gripped her elbow gently, and led her out of the ring of wolves.

"I am going to run for Alpha of all the packs present," he murmured low, though everyone around them had preternatural hearing, so it would have made no difference if he shouted.

"What!" she hissed back. "Are you crazy? What about the Alphas of the other packs?"

Aaron shook his head. "The three packs of New York State amalgamated when the Fae issued their warning, and Anton was the strongest Alpha here so he assumed control of all packs. They need me. The next Alpha can't be someone who runs and hides, because we'll be doing that forever. It can't be someone who will try and attack the Fae in retribution. We need to think this through. We need to work together with the Djinn to beat these guys, and I am the only one who isn't half afraid of you guys. I've seen the Djinn at their best." He smiled at Azar, and she squeezed his hand. "But I've also seen them at their worst." The boy had been tortured for days by the rogue Ifrit, just for the man's own sick amusement. He had definitely seen the Djinn at their worst.

Azar looked at Aaron's determined face, and she remembered Anton's words from what seemed like an eon ago. He'd told her that Aaron would be Alpha one day, she just didn't think that day would come so soon.

"When will you declare for Alpha?"

"Right now. You can't interfere Azar. Promise me?"

He wanted her to possibly watch him die? Was he nuts? "What if the old Alphas challenge you? Or Tao?"

From within Aaron's own pack, Jerry could have been Alpha, but with him dead, the next logical conclusion was Tao. Tao was huge, like a gorilla that ate a refrigerator. There was something in the were-wolf genetic pool that seemed to negate necks. Next to him, Aaron was like a twig in the wind. And if Tao wasn't enough, there were at least a dozen other linebacker sized wolves who might want the position, and that was just from within the original Sterling Forest Pack.

He gave her a hard look that was wise beyond his years, and she begrudgingly agreed to sit it out on the sidelines.

Aaron squared his shoulders and strode back into the circle of wolves.

He stood over Anton's dead body and let out a piercing howl that was chilling coming from a human throat, and the rest of the wolves joined the chorus.

"I. AM. ALPHA."

It was a statement filled with power and magic and it made her skin ripple.

Azar held her breath as their confusion cleared and one by one, the surrounding wolves kneeled in human form, or bowed down onto their forelegs as wolves. Everyone seemed to accept his claim, and the amount of power radiating off him nearly had her sinking to her knees. Where had all that power come from?

Tao gracefully went down to one knee, his head bent in supplication, and she let out a small sigh of relief. She knew Tao, knew that while he had brute muscle, he wasn't a diplomat, or a peacekeeper. Men like Tao thrived during conflict, which is why he made such a great Sentinel.

Everyone was kneeling now, except one big guy, and Azar's stomach clenched. He wasn't a Were she knew, and while he wasn't as big as Tao, he was at least a head bigger than Aaron, and twice as broad across the chest.

"I challenge you for Alpha," the man growled, his voice deep and scratchy, his voice box damaged in some fight long ago judging by the ragged scar across his throat.

Aaron inclined his head. "So be it. Before we start, we should take a moment to gather the bodies of our fallen kin, and return them to the earth, if that is agreeable with you?"

The man nodded, and Tao stepped forward to scoop up the body of Anton.

Aaron pointed to a small copse of giant sequoia trees to one side of the clearing. They didn't belong there, but someone hundreds of years in past had planted them and now they would stand sentinel over the dead.

"Anton loved those trees, and he could often be found working through great problems beneath their ancient branches. We will bury them there."

And so began the process of collecting the dead

and interring them into the ground. Azar stood off to the side, not wanting to interfere with their ritual. Jack had arrived after the fighting had finished, his face crumpled in sadness.

Jack's full title was The Green Man, Heart of the Earth, Keeper of Balance, and it was the balance part of that title which ensured that he was incapable of raising a hand in violence unless he thought it would do irrevocable damage to the balance of nature. As such, he was truly immortal, and couldn't be killed by any weapon of this earth. The only way that Jack would die would be if the Earth died.

Azar had never stopped to think about how hard it must be for him to see millennia of violence, of death and destruction, and know that he could only stand back and let it happen. He wrapped her in his arms and sighed against her hair, and she let him. She needed this physical contact as much as he did. Their blood sang together, a sad lament about the waste of life. His arms were strong and warm, and the steady thump of his heart against her cheek soothed her raw emotions.

People had started reemerging from the den; the old, the sick and the mothers. The pups would stay inside the den until all the dead were buried, before coming out for the memorial. Single women were encouraged to fight beside the men, however female wolves with young became the last line of defense before any attackers reached the pups. There was a certain level of wild ferociousness about a mother whose young were threatened. The level of ferociousness you got when there were seven mothers with threatened young would give you nightmares.

There were mournful tears over the bodies of the fallen, and there was a palpable grief in the air. Azar saw Dotty, the Matriarch of the Sterling Forest Pack, near the mouth of the den, and she walked over, leaving Jack and Lorcan at the edges of the trees.

"Dotty. I'm so sorry." Azar bowed her head before the older woman. Dotty looked older and frailer than she had the last time Azar had seen her.

Dotty nodded in return. "Thank you for coming to our aid. Without Oliver, you and your Fae," she nodded at Lorcan, "we would all be dead."

Azar knew she must be shaken because she rarely ever called Oliver by that name, instead preferring to call him Cable, his given name. She was the only one allowed to do it, a permission she used frequently, especially if she could get a rise out of the Werejaguar. When Azar had called him Cable, just once, he'd threatened to put her over his knee and spank her until she promised never to do it again.

Needless to say, she'd promised pretty quickly, although after last night's dip in the pool, she was beginning to think she should have been more stubborn.

"Speaking of Oliver, where is he?" Azar had been searching the bodies, half frightened that she'd see a big cat amongst the corpses of the wolves.

"Cable is inside entertaining the pups while we do what needs to be done." With another simple nod, the old woman walked away.

The dead enemy Fae, there hadn't been many of them, had all disappeared from the battlefield, taken away by Lorcan's men to be buried and given the proper Fae rites. When she'd asked Lorcan about it, he'd merely shrugged.

"Enemy in life or not, we are all brothers in death." And that was that.

Speaking of death, she searched around the milling people for Donovan. He wasn't hard to find in the end. The Weres cut a huge path around him, and he stood out like an island in a ferocious sea of grief.

Azar walked toward him, trying hard not to look into the eyes of the grief-stricken community. She had never been good with overt emotional displays, though she was getting better thanks to Bast and

Oliver. Even Jack was helping her get past her general standoffishness.

However, if there was a person who was the epitome of stand-offish, it was Donovan. He wasn't a person anyone would ever consider hugging. But today, she was feeling brave. Coming up behind him, she wrapped her arms around his body, holding on even though he didn't relax into her grip.

"Okay?"

He gave a derisive grunt. So, not okay.

They stood in silence for a little longer, watching the holes being dug, as bodies were placed side by side, each one touching the shoulder of the next, solidarity even in death. Each one was lovingly covered in white linen shrouds. Twenty-five dead, and another thirty were injured, some gravely so. She let her head rest between Donovan's shoulder blades, the muscles of his back practically vibrating with tension. Finally, a breath whooshed from his lungs and he rocked back against her, his body sagging.

"Jerry had been with me since The Onyx opened. Did you know that?"

Azar had the feeling he didn't really want an answer, or even platitudes. He just needed a sounding board. She shook her head.

"I couldn't find any other security to work for me, not Djinn, trolls, no one. Everyone took one look at me and ran the other way."

Azar couldn't say she blamed them. When she'd first met Donovan, she'd nearly peed her pants out of fear. He was a scary guy.

"And one day in walks Jerry, looks me straight in the eye and tells me he was going to be my head of security. Me, being the dick that I am, told him he could just fuck off. He had just stared me down, laughed and said he'd start the following night. That was almost twenty years ago now." He was looking at a point on the horizon, that place where memories ran like movie reels. She squeezed him tightly one more time, letting him know that she was here. They were a team now. Then she let go.

She was walking back towards Jack and Lorcan when something hit her in the back of the knees and she went down like a bag of rocks.

"Oof!"

She looked over her shoulder to see Kayla, her very favorite wolf pup, wrapped around her thighs.

"Azar! I was so afraid, and then they kept us in there so long, and Caleb kept saying not to cry like a baby, but I was frightened and I could hear yelling. Then Mr. Oliver came in as a jaguar, and let us all try and pin him, and everyone forgot that we were supposed to be scared. And now we are allowed to come outside, but everyone is really sad because a bunch of people are dead, but I only have my mommy and she was in the den with me the whole time, but I knew a lot of the wolves and I'm really sad too, but I'm happy to see you and I feel bad that I'm happy."

Azar squinted as she tried to take all of that in. She patted the little girl's pigtailed head.

"It'll be fine now. It's okay to be happy, even on the sad days. But you better catch up with your mom, so you can show your respects."

Kayla gave her another tight hug and left, sprinting to catch up with a tall, regal woman, who must have some Native American in her bloodline because she had a dark, wild beauty. Kayla was definitely going to be a clone of the woman in fifteen years.

Dusting the dirt off her knees, she walked toward the smiling face of Jack, who had seen her ungraceful face plant into the dirt.

"I am glad that you have the Black Prince here to watch your back if you can be blindsided by a puppy," he chuckled.

Azar made a rude noise. "Where was he when I needed him then, hmm?"

Jack held out an arm for her to hold, and she slipped her hand into the crook of his elbow. They walked toward the gathering of wolves, near the impromptu cemetery. "Lorcan felt it best if he went and saw to his troops. I promised him that I would call them back immediately if we were in any danger."

She looked at him in surprise. "Using telepathy?" She hadn't known they had that ability.

Jack shook his head, smirking. "With a cellphone."

Well, that was disappointing, and embarrassing.

She and Jack stood at the back of the crowd, and it struck her that this was the second funeral she'd been to in the space of a week. She had an ugly premonition that unless they did something drastic really soon, these funerals were going to become a weekly occurrence.

Dotty performed the ceremony, and in an odd blend of Norse traditions, European Christian rites and the ancient rituals of the Native Americans, she committed the fallen warriors' bodies into the earth, their spirits into the arms of the Valkyrie, and their hearts into the company of their ancient ancestors.

Azar had not known that the wolves attributed their lycanthropy to northern European ancestors.

Finally, after much chanting to which she didn't know the words, each wolf picked up a handful of dirt and threw it onto the graves.

Jack stepped forward, and bowed deeply to Dotty. "A gift, if I may?" Dotty nodded her assent, not searching for or desiring the permission of any of the Alpha candidates. She was Matriarch, and that position held its own power.

He bowed again, and placed one smooth hand on the overturned earth of Anton's grave. At first, nothing happened. But then Azar noticed that grass, verdant and lush, was beginning to push its way up through the leaf litter of the clearing. Soon, the ground was covered in a thick, green carpet, small purple flowers pressing just through the four inch tall grass. Then, Jack moved his hand, and a small tree sprouted beneath it. Raising his hand upwards, the tree continued to grow, reaching towards Jack's palm like he was the sun. Upwards and upwards it grew, its small trunk thickening until it was the width of a man's waist and well over six feet tall. Not yet finished, he put a hand on either side of the trunk, and the tree continued to grow. It wasn't a sequoia tree, in fact, it didn't look like a tree that belonged in this forest at all.

"Is that a yew?" she heard someone whisper, and that seemed right.

By the time Jack had taken his hands from the tree, it stood well over ten feet tall. Still a young tree, by yew standards anyway, it was strong enough to withstand most of what nature could throw at it.

Jack cleared his throat. "The yew was worshipped by the ancient druids. It was not just considered the symbol of death, but the transformation of life. It represents rebirth, and the perseverance of all things. This tree will watch over the fallen." He didn't raise his voice, but then he didn't need to. Every person there was held in rapt attention.

Without further ado, he turned and left the circle.

The wolves left the small grove too, heading back to the spot where Anton's body had fallen, sadness replaced by a shimmering energy. There was a power vacuum in their social structure, and nothing could happen until it was fixed.

It always amazed Azar how people could create a perfect circular ring when there was a fight to be had. She squished her way to the front. As much as the thought of Aaron getting beaten to death terrified and sickened her, she had to see. Oliver appeared beside her, and grabbed her hand, twining his fingers in hers. In support, or possibly to hold her back from leaping into the middle of the fight, she wasn't sure. Either way, his fingers were warm and reassuring, and she was glad she was pressed into his side.

Aaron peeled off his shirt, and she could see the healed burn that was the exact shape of her hand. She'd given him the scar cauterizing his wounds so long ago. He hadn't let them treat the wound, saying he wanted to keep it as a reminder of the brutality of people and the debt he owed to her. He had mentally healed a lot since then, but the handprint remained. The other guy peeled his shirt off too.

"Will they fight as wolves or men?" she whispered to Oliver, and she felt his lips near her ear, hesitant to break the tense silence that domed the group.

"As men. Our animals are always a reflection of our human form. A strong human, a strong wolf. But we consider the wolf the stronger of the two forms, so they'll fight as human. They have to prove they can succeed without the beast to rely on."

Hmm, complicated.

The two opponents circled each other, weighing and measuring. Then, as if by some unheard starter gun, they attacked in a flurry of fists and feet, the heavy thud of knuckles hitting flesh made Azar wince.

The earthy power that radiated from the two Alpha contenders was thick in the air, and already weaker members of the pack were whimpering and kneeling from the pervasive energy.

Aaron took a hard elbow to the nose, the crunching sound making her feel a little ill, and he hit the dirt hard. The other guy laid the boot into Aaron's ribs, grinning like a jack-o-lantern from the teeth that had been knocked out by one of Aaron's right crosses.

Another sharp kick, and she heard the crack of a rib. She stepped forward, ready to stop the brutality, but Oliver wrapped a restraining arm around her waist, his fingers digging into her hip even as his thumb stroked the bare skin soothingly.

Aaron leaned up and punched the other guy in the knee cap. He couldn't put enough force into it to do any real damage, but it threw the guy back a bit so Aaron could regain his feet.

Maybe it was being kicked in the ribs a couple of times, or the other dude laughing, but Aaron attacked like a man possessed, although his face was perfectly calm. He kicked out a foot and got the giant in his undamaged knee, and the guy crumpled.

Grabbing his opponent by the hair, Aaron threw several hard elbows at the guy's temple. One more mean right hook to the guy's cheek and the other Alpha was down on the ground, dazed.

"Do you submit?" Aaron asked. He didn't yell, or even raise his voice, but somehow the words reverberated through the crowd. The guy beneath him raised his chin, baring his throat. Aaron put his foot down on the man's windpipe, and Azar held her breath. She knew he wasn't a malicious person, but for a second, she thought that Aaron was going to crush the man's windpipe.

Instead, he moved his foot away, and put his hand down to help the guy up.

The defeated wolf shakily rose to his feet, and Aaron put a supportive arm under the guy's shoulders and they walked out of the circle together. His pack followed behind.

CHAPTER 4

*T*he guards watching the front of the den moved aside as Azar and her group strode up, but they watched them with a guarded expression, their bodies poised for any sudden movement.

Azar smiled and waved as she walked past, and Jack didn't seem overly perturbed by their inherent menace. Donovan scowled back, sending out his own waves of malice.

"It's like they've forgotten that we saved their asses a couple of hours ago," he grumbled, and she shrugged.

Once the Alpha challenge had been completed, Oliver had disappeared into the crowd of wolves that headed back toward the den in a wave. Azar and company had merely followed along behind the group. She wanted to talk to Aaron once more before they left, and she was more than ready to leave.

A woman who she recognized as Kayla's mother appeared in front of them. "The Alpha would like to speak with you." The inquiry may have sounded like a request, but the subtext was definitely an order. An Alpha was King amongst the Weres, his orders absolute. It was the only way to maintain order among a group of people who were closer to their animalistic natures than most societies.

Azar bit her lip to prevent herself from telling the woman to go fuck herself. She didn't respond well to orders. Instead, Azar merely nodded, and followed along behind the woman. After all, she'd wanted to see Aaron anyway, so she may as well humor the bossy bitch.

IF POSSIBLE, this den was even more confusing than the one that was hidden in Sterling Forest. For starters, this one was huge, like a giant ant's nest, with tunnels leading off in every direction every few feet. The ceilings were at least ten feet tall, the walls smooth, shot through with quartz. She ran a hand along the shining smooth surface of the walls. She knew instantly that these tunnels weren't natural, nor were they dug out by the wolves.

"What the hell used to live here?" She pictured those huge sandworms from Dune, and she began to feel very nervous.

"Long before there were people here, other beings made their home amongst the mountains. Things long dead, and I don't often admit this, but good riddance. Humans are by far my favorite of the Great Mother's creations." Jack sounded adorably guilty at playing favorites.

Azar patted his arm. "Yeah, we like you too, Green Man." The smile he gifted made her stomach feel like it was full of caffeinated butterflies.

The woman finally stopped, not too far from the entrance of the dens.

"I'll wait out here," Donovan growled. He wasn't taking Jerry's death well. She squeezed his arm. Kayla's mother gave him a bored look.

"Whatever." She pushed open a rudimentary door and ushered Azar and Jack in, closing the door gently behind them.

Aaron was sprawled on the couch, a cut across his eyebrow still seeping blood. It must have been deep, because while wolves didn't heal as fast as the

Djinn, they did heal significantly faster than humans.

"Want me to seal that up for you?" She held a finger towards him, the tip alight with a tiny flame. Aaron smiled, but shook his head.

"Nah, thanks though. I actually like my eyebrows."

"Do I need to bow?" Azar cocked an odd curtsy, and he just shook his head exhaustedly.

"Not you, Az. Never you."

He looked tired and battered, and she had to resist the urge to pat him on the back or hug him or something. "So, what now?"

He pulled himself up into a dignified position, completely serious now. "I'll have to call a meeting of the elders, discuss our next move. I have an idea, but I wanted to run it by you first, to see where you and the Djinn might stand."

She shrugged. "I don't speak for the Djinn, but shoot."

Aaron stood, and limped around the room. He hadn't magically gotten Anton's calm authority when he'd become Alpha, but he was young yet. Anton had been Alpha for decades.With time, Azar knew that Aaron would be one of the best Alphas the Weres had ever had. He was smart, fair and pragmatic. She had complete faith in him, now that the violent part was over.

He stopped his pacing in front of her, and she had to look up into his face. Hmm, maybe he was taking to his position of power better than she thought.

"I want to offer a place for you and your Fae here. If we are to survive this war, we need to band together. We've run and they found us, and nearly decimated all the packs in the Tri-State area in one hit. With you and the Fae here, we can be better defended, and they won't find us such easy prey."

That raised an interesting question that had been playing on her mind ever since she arrived. "How did the Fae find you here? Oliver told me that no one outside the pack knew the location of the safe den, even him."

Aaron's face hardened, making him look decades older and infinitely harder. "Becca."

She gaped. Becca. Of course, it had to be her.

Becca had been Aaron's ex-girlfriend, and the founder of the hate group Weres Against Djinn, who'd been responsible for the brutal deaths of several Djinn adolescents. She'd also wanted to stockpile the Great Weapons in an attempt to raise the wolves into a foolish war with the Djinn. But worst of all, in Azar's opinion, she'd hurt Aaron at a time when he needed her the most, when he was low and mentally scarred from his ordeal with the rogue Ifrit. Becca was spiteful, but she didn't think the girl was stupid.

"I don't understand."

Aaron sighed. "She thought that if we sided with the Fae, that we would be given exalted status and a 'primo spot to watch the Djinn burn'. Her words, not mine. They humored her, promising her glory until they found out our position, and then set about systematically destroying us. Their leader said it was merely a display. They wanted to show the world how easy it was for them to eradicate us from the face of the planet."

She was shocked. Becca was misguided, but every misstep she took, she did with the future of the pack in mind. But this, this was sheer recklessness.

"What to do about her betrayal is the first thing on the agenda for the meeting of the elders, but I'm going to push for her execution."

Azar jumped to her feet. "What?" She'd obviously misheard him.

"Her selfish ambition cost twenty-five lives, Az, and there may be more if some of the more critically wounded don't make it through the night. What am I supposed to do, give her a slap on the wrist? Just because she's my ex-girlfriend? This is the nature of wolves. You don't turn your back on a rabid wolf if you can put it down."

It was her turn to pace around now, trying to wrack her brain for an alternative. But deep down, the bloodthirsty part of Azar did think that Becca deserved it. So what if her intentions had been her own twisted version of noble? The road to hell was paved with good intentions.

Jack squeezed her shoulder. "It is the way of the world, Azar. Balance needs to be restored." He'd been silent up until now.

"I thought you didn't condone violence? Or do you get to make up the rules as you go? Would you have him start his time as Alpha with blood on his hands, as someone's judge, jury and executioner?" Her voice had started to rise. She didn't even like Becca, but Azar had been on the other side of the situation not so long ago, breaking rules for the sake of what she thought to be the greater good. So maybe she identified a little with Becca.

But Aaron wouldn't budge. "If you feel so passionately about it, you can come to the elders' meeting and argue for her life. Because I can promise you, no one else will."

. . .

WHEN SHE LOOKED around the room, there were a lot of red-rimmed eyes on faces she didn't know. That didn't bode well for Becca. Both Jack and Donovan had excused themselves from the meeting, but Oliver sat beside her for support. Although he didn't agree with what she was doing, he promised to have her back and he did. She was beginning to realize that perhaps she'd lost a little piece of her heart to the Werejaguar without even noticing. She curled her fingers in his under the table, and squeezed. He squeezed back, giving her a goofy grin the made her heart happy.

The meeting was brought to order. All the wolves bowed their heads in deference to Aaron, and he looked momentarily shocked. Luckily no one else could see it but her. He looked panicked, but steeled his spine and nodded respectfully in return.

"Thanks. I won't keep you too long from your mourning, but we have to decide what we should do in the face of this attack. Also, there needs to be a decision made about what to do with the traitor."

There were angry murmurs around the table. Tao walked in, as if he were waiting for his curtain call, frog marching a very pale looking Becca.

"Rebecca White, you are charged with treason against your pack, causing the death of twenty-five of your fellow wolves. Do you deny that you gave the enemy Fae our location?"

Brow-beaten and mourning, the girl just shook her head, her fringe falling over her tear stained face.

"I thought I was doing it for us, for the pack. We could be strong with an alliance with the Fae. Stronger than the Djinn." The words came out broken.

Dotty gave the girl a piercing look, one that would make a grown man wither. "Your arrogance and hatred nearly killed us all. There needs to be retribution for the loss of our fallen warriors. I put forward that she is executed immediately."

Normally amiable old Dotty was hewn from stone. In that moment, Azar better understood that brutality was a way of life within the Were community.

"I second this punishment," Aaron intoned. "Does anyone stand in defense of Rebecca White, formerly of the Sterling Forest Pack?" He looked directly at Azar, daring her to stand. Not one to back down from a challenge, she rose.

"I stand in defense of Becca."

The girl in question whipped around to face her,

her shock nearly comical. Well, it was a bit of an unusual turnabout.

"Becca thought, foolishly I admit, that she was saving the pack from us big, bad Djinn, and securing your future. So she was wrong, but she isn't the first to be caught unaware of the duplicitous nature of the Fae. The New York Adel compound stands as monument to the fact that most of them are slimy, lying sacks of shit." Oliver cleared his throat, and raised his eyebrows at her. "Sorry. All I am saying is that there has to be an alternative to death for the girl. She didn't do it maliciously, but she was blinded in her righteousness."

The face of an old man she didn't know was twisted in fury. "My son is dead because of her!" he shouted. "She deserves to be dead too."

Dotty hushed the man. "If you feel so strongly that her life is to be preserved, then you can have her, Azar of the Ifrit. Because she is no longer pack; she gave up that right as soon as she whispered our whereabouts into the ears of our enemies."

Becca looked stricken, though Azar wasn't sure if it was about being put into the care of a Djinn, or if it was because she'd been abnegated from the pack. Whatever. Azar's company wasn't as bad as having your head ripped off by Tao.

"Fine. She can watch the kids in my care."

Another elder Azar didn't know, a woman this time, spoke up. "You would trust this betrayer with your young?" Her tone made it sound as if Azar were being foolish, and she was probably right.

This got a rise out of Becca though. "I would never hurt a child!"

Aaron's hand slammed down on the polished conference table. "You almost got every pup in this den killed!" He took a deep calming breath. "All those in favor of abnegating the traitor Rebecca White from the pack, and giving her to Azar of the Ifrit say 'aye'."

Becca looked around wildly. "Please, Aaron. There has to be something else. I don't want to go with her."

Gee, that's what you get for giving a person a second chance at life, Azar grumbled to herself. "Well, if the girl would prefer to be executed, don't let me stop you."

Becca hung her head again, defeated.

"Bring me the brand," Aaron directed to Tao, who left the room and returned with a short branding iron in a small fire bucket.

Azar felt ill. "Is this really necess-"

Aaron silenced her with a glare. She bowed her

head, a respect she would have afforded Anton if he'd given her that look. This was Aaron the Alpha, not Aaron, the kid she thought of like a younger brother. As Aaron pulled the brand out of the bucket, she noticed the metal warping slightly. It was silver, not iron. It would be incredibly painful, in both her forms. And it would be for life.

Tao held Becca's face in his hands, and she madly tried to scramble away, but it was useless against the brute strength of the big Sentinel.

"Rebecca White, you have been abnegated from this pack, and every other pack in the continent of North America. For your traitorous acts, you will be forever marked with the letter A, informing any pack that may take pity on you that you betrayed your pack. From now on, you are dead to those who knew you."

With that, he pushed the brand into Becca's cheek and her scream made Azar feel sick. The smell of burning flesh cloyed the back of Azar's throat and she thought she was going to pass out. Oliver wrapped an arm around her waist, a silent show of support.

The brand, a rough A, stood bright and swollen on Becca's cheek, and Azar thought she could see the flash of tendons and muscle. Becca passed out from the pain and slumped to the floor.

"She is your problem now. I will let you know the outcome of the other matter we discussed," Aaron said and turned away from her. He was slightly grey, but he held himself erect. Azar could see the relief in his eyes, though. He would have executed her without hesitation, but deep down he was glad that it hadn't come to that.

His Alpha power mixed with the scent of burning flesh was getting under Azar's skin. She needed to get out of here.

Oliver bent over and picked up the prone form of Becca, and cradled her in his arms like an injured fawn.

Azar bowed deeply to Aaron, as was appropriate to his station when they were surrounded by his wolves. Weakness shown toward Djinn insolence could be the end of what he was trying to achieve. "Yes, Alpha."

She gladly fled the room and the dens.

CHAPTER 5

Only you, Jaanaman, could end up with your archnemesis as a pet.

"She's hardly my archnemesis," Azar grumbled, "more like an annoying pain in the ass. And she's not my pet. I kind of wish she was, then I could just dump her at the Humane Society like you would a psychotic dog."

"Pets are for life, not just for Christmas," Oliver teased, and she flipped him the bird.

They'd brought Becca back to Oliver's cabin, and tended to her cheek, the raw flesh in the grooves of the deep burn already trying to knit together. Oliver had told her to change to wolf, and Azar had shuddered when the bright red brand was still seared flesh even in her other form. It must have been so painful, but Becca held her jaw tight, never crying out. Azar could almost respect her for that.

She'd sent the woman out to the Fae in the woods, because she had no idea what to do with her. The elder had been right; Becca probably couldn't be trusted with Freya and Nevyn, despite her adamancy to the contrary. It wasn't a risk she, or Donovan for that matter, was willing to take. So, she got to be camp cook for the Fae, and Lorcan had sworn to Azar that the girl would be respected.

"After all, we may be loyal to our Goddess, but we are traitors to our kingdom too, are we not?"

Azar would have argued the point, but Lorcan wasn't entirely wrong either. It was all a matter of perception. Lorcan, the Black Prince of the Unseelie Fae adhered to the old beliefs. He believed that the Tuatha Dé Danann, like Jack, Nevyn and, to a far lesser degree, herself, were Gods that walked amongst the Fae. He believed that his Danu, the original Mother of the Earth, had created the Tuatha to maintain the balance of the world, and to control the feral urges for the Fae.

However, the rulers of the Seelie and the Unseelie courts had banded together to destroy every person with Tuatha Dé Danann blood in them and any powerful sympathizers. This genocide had the desired result of untethering them from the bindings that kept them within Europe. They believed that with the Tuatha Dé Danann out of the way, they would be able to rise up and become new gods, and not the kind, benevolent variety either. It was all subjugation or obliteration with that lot. And so it was war, between the Djinn, Were and the Fae, and within their own ranks; the army of the Black Prince fighting for his gods, and the combined Courts fighting for power.

Azar had once thought Djinn politics was complicated, but it was merely child's play by comparison.

Regardless, Becca was better out there where the Fae could keep an eye on her, and out of Azar's hair. She didn't think the girl was suddenly going to become her best friend because Azar saved her from execution. Any dreams Azar might have of braiding each other's hair and chick flick movie marathons were just pipe dreams.

She snorted at the thought; she had more impor-tant things on her plate than one self-obsessed were-wolf. She reached out mentally to Bast.

How are things with Killian? Bast had remained in the city, one because he wanted to personally keep an eye on the city, and secondly because, despite his non-corporeal form, he was still a senior member of the New York Adel, the most senior member after Killian, considering Joia had died in the attack and Mira was still in a coma.

Her heart hurt when she thought about Joia. They hadn't been friends by any stretch of the imagination, but Azar had respected the acerbic Sila, and she hadn't deserved to die that way.

Mira, however, had been the chief Adel in the North American region, respected and beloved, the quintessential iron hand in a velvet glove. Azar would definitely call Mira a friend. She hoped every day that Bast would contact her, and tell her that Mira had awoken from her long, unnatural sleep.

Though Azar hated to be apart from him, she knew Bast had to remain in New York City and attend meetings and conferences with Killian, trying to devise a strong defensive strategy.

Killian is at his wits end, and quite frankly, I don't blame the man. There was definite annoyance in Bast's voice. *Even now, the powerful members of each race bicker and fight over who should be in control, rather than focusing on the guillotine that's hanging over our heads. There's even been some talk of surrendering to the Fae and negotiating terms before the war gets any more serious.*

Azar scoffed. The time for negotiations was over. It had exploded in fiery rubble the moment the Fae had broken their word and attacked early. Who could trust the word of a race who went back on their deals? Though they are rumored to be unable to lie, they were very creative with the truth.

Out loud she said, "Aaron tells me that he is going to try and persuade the elders of the importance of the Were and Djinn joining forces."

Oliver growled a little, an odd feral sound coming out of her quintessential surfer boy. "He is Alpha now; he does not need to cajole the elders into getting what he wants. If he says jump, then the pack jumps."

That is true, but there is always a place for diplomacy in leadership. Being autocratic is a quick way to get yourself overthrown.

Oliver shrugged. "This is why jaguars are solitary. All the pack politics is enough to make a Were lose their fur prematurely. There's only one rule for Jaguars. If you can catch it, you can kill it."

The Djinn are worse than the Were when it comes to politics. If they catch something, they'll debate it to death before they can decide whether or not to kill it. But I believe that Killian would be open to an alliance. He had a lot of respect for Anton. Besides, we are not in any position to turn down allies.

It was left unsaid that if they didn't come up with a way to boost their numbers, or a cleverly constructed gambit, they were soon going to become Fae lapdogs.

Oliver was making scrambled eggs in the kitchen, shirtless of course. Trying to keep clothes on that man was like trying to put a cat in carpetbag. It could be done, but it was difficult. In truth, Azar didn't try too hard either. The guy was a joy to look at, all long, lean muscle and California sun tan.

It was fortunate he was hot, because his cooking repertoire was limited to eggs and anything that came out of a can. But he'd successfully occupied the kids by teaching them to play some game called 'Asshole', though when Donovan had given him a sour look, he'd quickly amended the name to 'Fibber'. The kids had been immersed in it for hours, dragging one or two of the household into a game every round, but most of the time it was Oliver. He was a lifesaver. Paranormal or not, kids were easily bored and whiney.

There was a knock at the door, and she was surprised to see Lorcan walk in, with Becca in tow.

Azar sighed and pinched the bridge of her nose. What the hell had she done now?

"Hey, what can I do for you?" She hoped they didn't need her to collect more strays, because she was pretty much at her limit now.

"It is bad to have someone at your back that you do not trust. I believe the werewolf has something that she needs to do. Something that she won't feel whole again without doing."

The big scar on Becca's cheek was healing, leaving a pink scar that was nearly perfect in its horror. Damn the girl for making a brand look like a fashion accessory.

Needless to say, Azar was shocked when Becca, her archnemesis as Bast had put it, kneeled in front of her, chin raised.

"I pledged my allegiance and loyalty to my Alpha, Azar Nazemi of the Ifrit. Her blood shall be my blood, and my life shall be hers."

There was a stunned silence in the room.

"Well, fuck. I didn't see that one coming," Oliver neatly summed up. He was standing there gaping like a fish, and Azar had no idea what to do. Was this like knighting a person? Should she whack the girl on the shoulders with her spoon? Or did she have to nip her neck like Aaron had done to his competitor in the battle for Alpha. Becca was still kneeling there, throat bared, obviously expecting something. Her eyes were downcast from Azar's out of respect for her Alpha, so she couldn't judge whether this was what she wanted or if she was pressured into doing this by Lorcan.

Christ, when did life get so hard?

In the end, Azar tapped the girl's carotenoid artery with her finger, threatening enough to soothe the wolf's beast without violence.

"I don't know what exactly this means, but thanks, I think. I don't want you to feel like you are tied to me though. Once this war is over, one way or another, you're free to go where you like."

Becca raised her eyes to hers, her muddy brown irises reflecting hopelessness as she pointed to the A on her cheek. "Who would take me? I am not like the cat." She pointed at Oliver like there was more than one big cat in her life. "I need a pack to survive. So for better or worse, you are my Alpha, unless you abnegate me as well."

Oliver scowled at the girl, and then kneeled in front of Azar.

She cursed. "Dude, unless you are about to propose, you better get the hell off your knees."

The shithead just grinned. "I pledge my allegiance and my claws to Azar Nazemi of the Ifrit, her blood shall be my blood, and my life for hers." He winked at me, "I couldn't be outdone by a wolf. I have a reputation to maintain."

She was actually tempted to strangle the sweet asshole. Instead, she tapped her fingers to the pulse point on his neck, as she had done to Becca.

Azar looked around the room, taking in all of its occupants. Becca and Oliver, her trans-species pack-mates. Lorcan, Commander of her very own army. Nevyn, her adopted Princeling and Demigod. Freya and Donovan, fellow mixed-blood abominations. Not forgetting the Green Man, Heart of the Freaking World. She just shook her head.

"I'm going to lay down. Call me if the world is about to end."

She trudged into one of the cabin's two bedrooms, flopped down onto the bed, and screamed into a pillow.

AARON CALLED THE NEXT MORNING, asking if she could arrange a meeting between the Were and the Djinn. She called Killian, who penciled them in for the following day.

Lorcan insisted on taking half his contingent of

men with them to the meeting, for protection. He'd wanted to bring Nevyn and the entire battalion, but they'd agreed on splitting the group and leaving half behind to guard the kids, along with Donovan, Oliver and Becca.

Oaths or not, it would take time for Azar to trust Becca enough to leave her alone. It wasn't that she was worried that the girl would run off; Azar half hoped she would. But she wasn't convinced that she wouldn't steal Nevyn and give him back to the enemy Fae, for whatever patriotic reason she had. You could never trust an enemy that thought they were the hero.

How everyone ended up in a private tea room of the Hilton though, that was a real mystery. It was almost like a bad joke. A Djinn, a Fae and a Werewolf walk into a bar. You think the werewolf would have ducked.

Unfortunately, once Azar's contingent had arrived, even leaving the Black Prince's army outside, the private room was nearly jammed to capacity. There was Aaron, and Tao, who she assumed was the Alpha's security. There were also four other Were who Azar didn't recognize.

There was Killian of course, and surprisingly Malee, but there were also several other Djinn in attendance, all of different races. Some races had one or two representatives.

She gritted her teeth when her eyes rested on Lila the Bitch. She was Ghul; a hedonistic race that lived to glut themselves on dead flesh and blood licked from feet of mortals. Gross. And Lila was the worst. Spiteful, opportunistic and breathtakingly beautiful. A terrible combination. It was proof positive of the injustice of fate that she lived while so many good Djinn had died in the attacks. Azar briefly wondered if she could get Lorcan to kill the *Barbie* doll bitch. What's the point of having an army if you couldn't use them to smite your enemies?

Luckily, Killian called the meeting to order before she could make a decision about putting out a hit on Lila.

"Thank you for coming on such short notice. You all know why we're here, so let's dispense with the formalities. It is my belief, as Director of the Adel, and interim Commander in Chief of the Djinn people, that all citizens of the paranormal community need to unite to fight this unprecedented threat. I have talked to my contacts in Europe, and they tell me that the Fae are steadily pushing out their boundaries, subjugating the inhabitants of their new lands, either as serfs, or as servants. Mostly only small border villages with few inhabitants, but they are edging closer and closer to larger cities with established Djinn, and Were, populations. This situation is the most pressing issue facing not only the Djinn, but every member of the supernatural community. For if one of us falls, then we will all fall."

As expected, there was a cacophony of objections, arguments, general exclamations and yapping.

Aaron boomed over the noise. "The United Packs of New York agree with the Director. Even banded together, we may not survive this war. Separated we are sure to lose everything. We pledge our sentinels and warriors to a coalition force. I have also approached the Alphas of other territories about sending their own forces."

The other Weres spoke amongst themselves. An older man, with a sharp hooked nose stood.

"We agree with the young Alpha. We represent the other large groups of Were in New York. Birds, Cats, Bears and Equine." She examined the man, trying to figure out which he was. Her money was on bird, based purely on the nose. Apparently, a man of few words, he sat back down beside Aaron.

Lila stood up from the end of the table. Bast had been wrong about Becca being her archnemesis; Lila was definitely her archenemy. The Moriarty to Azar's Holmes. The Joker to her Batman. The Burger King to her McDonalds. She hated the woman.

"This is ridiculous. Why mount a defense if we can't possibly win? These people," she pointed to Jack and Lorcan who were sitting beside Azar, "can flash into any place they want, and kill us in stealth attacks. They never have to assemble an army. They can just kill us off group by group. We need to be negotiating a treaty, not planning a war. Even with all the animals in America, we couldn't raise the numbers we need to defeat these Fae." She gave Jack and Lorcan another dirty look, and Azar began to rise from her seat. No one insulted her friends, especially not this scavenger trash.

Jack put a gentle hand on her forearm to stop her. She gave him a reassuring smile. "It's okay, I was just gonna blast the stupidity from the room."

Aaron laughed, and Lila sniffed.

"Try it half-blood. Your daddy isn't here to protect you now."

Lorcan stood, withdrawing his sword from its scabbard. "But I am and I promise you, I can eradicate you before you can draw your next breath, Ghul." Everyone in the room tensed, and even Aaron looked poised for a fight.

Killian slammed his hands down on the table.

"Calm down. Everyone is allowed to voice an opinion here, no matter how distasteful." Lila flushed, sitting, and Azar and Lorcan sat as well. "No one here wants to be a slave, Lila. No one. However, you do raise a good point about both their methods of attack and our numbers. Even with the Were community fighting beside us, we are vastly outnumbered."

"What's our numbers?" someone asked.

"The remaining Adel in North America is a hundred and twenty. Worldwide, perhaps six hundred. If we employ every able-bodied Djinn, we are looking at about two thousand, but most of those have no combat experience."

"I can gather around a hundred fighters from our ranks, but I won't leave the dens completely vulnerable by removing every person able to fight," Aaron added.

"The Avian Were are not much help in a fight, but we have vast numbers to help with reconnaissance and scouting. We can supply four hundred of our guard. The other Were represented here can send maybe seventy or so, in total. We are not as numerous as the Wolves either."

Killian nodded his thanks, and scribbled on the

notepad in front of him. "Is there a chance more of the Were will join us?"

Aaron shrugged. "Perhaps. But most will elect to run and hide and try to wait it out."

Running and hiding was beginning to sound good to Azar.

Lorcan spoke. "I have thirty in my guard, and they are at your disposal whilst ever Azar's cause is your cause."

It was clear to everyone in the room where his loyalty lay, though most didn't know the reason. Everyone knew that Azar had taken in a Fae child, though no one knew of Nevyn's royal bloodline. Then Lorcan had turned up with a small battalion, and not even Killian knew why. Azar planned to keep it that way; no one needed to know what happened in the Amazon.

"So you expect us to wage war with three hundred and twenty trained fighters, some birds and possibly a few thousand people to use as cannon fodder? This is your grand plan?" Derisiveness dripped from Lila's lips like poison.

Malee cleared her throat. "I might know of some extra support, if I can convince them to join." Everyone stared at her expectantly. "The Unbound."

"Excuse me? Who invited the other half-blood? One is enough," Lila spat.

Malee ignored her. "The Unbound. Those with less than half Djinn blood."

"You want us to pad our numbers with near mortals? You are out of your weak blooded mind, Malee." Apparently, Lila had been elected mouth-piece for the dissenters. Great.

"Most of them are trained in combat, so they're able to defend themselves against the Adel should they ever be found and an eradication ordered. There are a few half-bloods in the mix too," she explained and there was a grumble around the room. The Djinn didn't respond well to half-bloods shirking their servitude. Azar knew this first hand.

"Oh I'm sorry, not just near mortals, but deserters too," Lila returned, her face a vicious smirk. But Malee was used to sparring with more powerful foe than Lila.

"Djinn society deserted them first. Sorry they didn't come running back from the gutter to volunteer to work until they die." The sarcasm was strong with Malee. Azar loved that about her sister.

"These Unbound, they'll fight if we ask?" Killian seemed skeptical, and rightly so. If Azar had been kicked around by the Djinn her whole life, she'd tell them where to stuff their request for help.

"Maybe. It can't hurt to ask. Maybe I'll take Azar. She's somewhat of a poster girl for the group."

Seriously?

Considering she was still serving her Council ordained servitude on the Adel, they needed better role models.

CHAPTER 6

*S*he rode in the front seat of Malee's mini cooper. She'd left Jack and Lorcan behind, much to the latter's protest. He was determined to protect her, but she didn't need protecting twenty-four seven. Plus turning up to a secret hideout with half a team of highly trained Fae would probably send the wrong message. Malee had assured them of Azar's safety, but Lorcan hadn't been overly impressed. She'd felt like throwing a fireball at his head.

They'd left the city limits, and the Range Rovers were being replaced by pickups. Soon, they were in what appeared to be farmland on the outskirts of Stillwater, New Jersey. Malee turned onto a dirt road, over a grate, and past several cows that stopped chewing to stare at the interlopers. Azar waved, but they continued to stare at her with those huge, beady eyes. Ugh.

"What's with the cows?"

Malee shrugged. "This place operates as a corn farm. It gives the group money, cover and a lot of space away from prying eyes."

Well, she would never have thought to look for a group of fugitive Djinn in the middle of nowhere, shucking corn for dimes. When Malee had said they were an underground group, she'd actually expected them to be underground. Or at least in some dingy New York warehouse. She definitely hadn't expected this.

They pulled up to a ranch house, a huge sprawling building with big glass windows. The Kittatinny Mountains were the perfect backdrop, and the air was clear and crisp. It was beautiful.

A man and woman came down the stairs, both dressed in worn denim jeans and check shirts. The woman had a bright red padded vest over rolled up sleeves.

Malee got out of the car, smiling widely. She hugged them both, and Azar trailed behind her awkwardly.

"This is Mavis and Vincent Burke. They started

the refuge a hundred and fifty years ago. This is my half-sister, Azar."

Mavis stepped forward and hugged her. Azar tried her best not to be awkward, but she thought perhaps she was failing.

"Azar, it is a pleasure to meet you finally. We have heard a lot about you, from Malee and through the grapevine. What you did for that little Shaitan girl, getting us all some immunity, well, we couldn't be more grateful."

"It was nothing. Malee deserves the praise. She was great." Azar shifted from foot to foot.

Vincent Burke shook her hand hard, a firm, dry shake that matched his serious demeanor.

"Come in. We'll have coffee. Mavis makes a great coffee bundt." Azar followed behind the couple, who looked in their late sixties but were obviously much, much older.

The ranch house was immaculate, and they led them into a huge kitchen, a large marble island with a crystal vase of tulips on the counter that took up the majority of the floor space. A cake sat in an ornate cake stand. The whole space looked like it was straight out of a country living magazine.

Mavis fussed, making sure everyone had the

perfect cup of coffee and a slab of cake before they all sat down.

"So, what can we do for the Djinn?" Mavis said, her face losing its softness. Gone was the grand-motherly feeling, and in its place was a fierce intensity.

"You have heard about the attack, of course?"

"Yes. We are sorry about the death of your father," Mavis said sadly, petting Malee's hand when she let out a little sniff.

"Thank you. The Djinn, the Weres of New York, and a group of Fae rebels are banding together to fight this threat. But we are hopelessly outnum-bered. We were hoping we could get some support from the Unbound."

"We thank you for the title too. It's better than being called trash," Vincent's voice was gruff. They both sat in silence, the ticking of the old grandfather clock in the entry hall pounding like a bass drum.

Finally, Vincent cleared his throat. "Did Malee tell you why we opened this place, this sanctuary?" At the shake of my head, he continued. "Both Mavis and I are half-bloods. Mavis is Sila/Human, and I am Marid/human. We were the offspring of the first wave of Djinn copulating with humanity. We were watched, studied closely for decades, and tested against our full blood siblings. When the time came for the Anadari bracelets to be placed on our wrists, we stepped forward for our servitude willingly. We didn't know each other then, but we were in the same group of newly adult Djinn. To hear Mavis tell it, we saw each other across the room, and it was love at first sight. I won't argue. She was the most beautiful creature I had ever laid eyes on, and her heart, well you could see her humanity shining in her eyes. During that week, I courted Mavis and promised that when we were done, we would be together. The Servitude was non-negotiable back then, you know." The softness in his face suddenly hardened. Azar could see the power building behind his eyes. "They gave her servitude as the hand-maiden to the Troll King. When she came back after nine months, the humanity had burned out of her eyes, and our child had swollen her belly. Babies were a blessing in Djinn culture back then; we'd been growing more infertile for hundreds of years until children were so scarce and we were forced to cross-breed with humans.

"The baby was born, and he was beautiful. So beautiful. Nothing like the abominations they tell you about when two races cross breed. But he had no slave mark. Hell, he could have been a species all of his own. When the Councilors found out, they came into our house and looked at him, our beautiful son, and announced him an aberration. They..." he shuddered, and swallowed hard at the memory. "Then they took his body and left. Just like that."

A tear trickled down Mavis' cheek at the memory, and she reached over to lace her fingers in Vincent's. Fortified by the strength of his wife, he continued. "We continued with our servitude. We had no choice. As soon as our hundred years were up, we ran. We left behind the society that we abhorred, the families that didn't support us, and we came to the New World. We had more children after that, six in total, and raised them in secret. Every single one of them was perfect. They grew older and left, immersing themselves in the human world, hiding their abilities." Finally, a smile crept onto his face as he thought of his surviving children.

"But we looked at our empty house, and it was haunted by the memory of our beloved firstborn son. We decided that something needed to be done to help people who were in situations such as ours. We could give them a choice, a way to live. We whispered into the ears of people we trusted, telling them that there was a safe haven for these children, where they could be loved and protected.

We would help them learn to control their abilities and train them how to hide in plain sight within the human world. We've raised hundreds, if not thousands of children over the last hundred and fifty years. But we also got strays; the half-bloods who didn't want to spend their entire lives in servitude, those who feared the Djinn and their prejudices. We hid them until we were sure that no one was looking for them. Hell, some never wanted to leave, and have lived out their lives on this farm, helping our cause."

These people, these gallant, beautiful people, had done more for the Djinn than the Council had ever done. There was no way that she could ask them to defend a regime that killed babies because they didn't have the birthmark they wanted. Her fists clenched, and her jaw flexed until it ached.

"Fuck it. You owe the Djinn nothing. There's a storm coming though, and you guys need to be prepared. If we lose, there will be a new world order, and it won't be very forgiving."

Vincent laughed at her indignation. "We'd heard you were a bit of a straight talker. I'm glad the rumors were true. Let's take a walk, I'll show you our operations. It'll help cool the blood."

She left behind her cold coffee and untouched

cake, and followed Vincent out into the yard. Mavis and Malee stayed behind.

Vincent showed her the stables, the barn and the silos. He led her through the stock yards that supplied the homestead with most of their produce needs, from Mavis' kitchen garden to the flock of crazed chickens that ran at them like tiny little velociraptors.

When she finally knew more than she'd ever need to know about the evils of mono crops on soil health and the corn industry, and the smell of cow poo was starting to cling to her clothes, Vincent turned to her.

"It isn't that we don't want to help fight for our world. We do. We don't want to be subjugated to the whims of the Fae any more than we want to be subject to the unbending ruthlessness of the Djinn. But we would need something in return, some kind of recognition, greater than a half-enforced assurance that we can't be murdered in our sleep. There are thousands of less than half-bloods, Djinn with powers, albeit weak, who have to live life looking over their shoulder lest someone decide to end their life because of an old, outdated model of society. We do not need the servitude system anymore. The Djinn could make more than enough money in the human world to sustain us for hundreds of years. We do not need to pimp our young out to the highest bidder, forcing them to endure unforeseen horrors for a hundred years. It is barbaric. If we were to help, we would need recognition. A seat on the new Council. And the abolition of the servitude system."

Azar blinked, and blinked again. It wasn't that their terms weren't fair. Hell, the current regime was inhumane. What Vincent and Mavis were suggesting was right and just. Azar nodded.

"I'll put it to them. But I need to be able to sell it. What kind of force could you muster?"

"If I asked, and with the right incentive, I could raise a militia of about a thousand or so. Most have powers, but aren't very powerful. However, they have all been trained in hand to hand combat, though this isn't the foe they thought they would be facing."

"I'll try, Vincent. What you and Mavis are doing out here, well, you need recognition. I just, um, thank you," she said, tripping over her words. He clapped her on the shoulder and smiled warmly.

"You're welcome here anytime."

CHAPTER 7

*M*alee decided to stay at the farm with Vincent and Mavis. Azar had the feeling that the aging couple were more like parents than friends to Malee. Her sister was still grieving the loss of their father, so Azar could understand if she wanted to spend time out there in the tranquility of the farm, drinking tea and eating cake in Mavis' kitchen under the warm, loving gaze of the woman herself.

Azar headed back to the city to give the powers that be Vincent's ultimatum and listen to their inevitable outrage over the proposal.

She got to the turn off, one way taking her down the country roads back toward Oliver's cabin in the woods, the other towards the city.

She missed her little family. Spending time at a refuge for the unwanted had made her think of her own little troupe of misfits, and Oliver's proposal. She could lie to everyone else, but she refused to lie to herself. She wanted what he offered. But there was no way she could approach the subject with Bast. Maybe when he had his body back, and he wouldn't feel like she was replacing him. She sighed and turned off toward the city. She would go home tonight, maybe have another cookout and introduce Nevyn to S'mores.

She rolled down the windows of the Mini and indulged in the fantasy that she was free. She tried to picture her life as it had been a year ago, when she wasn't being hunted, or a slave to the Djinn. The latter was easier to imagine now that her Anadari bracelets had fallen off when Bast had come so close to death.

On the open road, she wasn't at war with an advanced race of warriors who wanted to rule them as malevolent overlords. Out here, right now, she could just be Azar the firefighter, pretending to be human. She missed the old days. Maybe if she turned west and kept driving, away from her responsibilities, she could outrun the war with the Fae, and keep running. She'd done it her whole life, so why not now? Did she feel any more loyalty to the Djinn than Mavis and Vincent? After all, she'd saved half of New York, and they'd given her fifty years of servitude.

The answer was no. She didn't owe them anything. But fifty years of servitude was better than a lifetime. And a lifetime of servitude was better than watching all her friends and family be killed or enslaved in the upcoming war.

She decided to swing past her father's house in Central Park. As Killian and Mira had been the only survivors of the attack, they'd decided that it was just as convenient to use it as a temporary hospital.

Much to Azar's surprise, she learned that Keeley, Killian's twin, was one of the Djinn society's most respected doctors. Actually, she wasn't all that surprised. She seemed to come from a family of overachievers.

She rang the doorbell and it was opened by a man she knew was one of her brothers, but was a stranger all the same. It was a testament to how far she had come emotionally that she wasn't freaking out right now.

When she'd learned that she had siblings, she'd been wary. When she'd discovered that she had ten of them, she'd freaked out. This one, she thought, was Roxx, the jewel thief. Internationally renowned jewel thief. Overachievers, no matter which side of the law they resided on.

"I'm Azar. I just wanted to see Mira."

"I know who you are," a laconic smile. "I'm Roxx."

"I know who you are," she mimicked, and he laughed.

"Guess you better come in. Keeley is upstairs doing Obs on the patient now."

Azar followed Roxx into the cage elevator. She catalogued his features. All her siblings were different, with one exception. They all had the long, straight nose of Saraf, their father; although some were straighter than others. Cy's had been broken by Casper when they were boys, and had a small bump in the centre and then turned a little to the left. They'd been a wild bunch, apparently.

Azar noticed that Roxx's nose was also crooked. Actually, it zig-zagged down his face.

"How'd you break your nose?"

He cast her a sidelong look. "Got it smashed in by a Werebear who owns a teardrop ruby the size of a goose egg. Or I should say, he *owned* a teardrop ruby the size of a goose egg." He grinned, making his nose screw up even more. He was gaunter than most of her other siblings, not as physically attractive. Small boned and pale, he brought to mind one of those wiry Amazonian monkeys that used to screech at her. He moved with a fluid agility though, more than any other Djinn she had seen. It was like he floated through a room, silent and sure. A ghost.

"How long are you in town?"

Roxx and his sister, Yasmin, lived in Europe. Ironically, she was a well-respected jeweler. Luckily no one had ever made the connection between the two of them in the human world. The Djinn didn't mind; as long as Roxx didn't steal their family jewels or get caught, who cared that he was stealing from the humans?

"We're here until we are no longer needed. There's a strange vibe about New York at the moment, like it's the epicenter of something big. I just feel like we're needed here."

He was right. The fact that the Great Weapons had turned up in North America, that they had chosen to attack here first, made New York feel like it was the eye of the storm. Maybe it was a misdirection, but then, maybe not. It hurt her brain to think about.

They stepped out of the rickety elevator on the second level of the house where the guest wing was situated. Roxx gave her a little salute and wandered off down the hall.

She paused out the front of the temporary hospital ward, peeking around the doorjamb. Keeley was shining a penlight into Mira's eyes, and then writing notes.

"Knock-knock?"

Keeley looked up and smiled genuinely. Azar had worried about whether her family would resent her when she'd suddenly appeared in their lives after being absent for so long. She worried that their happy faces were really belying a distaste for her half-blood, and they just put on a polite front for their father.

But with Keeley, she'd never had that worry. She was such a genuine person. Her concern was real, her laughter wasn't forced, and there wasn't an ounce of avarice in her. It actually made sense that she was a doctor. She had that kind of truthful earnestness.

"Azar, it is so lovely to see you. Are you here to check on Mira?" Her tone was concerned, and she looked at Azar intently, probably judging her emotional wellbeing. Azar smiled, and gave the woman a kiss on the cheek.

"I haven't been yet. Mira is my friend; I should have come sooner."

Keeley squeezed her hand, and then her face was professional again. "I can't find the cause of her unconscious state. I have ruled out head trauma, brain damage, internal damage, virus, bacterial infections and every poison I can think of." She chewed on the tip of her pen, its purple cap already containing countless teeth marks.

Azar sighed. She wasn't a doctor, or even an EMT. She could do CPR, but unless someone was bleeding, she was beyond useless.

Keeley picked up her notes and headed to the door. "I'll leave you guys alone. Talk to her. I'm not sure if she can hear you, but the studies say that it has a positive impact on recovery." She walked out and closed the door with a soft click behind her.

Mira looked like *Sleeping Beauty* nestled in the clean, white, silk sheets of the bed. She didn't look ill or injured, she just looked peaceful.

Azar sat down on the antique chair beside the bed.

"You know, you should probably wake up now, you've been lying around for long enough. The rest of us are working our butts off out here," Azar laughed, but it sounded strange echoing around the room, only the beeping of the monitors breaking the silence.

She sighed and rested her head against the backrest of the chair. "We could really use your help. The world has gone to shit and everyone is running around with no idea what to do. Well, Killian knows, but everyone refuses to listen to him. The Were have joined us, and a few Fae as well. I know you probably aren't really feeling all that magnanimous toward the Fae at the moment, but my Fae aren't bad. Lorcan is actually quite a nice guy, for the Black Prince of the Unseelie Fae. I kind of adopted a kid too, Nevyn. He's Fae as well. It's a long story. I'll tell you about it when you wake up." Azar reached out and took Mira's hand.

A jolt like electricity ran up her arm, and she tore her hand away. What the fuck was that? Hesitantly, she reached out again with one finger, and again she got zapped.

"Her sleep is unnatural."

The voice from across the room scared the crap out of her. She flew up out of the chair, but her foot tangled in the spindly legs of the probably priceless antique. She fell ungracefully onto her butt. She stared up at the person on the other side of the bed, and gaped.

Danu. The Goddess of the Fae, Mother Earth, was standing over Mira's bed. In New York City, without a Faery Circle, two floors above ground.

"What-t are you doing here? Not that I'm not happy you're here, because I totally am. Just surprised that's all."

Take a deep breath, Azar. You sound like an idiot, she chastised herself.

"You need this one. Her sleep is a virulent type of magic. The longer she is asleep, the less likely she'll wake up. I did not give my children this magic for it to be used for such evil," she spat out. A cross Danu was a scary Danu.

"Uh, yeah. Keeley implied that there was no physical cause. Can you help her?" She didn't want to hope, but if anyone could wake Mira, it would be Danu.

"Yes. That's why I'm here," she said slowly, like she was speaking to a dumbass. Well, Azar wasn't privy to the whims of Goddesses.

Giving her a smile so warm and full of love that Azar forgot her irritation at once, she motioned to Mira. "I'm not really here, on this physical plane, so I need you to ground me. Put one hand on her forehead."

Azar placed her palm on Mira's head, the silky

strands tickling her palm. She had the irrational urge to yell, "Leave this child, Devil Man!" like in those old school exorcist movies, but resisted. Barely.

"Please tell me that the next step doesn't involve kissing the enchanted princess, because I'm pretty sure I'll turn into a frog." She was getting giddy in Danu's presence, like she was drunk on cheap wine. Luckily, the Goddess just ignored her.

Danu placed her own palm on Azar's forehead, and started to hum. A low hum that whispered at the edges of her hearing, a beautiful tune that she forgot almost instantly.

A rush of warmth ran through her body, down into her blood, and pumped through her veins like honey. Her palm on Mira's forehead grew hot, and then it started to burn. That was a weird sensation for Azar, considering she'd never had a burn in her life. Except carpet burn.

Soon, the warm, liquid feeling grew uncomfortable, as the pressure built in her veins. Sweat started to pour from her forehead, and Mira's face grew a mottled shade of red.

She wanted to pull away, but some instinct told her that if she did, Mira would never wake up. So, she held on tight, and soon Danu's voice was thumping in her head, her hearing murky as if her ears were filled with blood.

Finally, Danu took her hand away from her head. Azar collapsed to her knees.

"Use it wisely," she said. Danu glowed so brightly that Azar's eyes began to water. She ran her wrist across her face, but when her tears cleared, Danu was gone. She stared at the corner where the Goddess had just been, confused, elated and exhausted.

A scratchy cough came from behind her, and she whirled around.

"Who was that?" Mira's unused voice was croaky.

"I'll explain later. Let me get Keeley in here to check you over." She stuck her head out the door and yelled. "KEELEY!"

She must have sounded a little freaked out, because Keeley came sprinting down the hall, Roxx close behind her.

"What is it? What's wrong?" Keeley pushed into the room and stopped so abruptly that Roxx ploughed into her back.

Mira was sitting up in bed, looking as if she'd just woken up from a nap rather than a ten-day coma.

Keeley didn't let her surprise keep her motionless for long. Taking in the woman before her, she was quickly checking Mira over, asking questions, and doing other checks.

"A miracle, eh?" Roxx murmured beside her.

She thought about the pain and the pleasure that Danu had pushed through her body. "Yeah, something like that."

Mira's return to the land of the living spread quickly around the paranormal world. By the end of the day, every Djinn in both North and South America had breathed a long sigh of relief.

Unlike Killian, who had been based in Europe for many decades, Mira was a fixture in the North American headquarters for over a century. She was like a balm for the worried masses.

Keeley insisted that Mira remain in hospice for at least another week before she immersed herself in the world's problems.

Personally, Azar was just thankful she was okay. She didn't think she could cope with going to another funeral this week.

Bast had arrived quickly, and filled Mira in on his situation. Bast and Mira had been partners once, in their early days at the Adel. They were still close friends, though it had always been platonic. Well, that's what they told her anyway. She couldn't see how that was possible; she might be biased, but Bast was so hot it hurt to look at him. Mira was also beautiful; her round face was angelic, her long blond hair perfect and she had lips that were a delicate cupid's bow. They would have been one of those couples that were so perfect you just wanted to spew on their shoes.

But Bast, for some reason that she really couldn't comprehend, loved her. When he left Mira's room, he found her up in the kitchen.

I want to know how this happened.

"That makes two of us. All I can tell you is that Danu came and somehow healed Mira. She just poofed out of the room with a cryptic message. I'm as confused as you."

He whirled around the room, the breeze from his path fluttering the flowers in their vases.

What was the message, Jaanaman?

Her toast popped and she slathered it with butter and strawberry jelly. "She said 'use it wisely'. Whatever 'it' is." She stuffed half a slice in her mouth and chewed. It felt like it had been forever since she'd eaten anything.

Perhaps she meant Mira?

Azar shrugged. She knew better than to guess the

inner workings of a Goddess' mind. She was just a passenger in the wild ride that was her life. She was too hungry to be angry about that fact right now, but she knew the anger would come.

She sat down at the large, slightly scarred kitchen table. It was the only piece of furniture in the whole house that didn't look like it had come out of a magazine. It just looked loved. There were scratches, gouges, red wine stains, and something that looked like permanent marker across one corner. Several of her siblings had grown up in this house. The twins, Killian and Keeley, and also Darius, Cy and Casper. Malee had been raised here too.

The rest of her siblings had been raised in her father's home territory in Turkey. Unlike most Councilors who usually had a residence in most territories, Saraf had only kept the two households, preferring to fly in and out, eager to return to his home.

Directly next to her left hand, there were six deep short gouges, and Azar lined up her hand so the holes were between her fingers. Yep, this had definitely been the boys playing five-finger-filet with their butter knives. She let out a small laugh. They would have been terrors.

She turned toward Bast's presence in the room.

She could find him like divining rod, despite him being invisible.

"Who knows what Danu meant? But she told me that Mira was important, that she had a magical sleeping sickness, and boom! She was awake."

She didn't want to tell him about being the conduit or the weird pleasure/pain. She'd keep that to herself for now.

She'd called Killian on her way to the brownstone, and he was coming over for dinner so she could fill him in on her negotiations with the Unbound. Vincent's ultimatum was a difficult one, but she thought that if she could get Killian on their side, they'd have a better chance of selling it to the rest of them. Two thousand years of archaic principles weren't easily going to be argued away.

Azar wanted nothing more than to go home to her little band of misfits.

"I need a nap," she stood to walk to the sink and rinse her plate. She was at her limit, emotionally and physically.

Taking the elevator down to the ground floor, she and Bast stepped out into her father's library. She was comforted by the wall-to-ceiling books. Although she'd never considered herself much of a reader, there was something embracing about being surrounded by a multitude of leather spines. A fireplace sat empty on one wall. A huge desk was pushed under a window, and she could picture her father there, working hard so that he could return to his desert home. Ashtoreth had flown back with his ashes yesterday. Now her father would forever be in the land that he loved.

She eased down onto the large chesterfield couch, and closed her eyes.

"Night, Bast. I love you," she whispered into the emptiness of the room.

See you in your dreams, Jaanaman.

CHAPTER 8

*A*t six, everyone started pouring into the brownstone. Keeley had ordered in Italian, and Azar had been able to hear the owner's angry shouting about an order so large with so little notice from clear across the room. After much cajoling on Keeley's behalf, the man had promised it would be there in an hour and a half, at the latest.

Casper and his wife, Renelle were the first home, and they hugged and kissed Azar as if they hadn't seen her in a year. Casper was definitely more in touch with his feelings than his brothers, who came in about ten minutes later. Cy kissed Azar's cheek, and Darius thumped her on the back affectionately. She hadn't had much to do with Darius, having only met him briefly before their father's funeral. She knew he was the oldest of the three brothers, and an Adel soldier in South America, on the same force as Cy.

Roxx emerged from the depths of the house somewhere, and several minutes later Yasmin appeared. She didn't look a lot like her brother, except her fine bones. She had high cheekbones, and the family nose, but she had brilliant green eyes that sparkled in her face like the emeralds she was so famous for setting. She quietly reintroduced herself, before going to sit next to her brother. She was a tiny birdlike woman in a family full of giants.

The two women that Azar simply referred to as "The Mothers" arrived in a flurry of activity, apparently having accosted the Italian delivery boy at the door. They came in carrying boxes of food, and the smell of garlic, roasted tomatoes and freshly baked bread wafted in with them. Azar's mouth watered, and she sat down next to Cy. The place next to her was deferentially left for Bast.

Killian arrived after all the food had been transferred to platters and the plates had been laid out. He'd shrugged out of his jacket at some point, and the sleeves of his black button-down shirt were rolled up to his elbows.

He looked at the empty place at the head of the

table but decided to take the space next to his sister instead, leaving the head of the table empty. The silence in the room was thick with unspent grief. But then, like the godsend she was, Mira rocked in, looking as calm and collected as she did every other day of the week.

There was a flurry of greetings. Even Darius wrapped her in a warm hug. The tiny Marid was well loved by this family. She sat down opposite Killian at the end of the table, and food was passed around.

"How's your Fae Prince?" Cy asked around a mouth full of garlic ciabatta. Azar could see his mother cringing from across the table.

"Which one? In my life you have to be more specific."

Cy boomed out a laugh. "The Princeling. I know how your Black Prince is, I saw him today."

"Oh?"

"With your Green Man."

Hmmph. Neither of the Fae are Azar's.

Azar may have been hallucinating from lack of lasagna, but Bast sounded a little jealous. She laughed it off, and hoped that no one probed into that line of thought anymore.

No need to get all huffy. I love you to the very depths

of my soul, she told Bast. She infused the words with all the love she felt for him.

I am not 'huffy', Jaanaman. I am not threatened by the Fae. Now she'd injured his silly male pride. She sighed, and spooned some bruschetta onto her ciabatta. She was just going to eat more and talk less. She purposefully did not think about Oliver's offer when they were swimming. She loved Bast, she'd never make him choose like that.

"Nevyn is fine. We are thinking about moving in with the Weres. Safety in numbers you know."

"Why don't you move in here?" Cy suggested, taking a sip of his beer.

Forks stilled around the table and everyone looked in Cy's direction, but pointedly avoided meeting her eye.

It was one thing that she'd invited herself to dinner, but it was an entirely different proposal to move herself and two dozen of the enemy into the family home. The wound of Saraf's death was still a raw, weeping thing and although they might consciously realize that Lorcan and his guards, Jack, and even Nevyn were friends, subconsciously their fear extended to all the Fae. Luckily, they didn't know she had a touch of the Tuatha in her blood too.

"Thanks, Cy. You are a great friend and a good

brother, but I don't think we would all fit in this place, no matter how many levels it seems to have. Can you pass the Chianti?"

Cy gave her a half grin and poured wine into her glass.

He dropped his voice. "You have just as much right to be here too, no matter what this lot say. Now Father is gone, this place belongs to all his children equally," he whispered so only she could hear.

Azar smiled and squeezed his arm, blinking back the moisture that threatened to gather in her eyes. "Thanks. But I don't want to make everyone uncomfortable. Besides, it's true, we wouldn't all fit."

"Yeah, you seem to collect strays like the pound. But I worry about you, out there in the wilds by yourself. I know you have Bast, as well as the Shaitan, for all that's worth. You need someone you can trust to watch your back."

The subtle racism in his comment raised her hackles, but centuries of persecution had definitely cemented the Shaitan's reputation. Still, Donovan was her friend. "The Shaitan aren't all bad, just like the Ifrit aren't all bad. I trust Donovan with my back, and my life. He may be cold, but he isn't heartless." She shrugged. "I'm not out there alone. For better or for worse, I am surrounded by people who are prepared to fight beside me. But thank you. Your offer means more to me than you can know." She only hoped he sensed her sincerity. She hadn't had family for long enough to throw their kindness back in their faces.

Cy just nodded. "Alright then."

The conversation moved on, Darius ribbing Cy about Vivian, another Adel soldier and Cy's current love interest. Cy just rolled his eyes and punched Darius hard in the shoulder. Azar winced when she heard the thud. Darius retaliated by slyly punching Cy under the table, corking his thigh. Cy grunted, drawing the gaze of his mother, Siobhan.

Both men sat up straighter and schooled their features under their mother's stern eye, eating and chatting away like well-behaved adults.

Azar shook her head. Apparently, boys will be boys even after several centuries.

The atmosphere was so friendly, so relaxed, that she could temporarily forget her troubles, or the fact that she was an outsider. Laughter echoed off the walls. This group of people knew love, and they loved well. No one could take that from them, not the Fae, and not grief.

The Chianti was drunk, the food was devoured with relish, and Roxx was entertaining the room with a story about how he'd gotten himself locked inside a safe belonging to a powerful Alpha in Bulgaria.

Killian caught her eye and pointed to the elevator. Dammit, she really wanted to know how Roxx got out of the safe. She excused herself politely, though everyone was wrapped up in the story and paid her no mind. She placed her dishes on the sink and then stood in the elevator with Killian.

It whirred to life and shuddered downwards.

"Sorry to drag you away from Roxx's story. Do you want to know how it ends?"

She nodded, though she doubted Killian would tell it with quite the same lyricalness as Roxx; Killian was a man of few words.

"The Alpha's mate goes to put away her earrings in the safe, and Roxx convinces her that he is there for her. He seduces her, takes her to bed and sneaks out while she's sleeping, her earrings and a few other gems stuffed in his pockets. It took all my influence to prevent Sashko, the Alpha, from tracking him down and eating his entrails. To this day, I don't think Roxx has been back to Bulgaria."

Azar shook her head. She wondered how many times Killian had stepped in to help Roxx, who was undeniably the black sheep of the family, but if what she'd seen at dinner was a true representation, a beloved black sheep.

"You're a good person," she said instead.

The corner of his lip quirked. "So are you. It must run in the family."

He opened the cage door, and it scraped. The old cage elevator had to be nearly eighty years old. The groaning noises it made were starting to freak her out. She'd decided to take the stairs from then on.

Killian walked toward the library, and tossed a fireball onto the logs that rested in the fireplace. Walking to her father's big desk, he leaned against its embossed leather top rather than in the expensive wingback chair.

She sat down on the chesterfield she'd had napped on earlier. She and the chesterfield were developing quite the relationship.

"You've had an eventful day; a secret meeting, a miracle healing and a family dinner."

"Oh my," she said laughingly. She'd prefer the lions and tigers and bears in *Oz*. "What I'd give to have a boring day once and awhile. Do my washing, watch *Dr. Phil* in my pajamas, you know what I mean?"

Killian raised an eyebrow. Hmm, perhaps not. He

poured them drinks from little square bar that sat on one corner of the desk. Scotch, she hoped.

She cleared her throat. "I spoke to Vincent, the Djinn in charge of the sanctuary, but not really the Unbound. They aren't gathering an army out there. It's more if a halfway house. They teach them to blend in with the humans and protect themselves from, well, us. But Vincent says that he could probably raise an army of a few thousand, trained in hand to hand combat. For a price."

Killian sighed, and for an instant, she could see the weight of the world resting on his shoulders like an iron mantle. "How much?"

"They want a place on the new Council."

Killian drew back as if she had struck him. Was it really that unbelievable? What did he think their price was going to be, a million dollars and a pat on the back?

"He also wants the system of enforced servitude abolished." She took advantage of Killian's momentary shock to pounce. "We have an opportunity here, a way for there to be a silver lining to this tragedy. We have the opportunity to right the wrongs of the old system. We no longer need to rely on the revenue raised by servitude to fund Djinn society. There is enough wealth in the world for the Djinn to live comfortably, hell luxuriously, without anyone needing to sell their body to obtain it. The system is outdated and unjust. It needs to go, and something better put in its place."

Killian pinched the bridge of his nose and screwed up his eyes. She felt guilty about adding to his burden, and then she thought about Vincent's story of the Council murdering that baby in cold blood. She was sorry for putting Killian in a tough position, but she couldn't let this opportunity pass her by. They listened to the fire spit and crackle, the room lit only by the small banker's lamp on the desk and firelight. It was peaceful.

"Okay."

She squinted, sure she hadn't heard him correctly. "What?"

"I said okay. You are right. Something good should come out of this clusterfuck. We are lucky, because as Commander-in-Chief, I have a fair amount of sway. But we still have to convince the elders of the races. They aren't Councilors yet, but more than likely, some of them will be. We are a race that is bound by our honor, so I hope that if we can get them to see we need the help of the Unbound, they will acquiesce to their demands now, and ratify them when we are victorious."

She only understood ninety-five percent of the words in his speech, but it sounded promising.

He continued. "We'll lead with the promise of an army, and I am fairly sure the most pragmatic of the group will agree. We will likely get some resistance from the Ghul, and perhaps the Sila. But the Sila are keen negotiators, and they will see the wisdom of the agreement eventually, despite it going against every convention we have."

"Then we get them to put forth their Council members then and there, so they will be bound by their word. This is wartime. We can't be without a Council at a time such as this," she added.

Killian gave her an amused smile.

"Political deviousness. That definitely runs in the family."

She held up her tumbler, the fire making the golden liquid inside shine like gem. "To a new world order," she toasted.

"To ensuring there is a world to make anew," he added, and the clink of glass was the only thing that could be heard over the crackle of the wood fire.

AZAR WASN'T SURPRISED that when she closed her eyes in bed that night, Bast was there.

He had the ability to visit her dreams, to create an oasis in her mind. Her ideal world, the perfect place to retreat from the harshness of reality.

Her oasis was always the same; they were in her homeland, on the green grass around a small watering hole in the desert. To the left would be a large white pavilion tent, its interior lushly decorated with silks. The breeze would be a light zephyr that would whisper through the leaves of the huge palms that dotted around the banks of the water. And always, always, Bast was there, waiting for her.

"You look so beautiful," he whispered, and Azar looked down to see she was dressed in a gauzy white dress that caught the wind, and swept away from her like a white train. It seemed distinctly see through as well. She wasn't convinced she had complete control over her oasis.

He was standing there without a shirt, just black linen pants that hung on his hips. His skin was so golden, it shimmered in the sun. Even the scars, a testament to battles that had been fought with paranormal foe, were just an accompaniment to his beauty.

Sadness overwhelmed her. She missed holding him so much.

He took her in his arms, smoothing her hair with

his hand. He felt good, even though she knew he wasn't real.

She pulled away and looked up into his deep golden eyes. She'd often scoffed when poets and pop singers wrote about drowning in someone's eyes, but she'd understood after she'd met Bast. They drew her in, and she could get lost in each deep, golden starburst.

She put her hands on his cheeks, and pulled his lips to hers. She kissed him fiercely, stamping him with every ounce of her love. His hands slid down to her ass and he lifted her up into his body. She obligingly wrapped her legs around his hips, holding him so tightly that she was sure they would meld into one. He dropped to his knees on the grass and laid her down. They'd made love so many times on this grass. It was the grass of fantasies, soft and fragrant. Grass made for lovemaking.

His hands roamed her body, memorizing their curves, and she nipped at his neck, drawing the scent of him deep into her lungs. She needed this, needed him.

"Please, Bast."

Normally they would play, draw it out until they were both a sweating jumble of flesh. But today, he sensed her desperation, magically disappearing their clothes until there was nothing between them but the warm summer breeze.

Sliding down between her thighs, he nipped the soft flesh that bracketed his head. She moaned deeply, tangling her fingers in his golden hair. When his tongue ran through her folds in one long motion, she squirmed. When he swirled his tongue around her clit, her thighs tensed around his cheeks. When he nipped the sensitive nub, she screamed. His tongue was like a whirlwind, and she was desperate for more. For everything. She ground her body against his face, and he held her still with one huge hand on her hip.

"Bast!" Her voice was a wild, desperate sound in the oasis.

He dragged his lips slowly up her body, as if he was worshipping every single inch of her skin until they were nose to nose. He cupped her cheek, and stared into her soul. There were so many words in his eyes, and she knew every single sentence began and ended with 'I love you'.

As he slid himself home between her thighs, she buried her face in his throat and whispered his name on each breath. They fit together perfectly, despite their imperfections.

He moved faster and harder, driving himself

GRACE MCGINTY

deeper, and soon her whispers became moans, and her moans became shouts.

They found a primal rhythm, and too soon, she could feel the pleasure knot inside her, before it unraveled and sent her spiraling into orgasm. Bast rode the waves of her release before finding his own, his guttural groan music to her ears. He collapsed in a satiated heap along her body, scattering tiny kisses across her temple and whispering endearments in Persian that she didn't understand but still made her chest swell.

When he went to roll off her, she clung to his sides. "Just a little while longer. I'm not ready for us to be two separate people again."

He nipped at her earlobe. "As you wish, *Jaanaman*." His pet name for her meant 'heart of me' and he stole a little more of her heart every time he whispered it.

Perfect sex in the perfect setting, and all she longed for were the awkward moments of reality. Misplaced limbs, sweat-soaked sheets, random bodily noises, the little moments that anchored you in the reality. These moments in her oasis were like a sad promise of what could have been.

"It will all turn out okay, won't it?" Here, with Bast, she could voice her fears.

He looked down at her, and she could feel him growing hard inside her again.

"I won't let it be anything else." He kissed her deeply, and began to move, and words were no longer necessary.

CHAPTER 9

"You overstep your position, Director!"

The pompous man at the other end of the table waved a beefy finger in the direction of Killian. Azar had the overwhelming urge to snap it off and feed it to one of Aaron's sentinels. The wolves seemed to be having a tough time holding their human form with all the palpable anger in the room.

The announcement that the Unbound wanted their own chair on the Council went over about as well as expected. However, the idea of abolishing the enforced servitude system got a better reception. Everyone seemed to agree that if there were other means to support their society, then putting their young through the rigors of servitude seemed unnecessary.

Now, the outrage in the room made her skin prickle. Every stupid question that was shouted in the small meeting room made her grind her teeth a little harder.

How could the half-bloods have the audacity to demand a position of power? Surely they didn't want to join the society? They'd already gotten immunity from persecution, what more did they want?

The easy bigotry made was going to make her snap. Cy was sitting next to her, keeping a supportive, and slightly restraining, hand on her forearm, fortunately. There was a good chance she would have kicked the little, round Jann's ass. Generally, she liked the Jann. She loved Bast, and his friend Danian who she'd gotten to know during her time in the Adel compound. She even liked the previous Jann Councilor, may he rest in peace. But this man, this bigoted dirt bag, was jumping on her last nerve. She sincerely hoped he wouldn't be the Jann's nomination for Councilor.

"My position, Phillipe, is Commander-in-Chief. What is your position, exactly? Are you the new Jann Councilor?" Someone scoffed, and the man's cheeks heated. "No, but I still care what happens to the Djinn under your leadership."

"The only thing I care about at this moment is our survival as a species. Your petty concerns can be resolved after our safety has been restored." He rose, squaring himself to his formidable height. "It is time the Djinn admitted that our old system is failing; our numbers dwindle every year, birthrates of full-blooded Djinn are declining at such a rate that children are becoming an anomaly in our world. We can cling to the old ways, try and maintain the purity of our bloodlines out of pride, until all we have left is that pride and the knowledge of certain extinction. We have an opportunity to embrace what we have been doing in secret for centuries. We breed with humans, and we produce offspring. These half, or even quarter bloods are an important part of our survival. You can admit that, or not, but it doesn't change the fact. The numbers of the Unbound rival that of the full bloods now, and they deserve a place in our society and on our Council. You can plug your fingers in your ears, and pretend not to hear the truth like a child, but you are doing our race no favors." His words echoed Jack's original warnings so closely, Azar wondered if Jack had a bit of the foresight too.

"We will breed with humans until there is no Djinn blood left running through their veins," a woman she didn't know added. She had a point, probably.

Killian nodded. "Perhaps. Or perhaps our numbers will be bolstered so much that there will be adequate spouses for us all, our reproduction levels will be restored, and we will no longer have to look amongst the humans for mates. It is not a situation that will work in the long term; most humans are too fragile to carry a half-blooded child to full term anyway. But from what I have seen, they have no problems birthing healthy quarter blood children." He was thinking of Freya.

Freya's mother had been a Las Vegas stripper, who had raised Freya until she was seven. There was nothing wrong with that woman apart from a bone deep selfishness. However, she had gained an immunity to Shaitan abilities, so that was something to be considered, although they didn't just go around using their abilities on the human population anyway. Their strict secrecy laws would definitely persevere.

The woman nodded, appeased by this explanation. She had to be a Sila, they were known diplomats. "You make a valid point, Director." She looked around at the other Sila in the room. One of these women would definitely be the Sila Councilor.

Although the process of choosing a representative was different for each race, all the possible candidates had converged on New York. Normally they could have done it in their own lands but this was a time of crisis, and for better or worse, New York was ground zero.

Finally, the Sila woman nodded. "The Sila will accept the Unbound's proposition."

Azar let out a little breath. It was a good start. The Sila were the natural politicians in the Djinn, and if they accepted it, the others would be swayed by their decision.

After that, it was like the flood gates had opened. Surprisingly, given their previous stance on half-bloods, the Shaitan agreed next. Her shock must have shown on her face. There were two Shaitan there, the waves of malice flowing off them were thick but unintentional. Being around Donovan had accustomed her to the knot of instinctual fear that occurred around them.

The Shaitan man looked directly at her. "Not everyone within our race believed as our former Councilor believed. Our numbers are now small, and without the half-bloods, there would be less than a hundred of us left in the world. We support interbreeding, and it would be hypocritical of us not to give them a place within the Council. Soon, it may be a half-blood who takes the Council seat for the Shaitan. Not today, but in the future." The man's voice was even and calm.

She inclined her head in deference. Of all the races, she'd expected resistance from the Shaitan, but it was one less hurdle. She looked hard at the two Shaitan men. She'd never met a female Shaitan, in fact, she'd never even heard of one, though they must exist. It was a question she wanted to ask Donovan, if she ever got back to the cabin. She missed the kids. And if she was being honest with herself, she missed the guys too. Maybe more than she should as a woman in a relationship.

Now, Azar looked around at the table, searching for the Ifrit Council applicants. She didn't know who got to vote them in, but it hadn't been her. She guessed they'd decided over in her home territory.

She'd thought that someone else from her family might go for it, Killian at least. But she'd soon discovered that in order to sit for Council, you couldn't be a member of the Adel. With their world being in such flux, there was no way that Killian would give over the reins. Casper was too young by

Councilor standards, and Darius and Cy were soldiers, not diplomats. Keeley probably could have stood up for the position, she was well respected as was Ashtoreth, who was in politics in Turkey. But she'd been wrong.

Joia would have been happy that there was finally a position of power that wasn't occupied by one of the Saraf's family. Thoughts of Joia filled her with sadness and rage. She would be avenged.

There were two Ifrit that she didn't know in the room, a man and a woman, both with heavily accented English. "We believe this, er, would be the best course of action for us all. Best to save the species before worrying about the purity, yes?" The woman said, and smiled at Killian.

Cy leaned in close. "That's Ezster, Killian's ex-wife."

Azar sucked in a breath. No way. "Is she running for Councilor?" Cy nodded, and Azar made a silent apology to Joia. Apparently, there was only two degrees of separation from her family in the Djinn world.

Three votes down for the inclusion of the Unbound in the Council, and the wider society, and her heart was beginning to thump harder in her chest.

"Over my dead body are we going to allow our bloodlines be washed away with human blood. Humans are food. It would be like mating with a pig." Lila gave Azar a dirty look, and when Cy removed his hand from her arm, it was clenched in a fist.

Killian threw them a stern look that kept them in their seats, and turned to face Lila. "Do you speak for the Ghul now, Lila?"

She threw him a smug look. "Yes, I have been voted in as the new Councilor for the Ghul."

Azar's heart sank. If they won this fight, she'd still have to leave the States. There is no way she could live in a country where Lila was in control. Their mutual hatred of each other was far too intense.

The world was split into territories, each race living and controlling one portion; the Sila ran the affairs of Western Europe and the Ifrit controlled Eastern Europe and the Middle East. The Jann had South America and the Ghul ran North America. The Marid ran Australasia and the Shaitan controlled the continent of Africa. They rarely ever interfered with each other's territory, unless it was deemed necessary by the remainder of the Council. That meant that Lila would have complete control over the workings of Djinn society in the US.

She swore softly in her mind, refusing to give Lila the satisfaction of seeing her rattled. Plus, she wouldn't be able to threaten her with death anymore. It would be considered treasonous now. Of all the goddamn bad fucking luck.

Killian's mouth tightened, but he inclined his head. "Congratulations. I look forward to working with you." He turned to the group of Jann down the table, and just like that, Lila was dismissed in a perfectly polite way. Years of political etiquette training obviously paid off.

"Oddly, and for the first time in known history, we are in agreement with the Ghul," the first Jann said, and the chubby little Jann, Phillipe, smirked. This was quite a turnaround. Normally the Ghul and the Jann fought like the polar opposites that they were. Azar had kind of been hoping they'd vote yes just out of spite.

"Blood lines and purity mean nothing to us in the current situation, but this is not a decision that should be made with a metaphorical gun to our heads. Due process needs to be followed. This isn't a decision for a kangaroo court."

Killian's face tensed, turning to granite. He slapped his hands to the tabletop, making her jump. "So be it. As Commander-in-Chief, it is my right to call for all the Council members, elected by your race, to be put forward and sworn in today. I have been gentle and lenient enough. We are at war, and we will still be making bureaucratic decisions as our people are slaughtered around us. Five p.m. people. Make it happen."

There was another uproar, but Killian ignored them and walked out of the conference room.

Azar took the timeout to call Vincent.

"Johannson's Dairy, Vincent speaking."

"Vincent, it's Azar." There was silence from Vincent at the other end of the line, but she could hear Mavis murmuring in the background.

"Okay, go ahead, Mavis and Malee are here too." Azar hadn't realized Malee was still out there, but it killed two birds with one stone.

"I'm hesitantly positive about the outcome. So far, three races agree with the ultimatum. It's down to the Marid. Killian has booted them all out to make a final decision on who their Council members will be. At the moment there are too many people involved and it's a shit storm to reach any decisions about anything. When the Unbound are given a Council chair, they are going to want a Councilor to fill it immediately. I think you need to come down here, Vincent."

There was a lot of muffled whispering.

"I don't think so, Azar."

"Pardon?" Surely she'd misheard.

"Both Mavis and I understand that it is vitally important that mixed-blood Djinn have a place on the Council, but I do not want to be the person in that place. Malee will come down before five."

Malee was going to be the Councilor for the Unbound? It made sense. She had been a crusader for half-blood Djinn for decades. She was young by Councilor standards, but she was passionate, and she knew what was right and just.

"Okay," Azar gave them the address of the hotel. "I'll meet her in the lobby. We are so close now guys, I can feel it in my bones."

After she'd given them a quick rundown of the meeting so far, and exchanged a few more pleasantries, they hung up and she walked back into the hotel, feeling hopeful that something was going to go right, just this once.

Cy found her in the lobby.

"I'm thinking extremely treasonous thoughts about one of our Council members at the moment," Cy admitted, and she laughed. She was glad she wasn't the only one.

"You got room at the barracks down in South

America? Because I'll be damned if I'm going to remain in the domain of Queen Bitch."

He wrapped an arm around her shoulders. "Let's go and have a few drinks. We'll put it on Big Bro's tab." Sounded good to her.

THE ATMOSPHERE MAY HAVE BEEN tenser in the conference room, but Azar was feeling as chilled out as she had in months. She and Cy had racked up Killian's tab a few hundred dollars, but at least now she didn't feel like jumping the desk and setting Lila's bleach blond hair on fire. Well, not much anyway. Let's call it a necessary business expense.

She was bracketed by her family, Cy on her left, who being full-blooded didn't even get tipsy on all that expensive scotch, and Malee, who'd arrived fifteen minutes earlier, looking confident.

Killian strode in and sat down, the general buzz in the room settling into hushed silence.

"Present your Councilors," he said without preamble.

The Ghul stood first, the man turning toward Lila and bowing deeply. "May I present Lila Alterman, Councilor for the Ghul." Lila smiled down at the man condescendingly, and then defiantly stared around the room, everyone dipping their head in deference. Azar just quirked an eyebrow at her. Lila sneered, and looked down her nose. If absolute power corrupts absolutely, she shuddered to see the effect power would have on the nasty Ghul. Lila finally sat.

The two Ifrit she had seen earlier stood, one being Ezster, Killian's ex-wife. The man turned to Ezster and bowed deeply.

"The Ifrit present Ezster Mardines, Councilor for the Ifrit." This time, Azar bowed her head to her new Councilor. Azar didn't know the woman, but she knew Killian. There must be good in her somewhere for him to marry her. She trusted his judgement. Cy also had nothing negative to say about his former sister-in-law. That was good enough for her.

The sole Marid got to his feet, and she had to stare. He looked ancient, and for a long-lived race, that meant that he was older than ancient, he was practically a fossil. They were also so rare that there wasn't another Marid to introduce him.

"I am Xavier, the Councilor for the Marid." Again, everyone bowed. Azar made a note to ask Mira about this man. He was obviously old-school, and that didn't bode well for the Unbound and their seat on the Council.

The Shaitan who spoke to her earlier, she didn't catch his name, was elected as the Councilor for the Shaitan, and he looked everyone in the eye before they bowed. Azar had to resist the urge to shudder.

The Sila, Rossana, who had agreed with Killian earlier was chosen as the Sila Councilor.

Phillipe, the little round Jann, stood and Azar hoped beyond hope that he wasn't their elected official. Lila and Phillipe on the Council would be disastrous.

She let out a relieved sigh when he turned to the older man next to him and put a hand across his chest like a salute. "I present Navid Navix, Councilor for the Jann."

And it was done. She stared around the room at the people who would shape the future of the Djinn.

"Good. I welcome you all. Now on to the first order of business for the Council, the proposal of the Unbound. For those of you who may have been napping, the agreement would be this; in exchange for approximately a thousand trained men, they would require the abolishment of the servitude system, and to be given a position on the Council. We have talked this to death earlier, so it is time for a vote. All in favor?"

Sila, Shaitan and Ifrit hands went up, and Azar

held her breath. Slowly, as if he was still weighing up the pros and cons, Xavier, the Marid Councilor, raised his hand.

"Adapt or die, no?" He looked at her and she bowed her head low. In reality, she wanted to jump on the table and do a happy dance.

Killian nodded. "The vote is four to two, the Unbound get their seat and the previous system of conscription is ended. We will have time to discuss the problems with that after the immediate threat to our world is obliterated. Will the Unbound put forth their Councilor?"

Azar stood, as did Malee. She opened her mouth to introduce her half-sister, but Malee began to speak first.

"Councilors, the Unbound put forth Azar Nazemi, of the Ifrit and the Unbound, as our elected Councilor."

Azar blinked, and gaped, and then blinked again.

Killian cleared his throat. "Azar, do you accept this role?"

She looked at Malee, and then at everyone else in the room. Could she be a Councilor?

"Are you sure?" she whispered at Malee, and the other woman nodded. "We all agreed. It should be you."

Dazedly, Azar looked at Killian. "I accept the role of Councilor," she said, and watched as the entire room bowed their head in deference, except Lila. Azar couldn't even enjoy the look on Lila's face, she was in that much shock.

"Good." Killian said, moving on. "As a second order of business, I would like to convene this Council as a War Council. Everyone in favor?" All hands rose. "Excellent. Then let's get down to saving the world, shall we?"

CHAPTER 10

*S*he drove towards Oliver's cabin in a state of bewilderment. The rest of the meeting had all been a little bit of a blur, but she assumed she'd answered questions, and made appropriate comments because no one stripped her of her Councilor status there and then.

Azar Nazemi, Councilor for the Unbound. Malee's voice saying those words kept going around and around in her head.

On one hand, she was honored. She had a real chance to make a difference to people like her and Freya and even Donovan. When she'd cornered Malee after the meeting just to find out whose bright idea making her Councilor was, her sister had laughed.

"Who else would we make Councilor, Az? You've done so much for the rights of mixed-bloods already; you gave the less than half-bloods protection and a name. They aren't just forgotten, collateral damage anymore. You convinced Killian, and then a room full of hard-nosed Djinn, that letting them have a Council seat was the only option. And that was during your servitude, of all times. Hell, you even got rid of enforced servitude. Imagine what you will be able to do with real power of a Council position."

Azar had wanted to argue. That was all just circumstance, anyone with half a conscience would have done the same thing. Not for the first time, she wondered if she had any control over her life at all, or if it was fate, preordained since her birth.

She was only fifteen miles from Oliver's love shack when a sudden cold sweat broke out along her skin.

Something was wrong.

Her heart pounded as she put her foot down, breaking the speed limit by a dangerous amount. She swerved around cars and trucks but she just knew that if she didn't get to Oliver's cabin immediately, something very bad would happen.

The landscape flew by in a blur, and she was glad

that she didn't see the flash of Highway Patrol. As she skidded into the driveway of the cabin, she could see the reason for the fear that was hammering her.

The Fae were attacking, and in large numbers. Lorcan's forces pushed them back from the house, but there were more of the enemy than the Black Prince's army.

She caught a brief glimpse of Oliver cutting his way through one of the Fae, but he was bloody and slow. She couldn't see Nevyn or Freya, and her panic ratcheted up a notch. She prayed they were in the house, but at this rate, they wouldn't be held back for long. Something needed to shift the balance.

Azar punched the windscreen, easily shattering it.

BAST!

I'm here. Bast's voice seemed strained, and she could see a tree fall down, trapping a Fae soldier beneath its trunk.

Tell anyone who is with us to pull back, I'm going to drop a surprise into their laps. In five...

She put her foot on the gas, and at the same time, she ignited.

Four, three, two...

Azar sent a flame through the air vents and down into the engine of the car.

One.

She ignited the gas tank so the car exploded in a fireball. Luckily, she was a Councilor now; they couldn't kick her ass for destroying Adel property.

She crawled out of the broken windscreen, her wings already unfurling from her back and her body encased in white-hot fire.

Fae were rolling on the ground, trying to put out their uniforms. Fireballs spewed from her fingers like molten death, and she encased those closer to her in flames. Lorcan's forces rushed forward to execute the downed Fae as they got to their feet, and the tide of the battle changed. But it was still too close for comfort.

Someone threw her a sword, and she caught it instinctively. But as soon as it touched her flaming hand, the shaft went up in neon blue flames.

Azar stood still, just gaping at it. Normal metal would have melted in her hand by now, but this sword still felt cool in her grip.

She looked over her shoulder and saw Jack fade back into the woods. A Fae in an enemy uniform crept up to him from behind, running him through with a sword. She let out a shout, but Jack just rolled his eyes and stepped forward, the sword sliding back out of his body.

Azar watched as the hole in his body just disappeared, and Jack turned toward his attacker, shaking his head. He said something to his assailant, then swung his forehead into the man's face, knocking him out.

She'd briefly forgotten he couldn't be killed by mortal means, being the Heart of the World, a true immortal. But he couldn't lift a hand in violence. She thought about the Fae's body going down like a sack of potatoes after that head-butt. Technically he hadn't lifted his hand.

Azar swung her sword in a circle, a move she'd only ever seen in the movies. The sword felt right in her hand, like an extension of her arm.

Two Fae ran towards her, and she pushed off her feet and into the air, slashing at one with her sword and kicking the other with her flame covered foot. All her clothes had burned away when she ignited.

A man in full regalia stepped in front of her. He had long blond hair to his waist, and a gold embroidered tunic.

"I have come to collect my cousin. Hand him to me, and I'll withdraw my troops without slaughtering the rest of your pathetic guard."

She pointed her sword at his chest. "I'm afraid we've never met. You are?"

He sneered at her. "I am Finlay, the new and rightful King of the Golden Throne of the Seelie."

Azar screwed up her nose. "Wow, that's a bit of a mouthful. I'm just going to call you Fin." She stepped forward, waving the sword haphazardly in his direction. Droplets of blue flame shook off, landing on the grass near his calfskin shoes. "I'm sorry Fin, but Nevyn isn't home right now. I'll tell him you stopped by though."

She thrust the sword at his chest and he stepped backwards, his own sword coming up to meet hers. With prolonged contact between their swords, the heat of the neon blue flame began to melt Fin's, making it droop a little, curving the blade.

"Seems your sword has a little erectile problem, Finny," she laughed.

Red, hot hate mottled Finlay's face, and he shouted something in Gaelic and sifted away. Soon, his soldiers followed, and Lorcan's troops were swinging their swords at thin air. Who fought with swords in this day and age anyway?

Azar sprinted into the house, and looked through the living room and kitchen, finding no sign of Freya and Nevyn anywhere. She got to the hall and found Donovan lying prone on the floor.

"Donovan!" She knelt beside him, looking for his

injury. There was a gaping wound in his side, but it didn't look dangerous. His face was beaded in sweat, his face pallid with death.

"Donovan! Hey!" Azar shook him, and his eyes fluttered open. He sucked in a breath, and so did she. Thank fuck. She ran her hand through his hair, brushing it away from his eyes.

"I'm fine. It's already healing. Just lost too much blood… and passed out… Find Freya." His voice was a raspy whisper, and she hesitated to leave him. "Go!" he growled, his onyx eyes flashing.

She shot to her feet, and ran down the hall. The door to the rear bedroom had been kicked in, and she ran in, sword drawn.

Two Fae had Nevyn and Freya cornered in the room, their only defense a shifted Becca standing in front of them, guarding her charges. Azar yelled, and stabbed one of the Fae in the kidney, and slit the others throat as he turned to face the new threat.

Both bodies sank to the ground, and Azar jumped over them towards the kids. Nevyn had Freya behind him, her gallant defender to the last.

Azar got a good look at Becca and sucked in a breath. She was wounded. Too wounded. Slash marks riddled her body, and as Azar watched, the wolf fell to her side.

She dropped down beside Becca, and watched as the wolf shifted back into Becca. The slashes were even more prominent in this form.

"Swords...were... silver," she gasped out. "I... didn't tell. This wasn't...me." Blood bubbled up through her lips, and her breaths made an awful gurgling noise. "I tried...I kept my oath."

Azar pushed Becca's hair out of her face and tears welled in her eyes. "I know, I believe you. You protected them. You're honorable. A hero."

"Tell...Aaron..." She sucked in a gasping breath, and tears pooled in the corners of Azar's eyes.

"You can tell him yourself. We'll get you to a doctor. You'll be fine."

Becca rolled her eyes. "I still...don't like...you." Azar laughed through her haze of tears.

"I know." She squeezed Becca's hand as the girl coughed up blood, spattering it over them both. Finally, she took one more shaky breath, and went limp.

Azar put her head on Becca's and sobbed. Becca had been her responsibility, her charge, and she'd let her die. Becca's death was on her, because she didn't know what the fuck she was doing. She was just blindly stumbling around, and people were dying. She was barely more than a kid.

Hush, Jaanaman, hush. This wasn't your fault, none of this is your fault. Rebecca got back her honor, died a warrior's death.

Azar wanted to scream and shout and rage against the world, but instead she said nothing. She laid over Becca's body until Oliver came, scooped her up and walked her out of the room.

It was dark when they landed on the doorstep of the Were den like a troupe of refugees, bloodied and a little shell-shocked. Donovan was still seriously injured, though he seemed to be healing well. Tao took one look at them from the checkpoint and had radioed ahead for medical assistance.

Aaron met them at the car when they pulled up, and pulled her into his arms. He looked around the faces in the car.

"Becca?"

A sob welled up in her throat, and she choked it back down. But the look on her face must have been enough, because his face was raw with grief before he pulled his mask of stern neutrality back into place.

"Come inside. You'll be safe here."

Lorcan bowed deeply toward her, and his army

disappeared into the woods. Jack stepped toward her, lifting his fingers to stroke blood from her face. He opened his mouth to speak, but then shook his head. His eyes were trying to say too much, but he just leaned forward and kissed her forehead, blood spatter and all. Then he left with Lorcan's army.

Donovan was put on a stretcher, although he snapped and growled about it. The woman they'd met the day of Aaron's ascension to Pack Master was there. Kayla's mother.

"Quit your grumbling, Shaitan. I'm not above knocking out an injured man." Donovan shot her his most ominous look, and she merely quirked an eyebrow. It took a brave woman to stand up to a Shaitan – brave or stupid.

The stern woman then looked Oliver over, and nodded toward the dens. "Infirmary, now." Oliver didn't even hesitate. He was off in the direction she indicated like a faithful puppy.

"Who's she?" Azar whispered low to Aaron.

"Halona. She's the pup Kayla's mother. She's also a nurse."

One side of her mouth quirked. Halona's bedside manner needed a little work.

The den was lit with wall sconces, and it made the place look warm and inviting. The halls weren't as busy as they normally were, probably because it was so late. It had an eerie stillness about it that both soothed and scared Azar. Although she didn't think she could handle much more action today, the quietness of the underground den reminded her of a tomb.

Nevyn had hold of Freya's hand. Nevyn hadn't let go of Freya's hand since the attack, the two kids squishing into one seat in the SUV so they wouldn't have to be parted.

Azar didn't know who was supporting whom, but she was slightly jealous. She needed someone to hold her hand through this; she needed Bast. But she couldn't tell him that. He was feeling just as much guilt as she. His inability to help defend his family had cut him to the very core of who he was. She wanted to just curl up in Oliver's arms, but that raised too many problems.

Dotty appeared from somewhere like an apparition. Azar was surprised to see Kayla behind her. The pup stepped around Dotty and wrapped Freya in a hug.

"Kayla and Freya became close friends while Freya was staying with us. They were nearly inseparable. Halona insists that Freya and the Prince stay with her while Donovan recovers. Kayla will show them the way. They will be safe, you don't have to worry about that."

She looked at Nevyn, and raised a questioning brow. Nevyn nodded sagely.

"We shall be fine, Azar. I will protect Freya, and I trust the Were. They have pure hearts."

She was loathe to have them out of her sight, but Dotty and Nevyn were right. They would be fine within the den. The Fae couldn't sift in, and there were hundreds of would-be protectors between them and the outside.

"Fine, okay. Be safe."

The kids shot away up a tunnel, looking distinctly more like children and less like victims of war. She envied them, the resilience of youth. Dotty followed along behind them, more slowly.

Aaron offered Azar his arm, and she took it gladly. It was hard to remember that less than a year ago, Aaron had been a college kid himself. Now he had the weight of hundreds of lives on his shoulders, and he handled it far better than she had, so far.

They ended up in Aaron's office, and he closed the door behind him. His mask of power slipped away, and he was once again the boy Azar knew and loved.

She slumped down on the couch and let her head loll backward.

"She wanted me to tell you that she died with honor, protecting the children."

Aaron sat down beside her, and crumpled, his face in his hands as his body shook.

He wept silently, for the woman who had been his first love, and then his first lover. The woman he'd abnegated from the pack, and placed in Azar's care. She rubbed his back soothingly, although she was crying along with him.

"It was a warrior's death. Oliver tells me she would have liked that."

Aaron sniffed and nodded. "She has always been fierce, if misguided. I can't help but feel as if this is my fault."

"I know the feeling. But we can't predict the future, and you couldn't have known. I couldn't have known." Her words were empty. Neither of them would unburden themselves of guilt that easily.

They sat in silence and stared at the ceiling for a while, lost in their own thoughts.

Finally, she turned to him. "They made me a Councilor today. I'm not sure who is meant to bow to whom now." It was a weak joke, but it made Aaron laugh.

"Seriously, they made you the Councilor for the Ifrit?"

"Geez, no need to sound so shocked, *Alpha*. Who would have thought a month ago you would be here, hmm? But in answer to your question, no, they made me Councilor for the Unbound."

He poured two snifters of whiskey from the decanter on the occasional table beside him.

"Well, holy shit," he said, handing Azar her glass.

She clinked her glass to his.

"That's a toast I can drink to."

CHAPTER 11

*A*zar shifted gingerly out of bed. The room they had given her was one near the back of the den, which ran for about two miles diagonally underground. Being toward the back, the room had an unfinished quality. The walls were still rough-hewn rock, the furniture the bare minimum of a bed, a desk and a rug. LED lights lit up the room in a glaring pale light.

Her back ached where her wings had emerged. Although she never felt their emergence at the time, the muscles of her back were always bruised and sore the next day, like she'd been dropped from a great height and landed on her back. It was an unfortunate side effect of her half human nature.

She grabbed a clean pair of jeans and a black tee

from her one duffel. It was all she could pack before everyone evacuated Oliver's cabin. Stuffing her feet back into her well-worn boots, she headed up the path toward the common room, near the front of the den.

Halfway up, she began to hear a commotion, and she began to sprint.

Not again.

She just wanted five minutes of peace to wrap her head around everything that had happened. She didn't want to be fighting Fae until she died of exhaustion.

When she came around the last corner of the hall, she noticed that all the Weres were centered on a single figure. Azar waded through the huddle of growling bodies, to see their prey standing there, hands raised and a grin on his face.

"You better call off your attack dogs, Az," Cy said, indicating the Weres that were edging closer towards lunging distance.

"Woah, woah everyone. This is my brother Cy. He's definitely a friendly. I'm sorry about this." Obviously, Tao and Aaron weren't in this group of Were. They would have recognized Cy instantly. "I'm sure he has a very good reason for being here."

The Weres begrudgingly backed away, but they

stayed on alert.

"You do have a very good reason for being here, right?"

"Sure I do. I just learned that my favorite baby sister almost got exterminated by the Fae last night, and you didn't call, or even text to say you were okay. I had to find out from Bast over my morning frappe." He frowned. "So I've come to watch your back. I mean, look how far into the dens I got before anyone noticed I was here? If I can do it, you can bet your ass the Fae can do it too."

He had a point, but Azar doubted that Aaron and the Were would appreciate being told so. It was a weakness in the den's defenses, and it needed to be sorted out. Cy was one of the Adel's best trackers, and he was practically invisible in the landscape if he didn't want to be seen. The Fae would have soldiers just as elite as Cy, and they needed to be prepared for that scenario.

"You better come with me before they decide they wouldn't mind fresh meat for breakfast." She grabbed Cy's arm and pulled him through the crowd. He magnanimously ignored the nips and snarls.

"We better go and announce your arrival to Aaron, and ask his permission for you to be in the den. And for the sweet love of everything holy, follow the etiquette. I know you know it, so don't pull that dumb soldier crap with me."

He snorted back a laugh, but nodded. He was awfully chipper today, considering he'd nearly just gotten some vital limbs torn off. She gave him a narrow-eyed look. "What's up with you?"

"Vivian agreed to marry me after this thing with the Fae is over."

Azar stopped dead. "What? Since when have you guys even been a couple? Congratulations! Looks like I owe Bast a fifty. I said there was nothing going on between you two."

His chest was puffed out, and his grin was so wide it threatened to split his face in two. "Since we've come back from the Amazon, we've been seeing each other every night. She's just perfect for me."

"Except she's a Sila. And you've known each other, what? Three weeks?"

"We went through training together, and have run a few ops over the years, but yeah this has been the longest we've been in each other's company. I don't know, Az, I've been around a long time, and I just know this is different. I knew almost instantly. We are like two pieces that match, even though we are from different puzzles, you know?"

She couldn't help but think of her and Bast. Yeah, she knew that feeling. Was it possible to have more than one piece missing?

"Well, I for one am really happy for you. Your brothers are going to give you some serious shit though. I hope you're prepared," Azar laughed. They stopped outside of Aaron's office, and she knocked. "Remember to drop your eyes, otherwise you're going to flare up his Alpha instincts and get your face chewed off. Your new bride won't take you if you aren't this pretty."

Cy rolled his eyes. "I know, I know. It's nice to know you think I'm pretty though. Spread the word."

She punched him in the arm. Aaron called for them to enter, and she flung open the door.

Leading by example, Azar bowed her head upon entrance, casting her eyes to the left to ensure Cy was doing the same. There was a blast of Aaron's ancient earthy Alpha power, completely at odds with his young voice. "Please sit."

Azar looked up and smiled, walking to the couch. Cy sat beside her, his long legs stretched out in front of him.

"How's it goin', Cy?" Aaron asked, sitting opposite them. There was a pot of coffee and several muffins on the coffee table. "Muffin?" She was starved. She chose one of the oversized pastries that seemed to be more chocolate than muffin. It was actually the size of a small cake. Cy took another.

"I'm good. Engaged," Cy replied goofily, his mouth full of cake.

"Hopefully she can teach you some table manners," Azar said, shaking her head.

"I thought Vivian had more taste," Aaron ribbed.

Azar raised both eyebrows. "Am I the only one that didn't realize they were an item?"

Both of the men nodded, and went on eating. She'd been wrapped up in her own life and her own problems, it had been one crisis after another for a while, but she made a mental note to try and stay up to date with everyone's lives.

"Cy wants to stay for a while. He doesn't trust my welfare to anyone but kin."

Aaron frowned, as if deciding whether to be offended. But the good-natured kid was still in there somewhere, and he just shrugged. "Sure, do what you need to do. One more fighting man never goes astray out here."

She was so proud of the man Aaron had become. He definitely had the ability to become a good leader. He was level headed, pragmatic but fiercely protective of his people. All qualities that made him such a great friend would make him a great Alpha.

"Your security out here is weak against paranormal enemies, Alpha," Cy addressed him respectfully. "I got all the way to your common area before anyone realized I was here, including the sentinels at the entrance. I'm good, but the Fae will be just as good. I would like to help you find the holes and prepare defenses, if you are agreeable."

Aaron's jaw tensed. No one would be happy that Cy had made it so far. If he had been Fae, he could have stealthily killed twenty-five Were before he'd gotten to the Commons. Tao was going to crack some skulls.

"Just tell me what you need, and we'll get it done." There was a knock at the door, and Aaron sighed. "No one tells you that you spend your whole day petting hands and solving arguments as Alpha. I can tell you it's not all prestige and glory."

"At least you're never cold at night," Cy ribbed.

Azar had seen the appreciative looks the females had been casting at Aaron last night. Aaron flushed bright red.

"I'll see you later, Romeo," she threw over her shoulder as she walked out the door. A pretty Were woman was waiting at the door. She had the longest auburn hair Azar had ever seen, it actually brushed the back of her knees, and she'd barely taken her eyes from Aaron to acknowledge them. Well, at least they now knew why Aaron spent so much time petting hands.

"So, Councilor Nazemi, where to now?"

"Ergh, don't remind me. I should check on my motley crew, I guess. Then, I don't know. I just don't know."

She'd never been in battle before. Well, a planned battle anyway. She'd avoided the human World Wars as best she could, and the fights she'd been in were mostly skirmishes. She didn't know how to prepare for an actual all out, balls to the wall, war.

Cy wrapped an arm around her shoulders, and hugged her close. For a large soldier, he was awfully huggy. Maybe it was just because he was so happy. Just thinking about Cy and Vivian had Azar shaking her head. They'd make a good couple, if they didn't get into an argument and battle to the death in the first year.

Vivian was one of the handful of people who knew that Azar had a drop of Tuatha Dé Danann blood in her ancestry. It wasn't a huge secret by any means, but it would put an extra target on her back if it got around. However, not even a whisper of it had made it onto the paranormal grapevine, not even Killian and her family knew. She didn't know why people thought she magically had a new Fae army, but she suspected they thought they were with her for Nevyn. Technically, they weren't wrong.

She asked for directions to the infirmary from a passing Were, who cast a suspicious glance at Cy before reluctantly pointing down one of the many tunnels. She hated being underground, but she was getting used to the crushing weight of the claustrophobia.

Cy walked along next to her, his eyes taking in everything and everyone like the trained soldier he was. He was looking for weak spots and security risks. She wanted to tell him that their only security risk was killed last night protecting her charges, but talking about Becca pressed down under an avalanche of guilt.

They stopped in front of a door with a large red

cross on the front. There was a pane of glass in the top half, and Azar peeked through to see if Donovan was still there. Cy's hair brushed her own as he looked through as well.

Donovan was indeed still there, scowling at the doctor, an ageing Were with hair like a skunk. His back to the door, Donovan had nothing on but a pale blue hospital gown and she could see a brief strip of his naked ass. They were arguing in low voices, and the Doc was waving a pair of tweezers from the sterile pack of dressings.

Azar raised her hand to knock, but stilled when Donovan shouted something at the nurse and dropped his hospital gown to the floor.

She gaped. She took in his long, pale body that was covered from neck to toe in tattoos. Even his ass. A Kraken ran over his hips; Azar could see the tentacles curling around toward his spine. Mostly black ink with shades of grey, there were a few splotches of color running through the tattoos. She stared harder and realized the color splotches were actually a Japanese style dragon that weaved its way through all the other tattoos, down, down, down over his glorious ass until its tail curled around his thigh. Holy hell.

She must have let out a squeak because both

Donovan and the Doc swung towards the door. Her hand flew up to her eyes, but not quite fast enough. Well, that answered a lingering question she had about the extent of his tattoo coverage on the front.

"Tell me when he's dressed," she muttered to a hysterically laughing Cy. He was doubled over and gasping for breath. Eyes still covered, she took a swinging kick at his shin and missed.

"Alright, it's G-rated in there again."

Not quite trusting that Cy wasn't messing with her, she opened one eye just a tad, and was disappointed to see Donovan back in his jeans, sans shirt. She pushed open the door.

Donovan gave her a loaded look, but she'd already decided to pretend she hadn't seen where the dragons head began.

The answer was on his dick. The head of his cock was the head of the dragon that ran over almost his whole body. Cy still had a bad case of the giggles, and Donovan glared.

"I've, er, come to check how you are doing."

The Doc pushed him back onto the hospital bed, and snapped on some gloves. No longer recalcitrant, he scowled and muttered as the older Were peeled off the previous dressing.

It was the Doc who eventually answered her.

"The patient is doing fine. An obstinate fool who refuses to stay in bed so he doesn't tear his stitches, but healing well enough."

Azar got a good look at the angry, red wound and had to agree with the Doc, he needed to stay in bed. If he was a full-blooded Shaitan, he would have healed almost instantly. But like her, he was half-human, and that meant they healed slower in comparison to their full-blooded brethren. They were also far easier to kill; something that sat uneasily on her conscience considering she'd just helped bargain for a small army of Unbound.

Cy was still struggling to maintain his composure, and Donovan was getting irritated.

"What's he doing here anyway? There's enough savage assholes running around in these dens as it is."

The Doc poked his wound with a finger, making him hiss out a breath.

"You should mind your manners while this savage asshole has his finger around your ouchie bits." The nurse holding the tray beside him let out a chuckle, but sucked it back when Donovan gave her his 'death' face. It was a scary expression, like your nightmares had stepped out of your closet and were here to make you scream.

Cy was barely controlling his hysterics now, and was beginning to make a sickly wheezing noise.

"Excuse me," he choked out and bolted for the door. They could still hear his belly laughs from the hall though.

Azar rolled her eyes. "Don't mind him. He's here to watch my back. He heard about the attack yesterday."

Donovan's eyes glittered like shattered black diamonds, and it was a dangerous sign that his rage was about to break loose.

"Calm down or I'll poke you with horse tranqs again," the Doc said, not looking up from where he was bandaging his wounds.

Deciding she was just making it worse, Azar took her leave. She patted Donovan's shoulder. "Stay in bed and rest. We need you fighting fit."

He sneered at her. "Who made you my boss? I don't remember being one of your pets, down on their knees swearing fealty." The mention of Becca was a deliberate one. That was the thing about the Shaitan, they always knew exactly which buttons to press. But Azar had been there too, ready to push everyone away. Luckily for them both, she was a stubborn bitch. She stared down at the wound in his side. So easily it could have been fatal. She could have been burying Donovan today.

"I'm not saying it as your boss, I'm saying it as your friend. I don't want to lose you too," she mumbled, her voice rougher than she wanted it to be.

Donovan reached out, grabbing her chin and lifting her face until his black eyes met hers. His face was softer, and his eyes held guilt that she knew intimately. Tugging her face forward, he pressed his lips to hers.

He kissed her.

Azar was too shocked to pull away. His kiss was tentative, but the longer she maintained the contact, the bolder he got. He kissed her harder, sucking her bottom lip into his mouth and biting it gently.

Following the shock was a wave of fear, but it was artificial. She knew in her bones she had nothing to fear from Donovan. She pushed past the fear to chase the next emotion. She knew what it was. It was lust.

Pure, unadulterated, drop your panties lust. She moaned and kissed him back, pressing her tongue back into his mouth as they fought for dominance of the kiss. She stepped between his knees and he gripped her hips tightly, pressing against his chest and the rapidly hardening, err dragon, between them.

Then she pulled back, gasping for air. *Bast.*

Bast. Bast. Bast. She had to remember that her heart was already taken. Someone else matched her puzzle piece already. The Doc was making himself busy on the other side of the infirmary, giving them some semblance of privacy. Shit.

Donovan was looking at her softly, but she turned and left before he could say anything else. She didn't want to air all their dirty laundry in front of a stranger. She walked down the hall in a daze

She met Cy in the hall. "Got yourself under control?" She asked, pretending her world wasn't just rocked moments ago.

He nodded, but there was still a stupid grin on his face. "I'm good. But speaking of under control, what's going on with you and Donny?" His tone was light, but she froze.

"What do you mean?" She cleared her throat and walked down the hall, pretending she had no idea what he was talking about. Did he see the kiss? She needed to talk to Bast before something happened that she couldn't undo. Or someone other than Cy saw. If Cy saw. Maybe he was just picking up on the sexual tension. Yeah, maybe that was it. If watching cop shows had taught her anything it was deny, deny, deny.

"I have eyes, Sis. And so does everyone else. You need to sort your shit out before it blows up in your face," he said, eerily echoing her own thoughts. Then he grinned. "Me and Vivian don't sound so crazy now, do we?"

Azar couldn't help but laugh. He had a point. They were basically the poster couple for healthy relationships in comparison to the mess that was her love life.

She smiled at her brother, opening her mouth to say something smart-ass back, but instead she just snapped her jaw shut and shook her head.

Lost in her thoughts, she ended up in the main area of the den as if on autopilot. There was a games room off of the common area, and Azar stuck her head in there first to see if she could find Nevyn and Freya. She knew they were fine, but she wanted to see it for herself.

Luckily, they were easy to spot, because Nevyn was levitating Kayla ten feet off the ground. Azar rushed into the room.

"Nevyn!"

His concentration broke, and Kayla plummeted to the ground. Luckily, Cy was there to catch her.

She rounded on the boy. "What are you doing? You could have seriously hurt her!"

Kayla wiggled out of Cy's arms and was over beside Nevyn in seconds. Then they both started talking at once, and Freya joined in, as well as a couple of the other pups. It all ran together in one slightly high pitch cacophony of noise.

"Everyone stop!" She took a deep breath and turned to Nevyn. "No more levitating of people, pups or kitchen chairs, okay?" She turned to Freya and Kayla. "I expect you two to know better. Do not encourage Nevyn to do things that you know your parents would disapprove of, because it won't be you who gets in trouble, it will be him. Do you want to be responsible for Nevyn getting kicked out of the den, hmm?"

They shook their heads solemnly, and all three of them were looking at their bare feet. She felt like the worst person in the world, but it was for their own good.

She sighed heavily. She hated being the bad guy. Parenting was hard. "Alright, off you go. But no more party tricks, okay?" Three nods, and Kayla threw her back a grin. They were off and out of the room, up to gods-knows what mischief. She needed caffeine and a doughnut before she could even contemplate being a grown-up again.

Behind her, Cy slow clapped. "You have maternal guilt-tripping down to a fine art. It's almost like you've been taking lessons from my mother."

Azar rolled her eyes. "I doubt it worked any better on you and your brothers than it did on those three."

They moved off to the kitchen, only to find the last person she wanted to check up on. Oliver was holding court, surrounded by a group of female wolves. A person would be forgiven for believing that there would be no attraction between dogs and cats, but Oliver was the walking, talking incarnation of seduction. Azar was fairly sure he could woo a nun out of her habit. He flirted like he breathed.

But for all his flirty man-whore ways, he wasn't the type of guy who needed the attention to survive. As soon as Azar walked into the kitchen, he grinned in her direction and excused himself politely from his fan club.

He smiled at Cy and then wrapped her in a bone-crushing hug, snuffling her hair a bit. It was a weird little idiosyncrasy that pleased the cat part of him, and made her heart do this weird flip-flop thing in her chest. Even knowing she should pull away, she spent a few seconds longer in his arms, just soaking up the warmth and joy that was Oliver.

Finally, Azar pulled away enough that she could check him over. The cuts on his arms and legs were healing slowly, but Lorcan had said that the Fae swords were steel that was struck through with silver and iron. It made them very efficient weapons against the paranormal.

"I'm fine, Az. Just a few scrapes. How's Donovan?"

She flushed bright red. "He looked fine. I mean, he is fine. Healing, under the Doc's capable hands."

Cy squawked with laughter again. Oliver quirked an eyebrow at them both, but let it go.

He walked over to the coffee pot and poured her and Cy a cup. It was a testament to how strange their life was that he didn't even ask why Cy was here, in a wolf den, a place that no Djinn had been in a century, until Azar and Bast had come out here six months ago.

Azar had been made a friend of the pack after she'd saved Aaron's life, which basically made her a pack member in their eyes, with all the associated benefits and pitfalls. She was the first Djinn in half a millennia to get that privilege, and it had put her in a unique position.

She thought of Danu's prophecy. Danu had always been adamant that Azar was the balance, whatever that meant, and had reiterated it to Jack so persistently that he'd come to New York to find her. When she'd gone treasure hunting the Great Weapons in the Amazon, she'd communed with the Goddess Danu for the first time. She'd seen herself sitting on a throne, a crown in one hand and a puppy in the other, two daggers strapped to her forearms.

She started a little as she realized that the prophecy was coming true. She was a Councilor now, which was kind of like a throne in the Djinn world. She had close ties with Aaron, and therefore the Were, which was the puppy in her hand. She didn't think the Were would have joined forces with the Djinn if Azar hadn't had that relationship with Aaron. Obviously, Nevyn was the golden crown, being the Heir to the Golden Throne, and he'd come with his own army. Azar had no idea what the daggers meant, but she was beginning to put credence in Danu's prophecy. Maybe she was the balance. She'd been dismissive of the concept, but evidence was piling up.

A cold sweat broke out over her skin. The fate of the civilized world couldn't rest on her shoulders. She was already weighed down with the lives that depended on her making good decisions; she couldn't deal with the pressure of the future of humanity too.

"Az, are you okay? You've gone this grey color."

She broke out of her reverie to see Cy and Oliver staring down at her with twin looks of concern. Oliver had his hands out, as if he was prepared to catch her if she should do something as unbadass as faint.

"Sorry, I'm fine. I'm just thinking."

"Did you hear anything I said?" Oliver asked, concern still on his face. He seemed to be struggling with the need to wrap her in his arms again, if the curling of his fingers was anything to go by.

She smiled at him. "No, sorry. I was a million miles away. What were you saying?"

The mug felt hot between her palms, centering her to the here and now.

"I said I had the strangest dream about your Goddess last night."

"Danu? How do you know it was Danu?" As far as she knew, no one but the Tuatha had seen Danu.

"Duh, she said 'I am Danu'. It was such a vivid dream too. She came into my room and talked to me, but her face was so bright, I couldn't see it, and she didn't seem to be talking out loud, but it was more like a whispered white noise, like blood rushing in my ears. She said she admired my loyalty, my strength and that I was so full of life. Then, we uh, you know…"

She laughed. "Only you would have a dirty dream about a goddess, Oliver." The way he'd described her had hit a little too close to the truth for comfort. But she couldn't imagine Danu sneaking into Oliver's bedroom for a little nookie, so it must have been just a simple dream. She'd spent too long with Bast, and had him walk in her dreams.

He flushed bright red, embarrassed. "It was the weirdest dream I've ever had."

"I wouldn't mention this to Jack or the Fae. They probably wouldn't appreciate you debauching their Goddess, even in a dream," Cy laughed.

Oliver looked affronted. "I'll have you know, I've never debauched anyone. We make sweet love, and then I make them breakfast in the morning, if they aren't a figment of my imagination."

She laughed and wrapped an arm around Oliver's waist, pulling him close. "You know I love you, right?"

Both men stopped laughing and stared.

"Not like that," she said quickly, probably too quickly, and flushed. *Liar, liar. Exactly like that,* a little voice taunted in her mind, but she wasn't ready to listen to it yet.

Oliver shook his head. "I knew what you meant." His look said she wasn't fooling him either, but he didn't press her in front of her brother. "It's just that in all the time I've known you, you've never admitted affection for anyone," he said, then quickly added. "I love you too, you know that."

Azar stopped and thought. She told Bast she loved him all the time, but probably not out loud. Other than Cy, she wasn't close enough to her new family to launch into soliloquies of love. When she'd been in hiding, she'd been isolated. She didn't want to love anyone in case she'd had to run from her life again. Being found and forced into her servitude had been a blessing in its own way. There was so much love in her life now that it nudged at every corner of her heart and filled it with life. It filled up the empty parts of her soul with happiness and meaning, and she hadn't even realized it.

"I see. Well, in that case, I'll try and say it more often." She turned to Cy. "I love you too, if that counts for anything. Your support, well, it means a lot to me." Azar smiled at the two men opposite her. "Is it strange that in the middle of a war and with everything else going on, I am the happiest I've ever been?"

Cy hugged her shoulders. "No, finding happiness in the dark times is the most powerful weapon against any foe."

HAVING CHECKED on her little troupe of misfits inside the den, and reassured herself that they were healing well enough, she collected a wrapped bundle of clothes from her room and left the internal cave system. She'd left Oliver to watch Nevyn and Freya, and ensure they didn't get up to too much mischief. Though she wouldn't put it past Oliver to join the mischief rather than stopping it. He was still as playful as a kitten, even at his age.

Cy followed her out into the woods surrounding the mouth of the cave system. "Just out of interest, are you going to follow me everywhere for the remainder of the war?"

Cy just smiled and nodded, and Azar sighed. Being alone was now a distant memory. They needed this over and done with so she could have a little me-time again.

Her Fae, as she thought of them, had set up camp on the edge of the trees. She marveled at their campsite. Apart from a fire, you wouldn't even know they were there. No tents, or even bed rolls. She looked up and realized why.

They slept in the trees, in cocoon-like hammocks, which were made of shifting green, browns and greys that made them hard to see with the naked eye. Lorcan jumped down from the branch he was sitting on, maybe fourteen feet in the air. He landed like a cat on the ground, his landing barely ruffling the undergrowth. It was pretty insane really.

She waved upwards at the rest of the Fae who still sat in the trees. "I still think this is a little crazy. What if you need to pee in the middle of the night? What if you sleepwalk? You'd go splat!"

Lorcan laughed. "It is safer in the trees. No one ever looks up. We are comfortable at great heights. Besides, going 'splat' as you say wouldn't kill us. Hurt a little sure, but we would heal any physical wound quickly. Maybe not the wound to our pride, however."

She eyed the trees, and shook her head. "Each to their own, I guess. Makes me glad that I have wings though."

Lorcan nodded to Cy, and Cy nodded back. Macho greeting completed.

"Where's Jack?"

"Communing with the Goddess." A look of envy passed over Lorcan's face. He adhered to the old faith, which worshipped the Tuatha Dé Danann and Danu herself above all, as the Giver of Life. Having felt the pure bliss that came from being in the presence of the Goddess, the envy was deserved. It was an experience unlike any other.

"We need to talk about what happened yesterday."

Lorcan's jaw firmed into granite. "We failed you."

Azar gaped. "What? No! You all fought admirably. We were outnumbered two to one. The reason everyone isn't dead is due to the efforts of you and your men. You have my sincerest gratitude." She looked up to the Fae who were still in the trees. "All of you. I know a lot of you suffered your own injuries yesterday, and I want you to know that I appreciate and regret every drop of blood you shed in defending the cabin."

Azar bowed low and deep, a courtly gesture that she knew would mean more to them than her words.

They all stood on the branches, perfectly balanced, and bowed low in return.

"You need not bow to us, Goddess, for performing our sacred duty." That was the sticky part of their relationship; their worship didn't sit well with her, but she let it go. They needed something to cling to in this time of uncertainty.

"That's not what I wanted to talk about. I wanted to talk about the guy in the fancy clothes, and to ask Jack about this?" She waved the sword above her head like a flag.

It seemed important to know why he had a sword that couldn't be melted by her flame, and probably find out what the heck it was made from.

Lorcan took a physical step backwards in shock. "Basatine."

There was a whisper of shocked murmurs from the treetops.

She sighed. "Seriously, does every weapon need to be named?"

"It is a revered weapon in our world, thought to be lost."

"There seems to be a lot of that going around these days. Lost weapons suddenly reappearing."

Lorcan held out his hand, and she handed him the weapon. Although Cy tensed behind her, she wasn't worried about Lorcan running her through with the weapon. If the Black Prince had wanted her dead, he could have killed her a thousand times over. He was stronger, faster, and more skilled than she was, and Azar could die from a normal old dagger to the heart as well as any mortal could. She was cursed with her near mortality.

"It was made by the same Fae weaponsmith as your Great Weapons, in a time long past. His name was Brandr, and he was as great a sorcerer as he was a weaponsmith. Each of his weapons were exquisitely made and the very fibers of the metal imbued with magical properties. That is why a single cut from Posidagi would have killed your consort if he hadn't become incorporeal, but you could slice off your hand and it would be like cutting yourself with any other man-made dagger. It is why the Courts are searching for the Great Weapons; they wish to study them in recreate Brandr's method, so as to equip their army with weapons that are made to kill the Djinn. It is magic long lost to the fog of time, and I doubt there are any left who are powerful enough to do it anyway, except perhaps young Nevyn. It was old magic, Goddess given magic, which the Fae have now forsaken." He shook his head at the folly of his fellow Fae. He swung the blade in his hand, making it twirl and slice through the air as if it were an extension of his body.

"But Basatine wasn't purposefully made for fighting against the Djinn. It was forged for an ancient king, and it is capable of killing any creature that walks, flies or slithers on this world and the next. It can cut through Fae glamour, and one side of the blade is dipped in iron, the other in silver. I cannot be broken. It cannot be melted by the flames of the fire demons, or Ifrit, which is why you could wield it in your full form. You have turned its strengths against it. It is a fine weapon for a Goddess." He swung it back and forth in a graceful flow of arcs and jabs, and then handed it back to her, hilt first, the blade resting easily in the flat of his palm.

The hilt fit perfectly in Azar's hand, like it wanted to be there. There was a sentience to the sword, and the thought made her want to drop it into the dirt. Instead, she ignored it and focused on Lorcan.

"It's a pity that I can't swing a sword to save my life. Why couldn't Brandr not have created a magical six shooter?"

There was a laugh from behind me, and Jack came out of the woods.

"The sword will do most of the work. You only have to learn how not to drop it. Because whilst it is a good weapon in the hands of a fire-wielding Djinn, it is also a very efficient weapon against you. Hold your sword, even in the direst of situations. That is the first and most important lesson."

Another Fae soldier dropped from the trees like a monkey, and handed Azar a leather sword sheath. Lorcan smiled and said something to the Fae man in old Gaelic. Not many of the Fae spoke English except Lorcan, and maybe three or four of the others, but they were picking up a few words here and there.

"This sheath straps across your back. It is better for concealing your weapon in these modern times. Just don't cut your throat when drawing it. May I?"

Azar nodded, sliding the sword into the sheath and he began buckling across her body. A leather strap ran under her chest, and a thicker strap ran up between her breasts and over her shoulder, keeping the sheath firmly in place and angled so she could easily reach the hilt of her sword. The weight of the sword was spread across her back, giving her freedom to move.

"Well, it's certainly a fashion statement, but boy does it do great things for my cleavage."

Every set of eyes in the woods went to her boobs, and she cursed her big mouth. Cy let out a groan and rolled his eyes, but Lorcan and the Fae were still appreciating the view.

Jack cleared his throat. "Indeed. But I think we have more urgent matters to tend too than your ample, well defined bust."

She flushed a shade of scarlet, but nodded. "I want to know about the Fae yesterday. Finley, the Rightful King blah blah blah."

Azar knew the guy must have been a real winner when both Jack and Lorcan's faces twisted in disgust.

"Finlay is an abomination. It was Finlay who ordered the death of Nevyn's family. He turned the Seelie Court against them, and they were murdered by some of their closest allies. It is only luck that I recovered Nevyn in time. It was Finlay who whispered blasphemous things in the ears of the Unseelie Court, inciting my own mother to turn against the Goddess. I had to fight men that I grew up with, because of Finlay the Deceiver." Lorcan spat on the ground, his face twisted in malice. Seeing the Black Prince of the Unseelie Fae angry made her glad that he was on their side.

"If we kill Finlay, will the Fae stop with their attempt at world domination?" Cy asked.

Jack shook his head sadly. "It has gone too far. The vast majority of Tuatha Dé Danann are dead, and we are untethered from the Emerald Isle. They are so drunk on their success, I doubt anything or anyone could stop them except at the point of a sword."

"Lucky I have a good sword then." She patted the sheath fondly. It was beginning to feel natural there. "Will you be okay fighting against your family, Lorcan?" She felt selfish that she'd never thought to ask. He'd given her everything, and she'd treated him and his army as a tool rather than living, breathing creatures with feelings.

"You have a sweet nature, Azar of the Ifrit, Child of Danu. But the Unseelie Fae are not like you and your family. We do not maintain close personal ties to our blood relations. We fight from birth for our place on the throne, and then if we gain it, we kill all those who try to take it from us. The fact that I survived childhood as a royal is almost completely due to a faction who wanted me to take the throne when I grew and therefore protected me, than any familial love. My men are my family now, and they stand beside me in this." Lorcan's face was proud as he gestured to the Fae in the trees.

It sounded like a very lonely existence, and Azar's heart ached for all those lonely little Fae children who had never felt love. Maybe that's why the majority of them were narcissistic and sociopathic enough to agree to the genocide of an entire race, and then world domination. They had no concept of love or honor. Except Lorcan. She hoped it wasn't too late for Nevyn.

She wondered if she could hug someone called The Black Prince, but decided against it. Despite her newfound affection, most interactions involving close personal contact still gave her the heebie-jeebies. Probably best just to hope he could see the compassion on her face.

Azar looked up again at the Fae in the trees, sitting up there like Christmas ornaments. She didn't even know most of their names, yet they'd be happy to lay down their lives for her. She believed that the Goddess planned her fate, and she was determined not to let the Goddess, or these Fae, down. But for the life of her, she couldn't see the end game for them. Did they eradicate all the opposing Fae? That was the majority of Fae kind. That would be genocide, then she would be no better than the Fae themselves. She could only hope she survived long enough to think of an end game.

"If it is okay with both of you, I'd like you to come to the War Council tomorrow."

"Really, Azar? Don't you think you should at least

run that by the other Councilors, or at least Killian first?"

She shook her head at Cy. "What's the point of being a Councilor if I can't make any decisions without asking the Olds? Besides, who could argue with the fact that they are an invaluable strategic resource with firsthand knowledge of the enemy?"

CHAPTER 12

*A*s it turns out Lila, Councilor for the Ghul, Major Pain in the Ass, could argue with the logic of bringing the allied Fae with her to a War Council.

"They shouldn't be here. For all we know, they could be spies. Hell, they could be playing double agents. You can't trust a single Fae because they will stab you in the back."

"I give you my word, Mistress, that there is not a single traitor amongst my ranks. We stand with Azar, the Councilor for the Unbound."

"Your word means nothing, Fae," Lila spat. "The fact that you have aligned with that half-blood trash-"

"Now, now Lila, is that any way to speak about

your fellow Councilor? Tsk. Maybe you need a lesson in Council etiquette," Azar sniped back.

Killian rubbed around his temples. "Councilors, please. As Director of the Adel, I agree with the Councilor for the Unbound that the Fae would provide good intelligence. We'll put it to a vote, very democratic like. But if we have to vote on everything, we may as well put the noose around our own necks."

"Of course you would side with your sister, Killian." Lila pouted prettily at him, and his jaw tensed fractionally.

"As the Director of the Adel, I am impartial. When I became Adel voluntarily, I made every race, and no race, my own. That goes for familial relationships. In this role, I am on the side of all Djinn."

"Perhaps we need a new Director? Seeing how your sister and your ex-wife now preside on the Council. Before it was just your father, but now the ruling parties of the Djinn society seem to sway in favor of your family."

The Councilor for the Ifrit, Ezster, scoffed. "So you suggest we get rid of the most experienced, most decorated Director we've had in nearly nine hundred years, in the middle of a war? Tell me again how you got to be Councilor for the Ghul, because it certainly wasn't for your political prowess."

"I think the more pertinent question is who she had to fuck to get the position? Maybe it was every-one?" Azar added.

"ENOUGH!" Killian yelled, and thumped down a fist. "Councilor," he directed to Lila, "if you wish for me to step down as Director, so be it. But we can put that issue to a vote after we win this war. To do so beforehand would be folly." He gave Azar and Ezster a stern look. "If we could please be adults about this? Our people are about to be slaughtered or enslaved, so if you could put your petty feuds on hold, that would be appreciated."

He clenched and unclenched his fists, and his face was perfectly calm once again. "A quick vote. All in favor of the Fae allies staying during the War Council, raise your hand." Everyone except Lila raised their hands. "Good, they stay."

He looked at Jack and Lorcan. "Please tell us everything you believe is pertinent to the allies winning the war. As you have probably gathered, we had no idea that there was a civil war amongst the Fae. The ultimatum and subsequent attack were unexpected. I have talked to my sources in Europe, and they too had no idea."

Lorcan looked at Jack for permission to speak first and Jack nodded. "Go ahead. Speak freely, you know more than I about the civil war, and the genocide."

"I have learned from Azar that the knowledge of Fae culture here in the United States is rather limited, which is understandable as you would have had very little opportunity to interact with us on US soil. We were once tethered to the soil of Europe, through magical means, and we recently realized this tether was kept strong by the Tuatha Dé Danann."

"Tuatha Dé Danann, Fae, what's the goddamn difference?" Lila asked.

With the patience of a saint, Lorcan explained. "The Tuatha Dé Danann are the children of Danu, the Goddess. Jack here and-" Azar gave a subtle shake of her head. She didn't want the Council to know she was part Tuatha if she could help it. Lorcan continued "And a few others, have special abilities. I am sure you know that Jack is the Green Man, the Heart of the World? If Jack dies, the world dies."

"That's a fairytale told to little children," Lila said.

The elderly Marid Councilor, who had been silent up until now, cleared his throat. "It is not a

fairytale I wish to test, wouldn't you agree?"
Everyone nodded, and Jack just smiled enigmati-
cally. He did enigmatic well.

The Marid Councilor waved a hand. "Please,
Prince, continue."

Lorcan gave the man a tight nod. "The Fae got
tired of being the second rung on the totem pole,
as you Americans would say, and decided that
they'd had enough of the old gods, and being
limited to the lands of Europe. They wanted the
world. The two Courts joined forces for the first
time in recent memory. They began systematically
destroying every person within their reach with
even a drop of Tuatha Dé Danann blood in their
veins. And it worked. Slowly we could move
outside the boundaries of Europe, hovering inches
above the surface. But as a side effect, the world
became off kilter; the weather became unpre-
dictable, natural disasters arose, wars broke out
across the human world. The Tuatha did more than
keep us tethered to our homelands. They maintained balance in the world."

This was the first Azar was hearing of this too.
She knew that Jack was intrinsically tied to the
world, but she didn't realize all Tuatha were bound
that way. Maybe even she was? She shook her head,

bringing herself back to the present as Lorcan continued to speak.

"But the Fae have never been known for their love of humans, and they were too selfish to see the effect they were having on the planet. A few of us still adhere to the old ways. The Goddess has given us this world to live on, but she could take it away just as easily. So we fought back. Once we had lost the element of surprise though, we started to get slaughtered. We saved who we could, and we ran. We ran to Jack, the Heart of the World, and he told us to put our faith in Azar of the Ifrit. And we have."

"Why Azar?" Someone asked, perhaps the Shaitan Councilor. She learned his name was Sephtis.

Jack fielded this question. "The Goddess told us so. We do not argue with the divine."

No one who had spent three-seconds in the company of Danu would deny her anything.

"Your Gods are not our Gods," Sephtis replied, but without malice and Jack nodded.

"This I understand, and there is a time and place for the theological debate that all gods are one god and it is just the worship that differs. However, for the sake of expediency, no one here is asking you to blindly follow the words of our Goddess. Please, do whatever you need to do. But Danu has asked us to put our faith in Azar, and that is what we'll do. Our loyalty, as it is, is not to the Djinn, but to her personally. It just so happens that her loyalty is to her race, and that is your boon."

"Along with the loyalty of the Weres and the Unbound. It seems that if Azar Nazemi felt the inclination, she could abandon us all to our fate," Ezster said. She glanced at her quizzically, as if she were trying to read Azar's true intentions by staring into her soul.

"The loyalty that has been given to me is a responsibility I take very seriously. The lives of the Were, the Unbound and the loyalist Fae mean no more and no less to me than the Djinn. Luckily for all, it behooves us to join forces. Now, tell us about the major players. Who is moving the chess pieces from behind the scenes?"

She couldn't help but grin when Aaron leaned close to Tao, and whispered, "Did she just use behooved in a sentence? Who does that?" Tao shrugged, but the corners of his mouth were curling upwards, kind of like a smile.

Lorcan considered the question, as did Jack. "The Royal families have the most power, both politically and magically. They can call men to arms, and to refuse their call is tantamount to treason. The punishment for treason is death. Their power is extensive, although individually, they differ in strengths. For instance, my mother Lustre, Queen of the Unseelie Court, is a master of illusion. She can make you believe that everyone around you is dead, or that you are drowning in snakes. However, she is weak in hand to hand combat and will probably stay off the battlefield, which is fortunate as she needs to see her victim to work the illusion magic. My brothers, the Blood Prince and the Golden Prince of the Unseelie Court, have similar destructive magic."

"Why is your brother called the Golden Prince? I thought the Seelie crown was called the Golden Crown," Killian asked.

Lorcan nodded. "Cian is half Seelie, half Unseelie. Mother liked to dally with the Seelie prisoners. A most unenviable position in our world until now. Luckily, his strength lies in making people love him, even as he is torturing them. It wasn't an ability that had ever been seen in the Unseelie Court, though there were whispers of an ancient king who possessed the ability centuries ago. I always believed that he'd developed the power early to survive being a mixed-blood in the Unseelie Court. Cian is, well, he's different to the rest of the family. No more or less cruel, but a product of his environment. He could have been a good ruler one day, if he wasn't born to the tender mercies of my mother." Regret creased Lorcan's normally ageless face, or maybe it was remorse or hopelessness. He obviously felt guilt regarding this Cian, it was etched across his face. He sucked in a deep breath through his nose.

"Oisrin on the other hand, the Blood Prince, was born evil. He killed a nursemaid when he was just three winters for fun. He can draw every ounce of blood from a person's body through the pores of their skin, until they are just a husk surrounded by a pool of plasma. It is actually quite gruesome to watch."

Huh. Sounds like the evil prince of the Unseelie and Lila the blood licking foot monster would be a match made in heaven. Azar glared across the table. More like a match made in Hell.

Everyone was trying to process the information overload that Lorcan had dropped on their laps. But apparently, he wasn't quite done with the Truth Bombs yet. "These aren't their only abilities; these are just the ones that they excel in. All of the royals, and even some of the nobles, can make minor illusions, open old wounds, sift from place to place, and heal ourselves and others to a certain degree."

Lila stared at Lorcan in a new light. "And what is

your talent for magic, Black Prince of the Unseelie Court?" She sneered out his whole title, as if to remind him that she thought he was scum sucking evil.

Lorcan just smiled. "I can kill people instantly, with a thought. The cells of their bodies start to die, and they fall to the ground." He stared hard at Lila. "Their bodies blacken and bloat with necrosis. It is why I am called the Black Prince, and it is why I am heir to the Unseelie throne."

Lila visibly paled for an instant, but then she was back to her resting-bitch-face.

"No King of the Unseelie?" Azar asked.

Lorcan shook his head, "No. My mother had him assassinated when I was but a boy."

Azar was especially glad that she hadn't grown up in the Unseelie Court. She'd thought the Djinn were bad, but that was like *The Hunger Games* year in, year out.

She already knew that Finlay had killed most of the direct line of royals to the Seelie throne except Nevyn. Finlay was a cousin, on Nevyn's father's side, which was why he became King after the genocide killed the rightful King and Queen of the Seelie court, as well as Nevyn's older brother and sister. After the brutal assassination of the Seelie Royal family, most of the Seelie nobles joined Finlay's cause and helped murder the rest of the Tuatha. No one knew what Finlay's abilities were.

Azar explained all this to the rest of the Councilors, trying to leave Nevyn out of it as much as she could. The Djinn weren't above using a child as a bargaining chip.

By the time they recessed the meeting, they'd gone over every ability, strength and weakness the Fae army had. They were allergic to cold iron, of course, which was why Killian had 'appropriated' an iron works in Jersey to start churning out iron daggers, swords and had someone working out the logistics on iron bullets. Although this might sound simple, the iron had to be cold iron, and therefore not worked to a heat that is high enough for it to lose its magnetism, or so Jack explained. The concept of metalworking made her head hurt, and she was happy to let the Djinn weaponsmiths do their thing.

The Fae also couldn't sift to locations under the surface of the earth, which is why the dens were safe, and most couldn't use their magic without seeing their intended victim. The average Fae soldier had very little magic though, just the ability to sift, and intense weapons and battle training. They were also more agile, faster and ruthless.

Azar's head hurt almost as much as her heart. How could they defeat anyone with such debilitating strengths?

Lorcan and Jack went to sit in Central Park during the recess, to immerse themselves back in nature. Being in the city surrounded by cement and steel was uncomfortable for any Fae. They took the opportunity to sit beneath a magnolia tree, and Azar crossed the park to visit her family and Mira.

When she knocked, she wasn't surprised when Roxx opened it again. He seemed to spend most of his days in the house.

"Azar! It's nice to see you. Come in. Keeley and Yasmin have gone shopping, but the unhappy patient is in the cinema room watching *Die Hard 2* for the seventh time. She'll be glad for the company, I think. Convalescing doesn't come naturally to our Adel soldier."

Roxx went to hop in the elevator, but Azar shook her head. "Let's take the stairs."

Roxx shrugged and they mounted the stairs together. Roxx, while slim, was impossibly athletic. He took the stairs two at a time, and Azar struggled to keep up. He was almost Fae in his litheness.

"So, how's your stay in New York going? Finding things to do?"

Roxx gave her a grin, big and wide showing perfectly straight white teeth. A small diamond glinted in his left incisor. It should have made him like a pimp, but instead it highlighted the devilish glint in his eye.

"It's going well. I've found a few projects to keep me busy."

Azar held up her hand. "Don't tell me. I don't want to be an accomplice after the fact."

Roxx laughed and shrugged. She could only imagine what her old contacts in the NYPD would think.

Thinking about her old life reminded her of her ex-boyfriend Keenan Reilly. Maybe boyfriend was too strong a word. Maybe ex-lover would be a better one. He was a Djinn informant now, but Azar didn't know what had happened to him since the New York Adel compound had fallen. With any luck, they would forget about him and he could finish out his life in peace. Well, hopefully it would be peace if they could defeat the Fae, or else it may be in a new form of subjugation that would make his attachment to the Djinn look like a play date. Azar didn't know what they had planned for the humans of the world, only the Djinn and the Were. But if they wanted to make them their servants and slaves, then it could only be worse for the humans who were even further down the food chain.

Now that she was a Councilor, perhaps she could get him released from his indenture. She made a note to ask Killian about it. He was in control of all the Adel intelligence resources. He'd do it for her. Killian liked her, maybe even loved her in his own brotherly way. Hell, she could order him to do it.

Roxx led them through double doors into the home theatre room.

"Seriously, Hollywood? A1 Jet fuel doesn't just flame up like that unless you are an Ifrit. Idiots." The grumbling voice came from somewhere in the darkness, and Azar recognized Mira's sweet dulcet voice.

"I'll be sure to write them an angry letter about it," Azar drawled, and Mira turned toward the door.

"Azar! How are you going? How's the War Council? What's happening on the outside world? Please convince Keeley that I'm fine and can leave the house before I go insane. I'm not made for bed rest."

Azar envied Mira's presence. Mira was only 5'3, but she was a powerhouse, and therefore seemed much bigger than her diminutive size.

A sly grin passed over the Marid's face. "Or

should I say Councilor? The paranormal world is abuzz with news of the Unbound's step up in the world. Congratulations." There was no snideness in her tone, she seemed to be genuinely happy that the Unbound had gotten their own seat on the Council, and that she was Councilor. Mira was ever the pragmatist, and she had always been fair and just. Azar should have known she would have been fine with everything that had happened.

"Just Azar, please. I need friends more than I need loyal subjects at the moment. How are you feeling?"

"A hundred percent. Actually, better than a hundred percent. I feel hundreds of years younger than I am."

"You don't look a single day over a hundred," Azar said with a smile. "Let me catch you up on everything. I could really use your counsel."

They walked around the halls of her father's old house, which partly belonged to her now, as she told her friend about everything that had happened, about the fight with the Fae, about Becca and moving into the dens.

They talked about the one problem she didn't feel comfortable talking about to anyone else. Bast had been gone since their battle with the Fae at Oliver's cabin. His own self-flagellation driving him away from Azar's side, and off on some 'mission' in South America to gather Adel troops, or something like that. He'd barely stopped to tell her that he was going.

"You must decide if your love is strong enough to survive the possibility that he will never be whole again," Mira said sadly.

She had been Bast's partner in the old days, when he was first in the Adel. They'd continued to be good friends after Bast had bought Coney Island Amusements from Mira's father.

"I love the man with everything in me. But he is pulling away. It's like he's preparing me for his eventual, permanent absence and it scares me, Mira. I can't live without him, which sounds pathetic and desperate, but he's been my rock, my tether after everything I've been through this past year. Without him I feel like I am just floating through problem after problem alone."

Mira patted her back. "Never alone, but you have to understand what this would be doing to his sense of self-worth. He cannot defend you, make love with you, or even console you when you are sad. Bast has always been a pillar of strength, and he has a kind heart even if he hides it most of the time.

This would be killing him as much as it is hurting you."

Azar sighed. She knew that, and had tried to reassure him over and over, but so much of her life had been out of control lately. She'd kind of taken for granted that he knew the depth of her feelings. Maybe she'd been wrong. Could she tell Mira about her other problem? Not that she considered Oliver a problem, or Donovan for that matter. But her feelings for Jack, Oliver and Donovan were definitely problematic. She slid her eyes toward Mira, and as much as she wanted to trust her with this, she couldn't.

"Perhaps we can find a Fae powerful enough to reverse the magic that was imbued in Posidagi? If we can reverse it quickly enough, he might survive," Mira mused.

"I'm not sure I want to risk Bast on a *might*."

They both sighed and walked in silence for a little longer.

"I better get back to the Council. Otherwise Lila will have them all rolling over and bearing their bellies to the Fae."

Mira laughed. "I'd heard Lila had been voted onto the Council. I can't say I understand the wisdom of their choice."

Ha, that was an understatement, but everyone knew Azar's feelings about the Ghul in general, and Lila specifically.

Mira walked her to the door, and they hugged. "I'll talk to Keeley about cutting short your convalescence. You seem fine, and to be honest, we need you."

Mira nodded sadly. "I know."

Azar walked back across the road, to where Jack and Lorcan were still sitting cross-legged in the park. They looked so very *other*. Jack earned his name as the Green Man, as he was actually physically green. Well, his skin was the pale color of moonlight, but it was kissed with green, like frost on green grass. His hair was a messy brown, sticking up in tufts. But his eyes were closed, and it was his eyes that marked him as something alien. They were large in his face, a moss green color, but the irises were huge, so no whites showed in their depths, like the eyes of an animal.

Lorcan's were the same, it was a Fae trait, but the rest of Lorcan looked physically human. Long, lean body, and a face that women found attractive, if the fan club he'd acquired at the dens was any indication. He was a little too feminine for her tastes. His eyes were a strange swirled blue and purple, like the galaxy through a telescope.

He was beautifully inhuman though, like a predator, and there was a part of the human flight or fight response that recognized that he was dangerous. Although in true New Yorker style no one batted an eyelid at their appearance, but they did take a wide berth around the pair. They both wore sunglasses when they were in public, so as to not alarm the humans, but it was like a Groucho Marx disguise. You still knew they were something else.

Azar didn't want to interrupt, so she sat down on the ground opposite them cross-legged, and closed her eyes too. She felt instantly calmer surrounded by nature. She wracked her memory to try and remember if being in touch with the earth had always made her feel this good, or if it was just since Jack had sat her in that Faery circle in the Amazon and showed her how to commune with Danu.

She sat with her palms on the grass on either side of her thighs and just let herself feel the energy that ran through all things. The energy created by people walking across the dirt, or throwing a football and the dog running to catch a Frisbee multiplied and ran through her hands. Even the grass, growing ever so slowly beneath her hands, sent a buzz through her palms. Life hummed in every square inch of Central Park, and it all flowed along its surface and into her body. All the pressure of life, the tenseness in her shoulders, and the weight of the world, left her for a moment.

Her body became a conduit for the sound of birds, the laughter of children playing, the music of the wind flowing through the leaves on the magnolia tree above her. It was too beautiful in that moment, and she thought she might break apart.

She felt someone watching her and her eyes snapped open. Jack and Lorcan were staring at down at her.

"Sorry. I was just resting."

Jack smiled. "Yes, for the last thirty-five minutes."

Azar's eyes shot to her watch. "Shit, shit, shit! I'm going to be late."

Lorcan smiled. "Hold my hand. I'll sift us there. Jack?"

Jack shook his head. "It is okay, Lorcan. Check in with your men. I will take Azar back to the War Council, even if I am pushing the boundaries of my interference limitations."

Lorcan laughed, a full, open sound that seemed to boom around her. "You gave her Basatine. I think you are jumping up and down on that boundary, my friend."

Jack laughed, and touched Azar's arm. He was always touching her softly, and with anyone else, such constant touching would freak her out. But with Jack, it felt natural, like her body needed the contact like it needed to draw breath.

He pulled her gently into his arms, wrapping his hand around her waist. She stepped another fraction closer, so her body was cradled in his, and gave in to the urge to rest her head on his chest. Why did being with Jack have to feel so right? Why did her love life have to continue to be so confusing? Jack's hands skimmed up her back until they sat on either side of her spine.

"Safe journey," Jack whispered, his face so close to hers that she could feel the small puffs of his breath on her cheeks. "Remember to brace at the knees."

"What?" Azar's confusion was short lived as she was hurtled through space, across town.

They landed in the alley behind the conference rooms that was doubling as the Djinn meeting space.

Azar nearly collapsed, but Jack's arm around her waist was bracing her tightly against his body.

She looked up into his large moss hued eyes,

and felt too warm. Her lips parted of their own accord, and his gaze slid down her face. He wanted to kiss her, she could feel it in her blood. He wanted to find a sun-dappled patch of grass, somewhere in the wild where silence and nature reigned, and lay her down and make love to her until she promised she'd be with him forever. But he never said those words, and she couldn't explain how she knew that's what he wanted. Did they have some kind of weird *Vulcan* mind meld thing going on? Because deep down, in a place that wasn't governed by what was right and wrong, that didn't give a flying fuck what society thought, that part wanted him too.

It was just the connection of the Tuatha. That was it.

Sure it is. I wonder if all these men would want you so much if they knew you were so delusional. The mean little voice inside her mind was back. The voice of reason.

Azar let out a cough, and stepped back. "Holy shit that was disorientating. I think I'm going to throw up."

"It is always strange the first time. You will adapt to it. It is proof of your Tuatha Dé Danann heritage though. If you had been anything else, your particles would have spread and you'd have disintegrated within minutes."

"Seriously? You didn't think to tell me that before we went half way across town?"

Jack shrugged. "I was quite sure you were Tuatha." He hesitated, a doubt creeping into his expression that she'd never seen before. It was odd expression on his normally confident face. "Azar, if I may, could I hold you for a little longer? I find myself more starved for touch than I originally anticipated. I did not realize how much I'd missed it, until I had the opportunity to hold you a little closer."

Azar hesitated. She didn't want to say no, even though she knew she should. She already had two giant problems, without giving into this...compulsion she had around Jack.

Fuck it. How much more trouble could she be in really? If Bast was going to be mad at her, cuddling with Jack was going to be way down the list. But still, she couldn't help but glance around guiltily, even though Bast was incorporeal, and she was not really doing anything wrong. When she was sure the alley was empty, she stepped back into Jack's arms and gave into the urge to lie her head on his chest. She listened to a heart that had beat for more years than she could comprehend, who had been filled with love and broken in two more times than was probably survivable by anyone other than Jack. A heart that was literally indestructible. He wrapped his arms around her, and hugged her tight to his chest, his fingers threaded into her hair, cupping her scalp. She let the feeling of peace wash over her in a wave. Let herself enjoy this one moment of calm.

"You know, Oliver said that Were women usually have many partners."

Jack made a deep, rumbling sound. "Indeed. Polyamorous relationships are found in many places in nature. There is nothing strange or wrong in the concept."

Did that mean he was okay with the idea? Would he want to be part of a polyamorous relationship? She was too chicken to ask. Instead, she wrapped her arms around his waist and just enjoyed the moment.

Because she was starved for touch too. They stood there silently, just letting life pass them by, even though she was late for the meeting, and that she had more guy trouble than any one woman had any right to have.

Finally, she took a fortifying breath and stepped away. "We should go, we're late."

He looked at her then, staring deep into her soul

in a way that felt heavier than it had a moment before.

"Yes."

She felt like he was saying yes to something greater than returning to a room full of stuffy politicians. But she didn't let herself hope.

CHAPTER 13

*A*zar watched the last van load of Were mothers and children drive away from the dens with a feeling of relief and trepidation.

The Council, on the advice of Lorcan, decided that they would move their entire army into a defensible position, and wait until the Fae attacked. Separated, the different races were easy pickings for the much larger fae army, who could sift in, kill them off, and then sift out again without breaking a sweat.

However, if everyone came together as one Allied army, the Fae would have to sift in much larger, more noticeable numbers. They would lose their element of surprise, allowing the Allied army to defend. At least, that was the gist of the reasoning. Azar was no military strategist.

The dens were put forward, as the army could be housed underground, preventing sifting. Aaron had been hesitant at first, but eventually agreed on the proviso that all the women and children be moved to a safer, secure location.

It had taken three whole days to arrange the evacuation. The army would move in this afternoon. Then all that was left to do was train and wait. Every day the Fae didn't attack frayed her nerves a little more.

She looked down at Nevyn, who stood at her side. They'd decided that sending Nevyn with the Were was too dangerous, for both him and the Were. So he'd stayed. Freya insisted that if Nevyn got to stay, so did she. Donovan had cajoled, threatened, used his parent voice, but the girl had stood fast. She would only go where Nevyn went.

Being grownups, no one had given in to the demands of the child, and they'd stuffed her in the first of the vans to leave. Azar had waved goodbye and watched Freya's face pressed against the glass of the window as it drove away down the dirt track with relief and sadness.

It was short lived. Twenty minutes later, a distressed Were woman, whose name Azar had already forgotten, called and said Freya had jumped out of the window at a T-intersection and ran like the wind back toward the dens. Azar had sent Oliver out to find her, and he'd brought her back looking fearful, but with a stubborn set to her chin. So they'd let her stay.

Donovan had looked just as relieved, although he gave the girl the scolding of her life. The scolding of a Shaitan parent was something to behold, but Freya had just looked at him with her big, black eyes, framed with those long, sooty lashes, so like her father's, and he'd relented. So, they'd been given strict rules and placed in the safest den room in the place.

Lorcan had volunteered to teach Freya how to wield a knife, for the direst of circumstances, and Donovan had begrudgingly agreed. Even Azar had been horrified by the fact that this was a practicality of war.

Nevyn was already well versed in the dagger and the sword. They'd given him a light short sword, and he'd gone through a set of exercises with the grace and fluidity of all the Fae.

He still had the short sword in a sheath that was belted around his waist.

"Nevyn, do you know what your magical super-power is?" Azar had thought about asking Lorcan if he knew, but it seemed wrong somehow. The boy was far older than his cherubic face appeared.

"I can sense other Tuatha Dé Danann and Faery circles from great distances." He looked up at her with eyes the color of storm clouds.

She nodded. "I meant your Fae abilities. The ones you inherited from the Fae side of your family."

Nevyn shrugged. "It isn't a very good one in battle. I can see into a person's soul and know their hearts. Mother told me it was an ability that hadn't ever been seen before."

Azar wouldn't have been more shocked if he said he sprouted six heads and did the hula.

"Really?" she squeaked out. She suddenly felt very exposed. He gave her a reassuring pat on the arm.

"It's okay, Az. Your soul shines golden. Your heart though, it is hurting. I'm sorry."

She ruffled the boy's hair and held back tears. "Thanks, buddy. You'd tell me if there was anyone you were worried about, right?

Nevyn nodded. "No one is pure of heart and soul. Except Jack, but he doesn't really count. But I hardly see anyone with a black heart and soul. Sometimes one or the other, like Mr. Donovan. His soul isn't black, but it's dull, like someone smeared mud all over it. But his heart is pure, and that is good enough for me. Freya has a beautiful heart and soul, but they aren't pure either. Close enough, though."

The fact that Nevyn could judge people on such an intimate basis had to be hard for the child. Because heaven knows, there were some black hearted people in the world whose soul she'd never want to see.

They walked back towards the entrance of the den. "It mightn't be the best magic for battle, but it will make you a fine and fair King one day."

He just nodded sagely and walked in ahead of her. "I'm going to find Freya and teach her to fight." With that, he was gone down into the multitude of tunnels.

She walked down further into the network of caves looking for Bast. He'd returned this morning from his trip to South America, and had brought the majority of the South American Adel garrison with him. They'd put the vulnerable Djinn into hiding also, as had the Unbound. Those with little combat or battle experience, those too young or too old to fight, all went into undisclosed locations. Vincent and Mavis went with the Unbound, and the Council members had been dispersed back to their own countries. As far as the Fae were concerned, everyone had gone deep underground in a way that only species that had spent their entire lives in hiding could.

Speaking of hiding, she finally found Bast in their room. She was drawn to him like a magnet, and it pulled her down the hall towards the small room they would share. Their relationship was rocky, to say the least, and she needed to clear the air. She wanted to show him that he was the love of her life, no matter his form. No matter who else held a little piece of her heart.

She walked into her room, and shut and locked the door. She knew he was there, but kept quiet. Instead, she slowly started to strip off her clothes, walking around the room as if she were there by herself. She felt a breeze slide lightly against her ass, and a smile tilted her lips. She jumped into the shower, feeling his eyes the entire time she soaped her body, spending extra time on her breasts.

Stepping out of the shower, she ignored the towel hanging on the railing and just walked back into the bedroom.

I know you know I'm here, Jaanaman.

"Oh, Bast, when did you get here? I was just about to change into my workout gear." She bent over her duffle bag, waving her ass provocatively, and was rewarded by a low growl. A soft whisper of a touch ran down her spine, and she bit her lip.

You are a terrible liar, Azar. But I forgive you. Actually, if you stay in that position, I will forgive you almost anything. Bast let out another low groan. *Wait until you close your eyes tonight, because I will make love to you until you beg, little tease.*

Azar pouted. "I don't want to wait until tonight. I want you to make love to me now."

There was silence, and Azar could picture his face, perfectly neutral as he pondered the idea. While he was thinking about it, she wandered over to the bed, her hips swaying provocatively. She laid down on the bed, trying to look bored, but probably failing miserably. She arched her back as if she were stretching, pushing her bare breasts into the air.

There was a whispered oath in the air, and her body felt like it was blanketed by warmth, the pressure across her body deliciously dense. She closed her eyes and imagined her lover there with her. It was easy to do, as he whispered odes to her beauty in the old tongue.

Small puffs of air littered her still damp skin, up over the curve of her breasts and then on each of her wet nipples. They peaked eagerly, and the swirls of air traced the circle of her aureolas. The flow of air moved lower, dipping into her navel before continuing lower. The pressure increased as it reached lower, and it was firm when it passed over her clit, making her writhe on the bed. The pressure drew away, and she gave a small mewling noise. It returned again, but with even more pressure, rolling in small circles until she was panting.

It drew away again, and then it was inside her, thick and full as if it was Bast himself.

"Yes," she whispered as Bast began to move, and then there were a million small points of air all over her, sucking at her skin like tiny mouths, over both her nipples and her clit, as the fierce pressure drove in and out of her body, thick and fast. She lost herself in the sensation, the absolute otherworldliness of it all and soon she was panting his name over and over as her climax whispered at the edges of her body.

"Please, Bast, please!"

He answered her pleas by creating a hard, sucking sensation on both her nipples and then driving himself home with such force that he rocked her across the bed, over and over until she screamed his name, the pleasure rushing over her body and wetness flooding down her thighs.

She just lay there in the room, panting, Bast's presence pressed along her like a second skin.

"That was intense," she puffed out through a throat that was croaking from her screams. "Lucky these walls are solid rock."

You are clever beyond measure.

"I'm sure I have no idea what you are implying." She smiled at the ceiling.

I love you so much, it pains me not to be able to touch you for real. But this, to know I can make your body sing without having one of my own, it makes me very happy.

She smiled lovingly, feeling his gaze on her face. "I love you too, Bast. You. Not your body, or your face. I love your heart and soul. They are all that matter to me in the end. What I can't stand is when you distance yourself from me. You have to promise me you won't do it again."

I am always with you, he whispered.

"Wow, this conversation is beginning to sound like a Disney movie with the talking animals," she laughed, rolling onto her stomach. She had time for a quick nap, right?

I don't know what kind of Disney movies you've been watching, but what we just did has never happened between the two talking cats in any Disney film I've ever seen.

Her chuckle bounced off the walls as she closed her eyes and drifted into her Oasis, where she could lie in the arms of the man she loved for just a little while.

She couldn't rest, though. She needed to ask him something. It felt important, but she'd only just got him back and she was terrified. Terrified she'd lose him, and if not him, something else beautiful and special.

"Bast?"

He looked down at her, and she was glad she was doing this here where she could see his face.

"Yes, *Jaanaman?*" He snuggled his face into the crook of her neck.

God, how did she even phrase this? How could she tell him what she wanted without destroying everything they already had?

Sensing the tenseness in her body, he sat up on his elbows until he was looking down at her, two little frown lines etched between his eyes. "What is it, Little Flame?"

Azar smiled at his old nickname for her, but it only made this next part harder.

"Oliver kissed me. When we were sober, I mean."

Silence.

"And Donovan. And Jack wanted to kiss me, has wanted to kiss me for a while now."

More silence. Her heart began to hammer in her chest as panic at his lack of reaction. She'd started now, so she had to finish. "And I wanted them to kiss me, and it is so fucked up because I love you. You own my soul, but they own a little piece of me too, somewhere deep down and I can't shake it. I've tried to ignore it, but I can't. It's shit timing, and a shit thing to do to you, but you have to understand, it has nothing to do with your problem," she winced. "Our problem," she corrected, but it was too late.

Bast sat up, and she wanted to drag him back down into her arms. "What are you saying, Azar?" His use of her name hurt her. "Do you want to be with them?"

She shook her head, but even that was not right. "I want to be with you. And with them. I don't want to choose. You each give me something I need, and I don't want to fight against it."

He stood and started pacing, but he didn't say anything. His silence was becoming unbearable. "Oliver said that the Were have polyamorous groups. That there's enough love to go around."

Bast whirled toward her. "Did he?" He raised an

eyebrow, but the rest of his face was the neutral Jann mask that drove her so crazy.

Azar gritted her teeth "He respects you, Bast. He's a friend. But he loves me too."

Bast's shoulders hunched as he deflated. "And do you love him?"

"Yes," she breathed. There was no doubt in her mind. Not like with Jack and Donovan. She knew she loved Oliver unconditionally, as he loved her.

Bast flopped down on the sand beside her, and her heart threatened to beat out of her chest. What she was asking of him was selfish. If he'd asked the same of her, she would have been throwing fireballs at his head.

But in the next moment, Bast proved he was a better person than she could ever be. "I knew I should have made him a cat skin rug when I had the chance. It was inevitably going to come down to this. Any person with eyes can see it when you are in a room together."

She held her breath, just waiting. "Oh?" He stared, appraising her with an intensity that made her quake. "You know that it doesn't mean I love you any less, right? I love you so much that when you weren't with me it is a physical ache in my soul. I have enough love for you all. I swear this to you," she babbled.

She sounded desperate, but she didn't care. This was important. They could all die tomorrow, but she needed this small window of happiness.

"I know, *Jaanaman*. For you, I would do almost anything, even share the one person I love beyond all others."

"Barry Mannilow?"

He smiled at her, and she felt the pressure in her chest ease. "Barry Mannilow, and you. Tell that Cat that if he breaks your heart, I will break his face. That goes for the others too." He laid down and pulled her into his arms. "Now come here and let me have this final moment where I can have you all to myself."

CHAPTER 14

As much as she had wanted to, she hadn't had time to tell Oliver or Donovan about Bast's tentative agreement to their little proposal. The place had been a mad house from the moment she'd stepped from her room.

There was an uneasy tension within the dens. The different armies had begun to arrive. The Adel from different regions, the Unbound, and the Weres who wanted to join the cause had begun pouring in, and each one needed to be interviewed, and given a thorough security check. They'd learned their lesson with Becca.

But with so many distrusting people in one area, it was like a powder keg waiting to explode. The full-blooded Djinn had years of prejudice to work against, and snide remarks could sometimes be heard in the halls, towards the Unbound, or a Were or sometimes even one of Lorcan's Fae.

She and Aaron had broken up so many fights in the last twenty-four hours that if it kept up she wouldn't have any energy left to fight a war. When Killian had arrived a few hours earlier, it had helped to keep the Djinn in line.

With the arrival of the other Adel, Cy's lady love Vivian had arrived, and Azar hadn't glimpsed her brother since. She couldn't blame him. Absence makes the heart grow fonder, or the balls grow bluer. She knew where they had been for the last day, at least.

With so many soldiers in one place, there was machismo enough to spare. That definitely included the man in charge of leading the Unbound troops. Ethan was much older than he looked, which was about twenty-one, but he was apparently in his late seventies. Definitely a half-blood then. Azar had no idea what race.

The guy had strode in with his troop, about thirty men all in all, and shook hands with Azar first, and then Killian.

"Councilor," his voice was low and effortlessly sensual, at direct odds with his stern face. "I'm

Ethan, the elected Captain of the Unbound troops. At your service."

He was about her height, maybe a half an inch or so taller than her six feet and his body was clad in black cargo pants and a tight black shirt. If there was an ounce of fat on his body, Azar didn't know where it was hiding. He had black hair, dark chocolate brown eyes and caramel colored skin. Maybe Latino? He stood at attention when he spoke to her, so definitely military on the outside.

"Thanks for coming."

He was looking at her respectfully, but every now and then she caught his eyes wandering over her body. He was hot, there was no doubt about it, but she had enough trouble already. Why was she getting a weird sense of déjà vu at the thought?

"We have something worth fighting for. More will join our forces throughout the day," Ethan said, his tone returning to strict formality. With that, he gave her a respectful nod and started shouting orders at the troops he'd brought. They were all military from what she could see, and Azar again wondered about what they did in mainstream human society.

An Adel soldier made a snide comment that Ethan and his troops ignored. Killian growled something at the offending Adel, and the man had the good grace to look guilty.

Azar walked with Killian toward the meeting rooms, which had been set up as a War Room. "I thought that a common enemy would bring them all together, but all they seem to be doing is fighting amongst each other like school children," she sighed.

Killian shrugged. "They will come together after the first battle. Blood has a way of solidifying an alliance."

"If they don't kill each other first," she grumbled. They might just do the Fae's job for them at this rate.

Halfway down the tunnel, she began to feel a little claustrophobic. "I'm just going to head outdoors. Being in the tunnels all the time is making me feel a bit off."

Killian nodded knowingly, continuing down the hall with a small finger wave. She backtracked through the tunnels and out one of the side entrances.

When she stepped into the sun, she sucked down a large gulp of air. The walls no longer pressing in on her, and she felt like skipping across the meadow.

They'd set up a practice ring in the center of the field, and a group of Were trained against Lorcan's Fae. Most in wolf form, they were outclassed one on one. But if there were two wolves against one Fae, their odds were better. Eventually the Fae still overcame them, but it was a closer fight.

There was a large crowd around the training soldiers, some watching intently, others laughing and joking with their comrades. She saw Nevyn and Freya sitting side by side on a log, watching the fighting, and Freya had half a dozen small knives in her hand. Throwing daggers.

Freya bit her lip between her teeth as she lined up what appeared to be a pillowcase stuffed with gods-knows-what. There was a bullseye painted on the middle of it, and she pulled back her arm with fierce concentration before letting the small dagger fly. It landed dead in the center of the bullseye.

She wandered over, clapping.

"Well done! That was a great shot"

Freya flushed, the pale skin over her cheekbones turning pink. "Thanks, Az. Enya gave them to me, and Nevyn taught me to throw them."

Nevyn grinned. "I am not as good at throwing the daggers as Freya. I am better with the sword."

"Who's Enya?"

Nevyn gave her a disapproving look. "My tutors told me that a good leader strives to know the name of every person in their court. Enya is one of the Black Prince's guard."

It was Azar's turn to flush red. "Sorry, but in my defense, I have met hundreds of people today alone. Names were never my thing. Is she the one with the curly red hair?"

There weren't so many female Fae in Lorcan's guard, and they all dressed the same; men, women and Princes.

Nevyn gave her a knowing look and Azar sighed. "I'll make more of an effort, okay?"

He smiled, throwing a dagger toward the target. It swung too far to the left and landed on the very edge of the pillowcase. He sighed with disappointment, and Freya threw another one, so it landed snug against his. The pillow burst open and a shower of leaves, feathers and dried grass flew out.

They smiled at each other, then they began to laugh hysterically until they fell off the log and onto the ground. Azar gently pried the daggers out of Freya's hand as she curled in a ball of giggles. She laid the daggers far enough away that they weren't likely to stab themselves accidentally.

She left them rolling around in the dirt, gasping for breath, just being children, and she couldn't help but smile at their childish giggles. She walked over to Lorcan, who was standing on the edge of the ring, watching his soldiers train.

"Care to spar?"

"I'm not sure that would be appropriate, Goddess. I would not wish to injure you accidentally."

"Pfft, maybe I'll injure you accidentally. Besides, I need to practice fighting with my super special sword."

"Basatine," he corrected.

"Sure, Basatine. Because I can promise you, my sword experience is next to zero. Give me a gun and I could probably shoot you seventy percent of the time. But with a sword, I'm just as likely to chop off my own leg as stab my opponent."

Lorcan considered her statement. "Basatine is not like a normal sword. It has been blooded. It remembers how it has been wielded in the past. Just hold on and it will do the work. But you are right, it would be pertinent to teach you the basics of the sword."

Fighting stopped as they strode into the ring, and everyone moved off to the sides. Azar didn't know if she wanted everyone to watch as she got her ass handed to her. She drew Basatine out of the back holster.

"You should be in your other form. It will be the form you'll most likely be fighting in, and you should try and find your balance there."

She looked down at her workout gear. It was the only one set she had with her. If she left them on, they would turn to ash in seconds. She was among a group of people where public nudity was a natural part of life, especially the Weres and the other Djinn.

She sucked in a breath and removed her clothes. She held Lorcan's eyes, daring him to look down. He held her gaze chivalrously. There were mere seconds between standing in her underwear in the field, and being completely encased in flames, but it felt like the longest three-seconds of her life.

In Ifrit form, she was a sight to behold. Unlike a full-blooded Ifrit, whose whole body morphed into the very visage of a demon, she maintained her human shape. Well, except for the large batwings that unfurled from her back. Her hair stood on end, each strand an individual flame, floating upwards like a candle. Flame rippled over her skin like a fiery cloak.

Now the sword in her hand was ignited too, blue flame traveling over the hilt and up to the very tip.

She stood with her legs braced wide, the sword resting in her hands like it was an extension of her arm. Lorcan drew his own sword, a huge claymore looking thing that was decorated up the sides with etchings of crows.

"Pretty sword," Azar commented, and Lorcan bowed low.

"Thank you. It was my father's. Are you ready? We will just spar for a little while so I can judge your level of skill. Some of my men said you acquitted yourself well against Finlay, though he is no great swordsman."

"Sounds fine. Do I say ready, set, go?"

Lorcan just laughed, stepping forward and taking a halfhearted jab at her stomach. She danced backwards, away from the sharp tip. "Are you sure you should use your fancy sword. I wouldn't want it to melt."

"This is the twin to yours. Brandr created one for each of the Kings of the Fae. It will survive."

He swung again, and the sword came up to block it naturally. He dropped his shoulder, bringing the sword under Azar's guard and up toward her left thigh, and she dropped her sword again to block it, the clanging of metal reverberating around the open space.

She danced backwards out of his reach, tempted to just use her wings and fly up into the air. But she was here to learn, so she stepped forward, ensuring her weight was balanced on her back foot, and swung.

The sword took off by itself, slicing at Lorcan's torso, before swinging up and around at his head, making him dance backwards on the defensive. Glancing off Lorcan's blocking blade, she swung back down toward his left-hand side, aiming for his ribs. The sword moved, position after position, until their speed was so quick that the crashing of metal swords, hers alight with blue flame, was as quick as Azar's racing heartbeat. She didn't overthink her steps, just let the sword and her instincts direct her.

But still, their speed increased until they were a blur of movement, and her muscles were aching.

"Stop!" Azar panted.

Lorcan's sword halted mid blow, and as soon as his sword lowered to his side, Azar's flame went out and she collapsed down on the ground in a heap, panting for breath.

Her blood thundered in her ears, and when Lorcan offered her a hand up, she thought about refusing. She seriously contemplated just lying in the middle of the field, naked and having a heart attack.

The thundering in her ears decreased, and she finally heard the sound of applause. That was what made her get to her feet. She was lying naked, face down in the dirt, in front of at least a hundred people. Lorcan pulled off his tunic and offered it to her, and she was satisfied to see that his own perfect body was glistening with sweat.

She jumped to her feet, pulling the tunic on mid motion. It hung down to mid-thigh, but it was conservative enough. She pulled on her yoga pants as well.

She shook Lorcan's hand. "Thanks."

He shook his head. "My pleasure. I have not had a sparring partner of such skill in a long time. With Basatine in your hands, you need no further training. Listen to your weapon and your instincts, and you'll be victorious in all your battles."

She picked up Basatine's sheath, and slid the weapon away. She'd oil it later.

"Let's just hope that it stays in my hands. In the hands of the enemy, Basatine could be quite the adversary. Now, I am going to go have a shower and collapse somewhere. Thanks for the tunic. I'll have it laundered and returned."

He waved away her thanks. "Whatever I can give is yours for as long as you need it, Goddess."

"Just Azar, remember?" She didn't want paranormal ears picking up her little secret.

Lorcan bowed his head. "Of course, Azar."

She limped her way back towards the mouth of the den, through cheers and exclamations. She needed a bath, or a massage, or an entirely new body.

Oliver met her a few feet from the door into the cave system that housed the dens.

"I gotta say, that was quite the exhibition, Az."

She only had to take one look at his stupid big grin to realize he wasn't talking about her sword skills.

"I hope you took a mental picture, because you're never gonna see that again."

He laughed. "We'll see. But seriously, I didn't realize you had such swordsmanship."

"Me neither."

Hobbling downhill on aching thigh muscles was like torture.

Oliver wrapped an arm around her shoulders. "Want me to give you a piggyback ride back to your room?"

Azar almost collapsed with relief. "Please." She strapped on her sword sheath, fitting it snugly across her back.

She wrapped her arms around his neck and he hoisted her onto his back, holding her thighs.

"Mush, mush!" She pointed down the hallway.

"I am not a husky!"

She laid her head against his. "I love you, you know that right?" The words came naturally with Oliver. They fit like they were always meant to be together, without the angst and the what-ifs. They just felt right.

She was desperate to tell him that Bast had said okay. She wanted to push him against the wall and kiss him so that the whole world would know. But there was a time and a place for that discussion and in the halls dressed in another man's tunic was neither the time nor the place.

He squeezed her thigh. "I love you, too. But you better hold on."

With that little warning, he ran full speed down the hallways, dodging people and shouts, bumping off walls and archways, until Azar was laughing so hard she could barely hold on.

They got back to her room, and he dumped her on her bed, flopping down next to her. She couldn't feel Bast in the room, so she assumed he was with Killian in the War Room. He was taking over reconnaissance and scout duty with the Werebirds.

"I think I'm more bruised after your piggyback ride than I was after my sword fight," she grumbled half-heartedly. Oliver was staring up at the ceiling, a goofy grin on his face. "Don't let me keep you from your adoring fans."

He gave her a quizzical look, as if he didn't actually know that the female Weres were constantly throwing themselves at him.

"You know, the posse of female Weres that follow you around? I'm pretty sure I can hear them loitering outside my door now, cursing me with every form of venereal disease known to man because you are in here with me, on my bed. Little do they know, right?" She wanted to test him, because she wasn't sure he wasn't out of his mind. What kind of man wanted to share a woman with three other dudes?

Oliver just laughed. "Nah, Az. I don't sleep with the Were girls. Now, a fiery Ifrit with a body made for sin, well, that's a different story."

"Is that right, Cable? Met many sinful bodied Ifrit lately?" she asked, raising her eyebrows.

"What did I say would happen if you called me Cable?"

Her eyes hooded. He'd promised to spank her if she called him Cable. She didn't think that was much of a deterrent.

"Why no Were girls? Not that I'm harping you on

or anything, but some of those women are attractive, and it's unlike you to turn down a beautiful woman."

If he was breathing, he was flirting. It was just in his nature. She knew deep down that it didn't mean anything. He flirted with Dotty. Hell, sometimes he flirted with Donovan, and they were both straight. It was just his general demeanor. He was sensual and playful, and he loved to make people blush. She understood that.

"Well, I can't help it. My self-esteem has been crushed because you refuse to be mine."

This was it, the moment to tell him, but there was just one more thing she had to know. "Seriously, why no Were women?" This time, she wasn't teasing either. It wasn't a test, but it seemed important somehow.

His face turned serious, more serious than Azar had ever seen it.

"I feel like it would be disrespectful to my mate."

"Your what? Mate! What the hell?" Holy shit. She tried not to jump to conclusions, but growled out, "You better start talking, Casanova."

He screwed up his face. "I promise I'm not messing around on the little woman at home or anything like that. Do I have to?" Azar nodded and he sighed. "Fine, I'll tell you, but you owe me two hundred strokes of my fur with that soft boar bristle brush you have."

"That brush cost me seventy bucks!"

He shook his head resolutely, and she relented. "Fine. Two hundred strokes."

He still looked a little reluctant, staring at the ceiling. "It's you, Az. You're my mate. It's always been you. My Jaguar knew it from the moment I stepped into your apartment and scented you. Then you punched Reilly in the face, and the human side of me wanted you bad too," he smiled at the memory. "I thought it was just lust, because let's face it, you are so fucking hot it hurts. The Jaguar knew it was more, I was slightly slower to catch up. When I couldn't get ahold of you after the compound collapsed though, I realized what I felt for you was more than an epic case of blue balls."

She gaped, her body tensing where it rested against his. Oliver buried his face in her hair, and she could feel his heart pounding in his chest. "Don't stress. I understand you're with Bast, and I would never purposefully mess that up for you."

"I told Bast about your proposition." Now it was his turn to tense.

"And?" His voice gave nothing away, though he couldn't mask his body's reactions.

As an answer, she leaned up and caught his lips with hers. He bundled her closer in his arms, and kissed her back. His heart thundered under her chest with hope. She let her fingers roam up into his hair, and her tongue teased his. He kissed like he lived; playfully and with so much passion it threatened to overwhelm her. His hands slid down her back to her ass, and he pulled her back on top of his chest, and she could feel the hard length of his cock against her thighs.

"Az," he whispered against her lips. "Damn, I didn't want to hope. I know how much you love Bast, and how much he loves you, and I thought it would never, you would never…" He was tripping over his words as he peppered her face with kisses. His face was split in a huge grin that just made her heart happy. "Have you told Big D?"

She laughed. "If you call him Big D to his face, I'm not sure if he'd take it as a compliment or bite your head off. But no, I haven't told him yet."

He rolled her over, lying on top of her and pressing her into the bed with his long, lean body. Heat pooled low in her belly. She touched all the skin she could lay her hands on and he groaned as she scratched her nails up his back.

"God, that feels so good. But we need to stop."

She pulled back and stared at him incredulously. "Are you kidding?"

He sighed and kissed her again, a long searing kiss that she felt right down to her core. "I wish. But you have a strategy meeting and we should tell Donovan. And Jack."

Azar's fingers still on his back. "Who said anything about Jack?" She'd told Bast, and maybe even Jack in a very round-about way, but she hadn't even mentioned her feelings to Oliver. It had always seemed like rubbing salt into his wounds. Until now. Until them being together was not only a possibility, but maybe even a reality.

Oliver just gave her a knowing look and rolled off the bed. "Please. Every time you are near him you give him this big, adoring, puppy love look. If I wasn't so secure, I would have been jealous. But he's a good guy, and he gives you the same longing looks that I know so well, so I'm cool with him being part of our happy little family."

He stretched his back, and Azar's mouth watered at the sight of his V and the impressively large bulge still straining against his zipper. "Aw, Az. You gotta stop looking at my dick like that, or all my good intentions are going to fly out the window." She was tempted to insist he do exactly that, but then she remembered that she was a Councilor now. People depended on her. Lives depended on her.

She sighed and rolled out of bed too. She walked over and wrapped her arms around his waist, tilting her mouth up for a kiss.

"Don't tell Donovan without me?"

He shook his head, and kissed her like his life depended on it. "I'll wait for you. Always."

*a*zar stared at topographical maps and pretended to know what the hell she was looking at. The large wooden table in the center of the meeting room held all sorts of these maps, as well as other detritus needed to help them win the war. Border and scout reports, weather reports, maps of every size and shape, not just of the above ground landscape, but of the tunnels themselves. Notes had been made about areas that could be fortified or booby-trapped. There were productivity reports from the iron-smelting plant in Jersey. There was a surveillance covertly hidden above the dens, and someone had hacked a satellite so they could get regular images of the surrounding terrain. Despite the home turf advantage, everyone was worried that the level of cover would hide a multitude of sins, or in this case, a Fae army. But Bast had scouting parties working around the clock, and so far, they had reported no movement.

The lack of action by the enemy Fae was making Azar nervous. She felt like one of those cartoon characters that was left holding the stick of dynamite, and watching the little flame run down the fuse.

But the longer the Fae waited, the better prepared the Allied army would be for any eventuality. Reports were coming in from all over the globe saying that the paranormal population had gone underground. They'd disappeared from the face of the planet, shut up shop and began to move as far away from Europe as possible. Since the American Djinn and Weres had joined forces, most of their international counterparts had followed suit. There were reports of century old feuds between the Weres and the Djinn in Yugoslavia having been called a truce so they could join forces against their common enemy. The Fae had made an error in their high-handed tactics. They'd given the rest of the paranormal world something to rally against, to heal old divides and create a new world order. The enemy of my enemy is my friend.

There was always the chance that the Fae would ignore them here in North America in favor of conquering their neighbors first. Azar was guiltily hopeful that it might be the case. None of her loved ones were in Europe, although she did have quite a few members of her family in Mardin, Turkey, the traditional seat of the Ifrit. However, she'd only seen most of them from a distance, or said a polite hello. She was more invested in the hot dog vendor in Central Park, in her little family of misfits who were right here, right now.

But she was Councilor for the Unbound now, not just the ones out at Vincent and Mavis' farm, or even just the ones spread across the US. She was the Councilor for all the Unbound spread across the world; the ones hiding in plain sight, and the ones who spent their lives looking over the shoulders, running from assassins and race purity fanatics. She needed to do her best for these people, her people, but first she had to keep them safe. She'd told Vincent to reach out to any contacts he might have in Europe, to tell the Unbound to lay low for now. She could protect them from the opportunistic Djinn here, under her ever-watchful gaze, but she couldn't guarantee that the purists from the races wouldn't take the opportunity of wartime lunacy to 'tie-up' some loose ends. So, unless the Unbound wanted to fight, she advised them to remain hidden. Once this thing with the Fae was all done and dusted, and the position of the Unbound was more concrete, then they could come out of the closet, so to speak.

There was a brief whisper of wind across her neck, as gentle as a kiss, and she smiled.

How do you always know when I need you?

The air pressed close around her, and the scent of Bast filled her senses, calming her.

Half of my heart is yours. Plus, you always chew your lip and you get these little accordion lines between your eyebrows when you are worrying.

She rubbed the top of her nose, smoothing the lines. There was a certain comfort to talking to Bast in her mind. She could tell him her fears without saying them out loud. Words gained power when spoken aloud.

There's too much. The Fae, the Unbound. I'm drowning over here. I actually miss being a slave in the Adel, with nothing better to do all day than roll around on the ground with you and call it "training".

His chuckle was low and sultry. *It was quite an enjoyable training technique. Though there is a lot of talk about your swordplay with Lorcan in the training ring, so I must not have done a bad job.*

Azar searched his tone for anything resembling jealousy, but there was nothing. Bast in his glorious human form was as confident as any golden eyed, golden haired, golden skinned Adonis could be. But he'd been losing his self-esteem a little more every day since he'd lost his human form.

After her big reveal about Oliver, Donovan and Jack, she'd expected him to be a little possessive, but so far, he'd taken it in his stride. Apparently, Oliver had tracked him down and they'd had a talk, though neither of them would tell her what was said.

You have nothing to worry about with the Black Prince, my love. He's not my type. Though everyone else didn't share her point of view. The Black Prince of the Fae had definitely made an impression on the female, and some of the male, population of the den. He even had his own fan club now.

She remembered his story about Lorcan's brother, Cian, who could make people love him. She wondered if Lorcan had a little of that ability himself.

When she'd asked him if it was because Cian was very beautiful that people fell in love with him, Lorcan had shaken his head.

"It is an illusion, akin to that of your Shaitan. Instead of causing pain and fear, he can make people love him just by spending time in his presence. The longer you spend with him, the greater your feelings for him grow, until you feel physical pain if he isn't looking at you."

Cian's powers seemed so like Freya's that Azar couldn't help drawing comparisons between the two. She'd never thought that channeling love, as Donovan had taught Freya to do instead of channeling the natural fear that permeated from the Shaitan, could actually be a bad thing. It had given her another thing to worry about.

Now, Lorcan was standing next to Aaron, pouring over the indecipherable topographical maps. They seemed to be able to read them fine, and not for the first time, she wondered what the hell she was even doing here. She knew nothing about war, or strategy.

Am I the army mascot? She asked Bast.

No, Jaanaman, if we had a mascot, I think it would be a platypus.

What? Azar thought back to all those hours watching National Geographic on cable, and tried to recall what the platypus looked like. Some freaky Australian animal that looked cute, but could kill you. Typical.

Why a platypus?

He chuckled in her mind. *Because it's a little bit of everything. A bill like a duck, a body like an otter, it lays eggs like a chicken but it's a mammal. It is such a bizarre creature, yet it works. A little like this army. You are here because you have a big heart, and when all we are thinking about is winning, you inevitably think of the human cost. Plus, you are far more strategic than you give yourself credit for. You think outside the box. You are far more than a pretty package, my love.*

She rolled her eyes at the comment and but still blushed. She wasn't so delusional that she doubted the aesthetic pleasantness of her features, but compared to some of the beauties that were produced by the agelessness of near immortality, she was a plain Jane. Compared to people like Mira, and even Lila the Bitch, she was as attractive as a potato.

One of Lorcan's Fae soldiers rushed into the room, and over to his Prince. Whispering in his ear so low that not even the super hearing in the room could pick up a single word, whatever he said to Lorcan made the Black Prince tense.

Like the predators they were, every person in the room turned towards the pair of Fae.

Lorcan dismissed the soldier with a glance. He

didn't flinch under the everyone's collective gaze, instead he met the eyes of every person there; Killian and Aaron, the all-knowing gaze of Jack, even the somewhat less penetrating glare of Ethan, the Captain of the Unbound.

"I have had news from my spies within the Courts. The Seelie Fae are amassing their army. My source believes they are preparing to attack each individual strong hold like the conquering armies of old. But they plan to start in North America first; they believe that a crushing defeat here will lead to other resistances surrendering."

Azar felt... relief. Knowing that they planned to attack was better than waiting with the guillotine ready to fall.

Killian gave the Fae Prince a hard look. "That is not what has rattled you."

He nodded. "No, rather it was the information that came out of the Unseelie Court that has unsettled me. The Unseelie have coerced the Goblin King into contributing numbers to their forces. This adds an army of at least another thousand soldiers. We cannot match an army of that size."

Azar sat down on the floor and resisted the urge to cry. They were doomed.

The silence around the room spoke volumes.

What did they do now? Did they just give in, and pray that a life as a handmaiden or a slave to the Fae wouldn't be as bad as it seems? Did they fight and die against a Fae/Goblin army? She didn't have the answers.

"What do we do?" It was Aaron who asked, but it was the million-dollar question.

She looked at Jack, whose face was unreadable.

"I will go and ask the Goddess." With that, he left.

"Does anyone have a plan that doesn't revolve around a mythical deity?" Killian asked.

If only Danu could fight. I'm pretty sure our Goddess would trump their goblin army, she thought.

Mythical deities. The thought caught in her mind. Then it grew into something terrifying.

"I have an idea!" She shot to her feet, and everyone turned to stare. "We release the original Djinn. Do the pledges, and set them free. They have a Goblin army? Well, we'll have actual forces of nature."

For a heartbeat, you could have heard an eyelash fall in that room.

See, right out of the box, Bast chuckled. *And you wonder why we keep you around.*

It was Aaron who spoke first. "Just to be clear, you want to release the Balraka? The same Balraka that you prevented from being released six months ago, and nearly died in the process? Am I getting this right?"

When he put it like that, it seemed crazy. Ha, no matter how you put it, it sounded cray-cray, but it was so insane it just might work.

"Yes. We release them all at the same time; Balraka, Oris, Thanamen, Lilith, Tel and Kuma. All of them. If we time it right, they will be released, and be attacked immediately. They will obliterate the army before anyone knows what the hell is going on."

"And when they are finished stomping the Fae/Goblin army, they'll turn their wrath to us. There is a reason they were locked away in the underworld, Azar. They are unstable and very powerful. We could be swapping certain, painful death for a more certain, more painful death," Cy argued.

He had a point. "We only need to keep them focused and busy until the pledge wears off and they are pulled back to their cells."

"The idea is lunacy. To draw them all out at once, we'd need all the great weapons. We only have four of them," Cy said, determined to play the devil's advocate. "The Fae have the rest, god knows where."

"I know where," Lorcan answered. "The Queen of the Unseelie has one, and Finlay has the other. My sources tell me that the great axe Zindagi hangs above her throne in the throne room. The Katar, Umedesta, hangs above Finlay's bed, when it isn't being studied by his sorcerers."

"So what's the plan to get those? Are we going to go, knock on the door and ask for them back?"

Azar gave Cy and Killian a huge smile. "No, we are going to steal them back. It's lucky we know the best thief in the world, isn't it?"

"Roxx," Cy and Killian said in unison.

"Roxx," she repeated, nodding.

Roxx shook his head.

"Hell to-the-mofo no! It's impossible. No, it's beyond impossible, it's suicide. Hell, if I survive that, there's a good chance that Kuma will eat me when she's released anyway. I don't have a death wish."

Kuma was the Ancient Marid, the counterpart to Balraka. It was said that Kuma could snap freeze whole continents. Apparently, the Sahara Desert had been a beautiful grasslands until one of the local tribes had insulted her in some way, and she'd drawn every ounce of moisture out of the ground, causing it to become a desert wasteland that ensured the extinction of that tribe and many others. You didn't piss off Kuma.

"You wouldn't be going alone. I'd be there, as well as Lorcan and his best guards."

"Very comforting. You want me to break into a *Sidhe* filled with enemy Fae, and steal a weapon that is hanging above the bed of the Seelie King."

Azar had learned that *Sidhe* was the official term for the Faery mounds that housed the Fae in Europe. The fact that Roxx had already known that led her to believe that this wasn't the first time he'd considered breaking and entering into the Fae strongholds.

"Think what a challenge it would be. You would be the only Djinn in our history to do such a thing and succeed." If all else fails, appeal to their vanity, that was her motto.

Roxx thumped his head down on the conference table, upsetting a stack of scout reports.

"Fine. If I'm going to die, I may as well go out with a bang. When do we do this daring raid?"

Azar clapped him on the back. "Tonight."

He shot back up and stared at her incredulously.

"Tonight? It takes months to plan a decent heist." He looked at his watch. "Not thirteen hours. How are we even going to get to Ireland in that time?"

"Two words. Private. Jet. I'll fill you in on the rest on the way."

Roxx gave a sigh and she hustled him out of the room. They were set to take off in forty-five minutes. There was a lot to be done, and little time to do it in.

CHAPTER 16

*L*orcan and six of his elite guard met them at the airport in Dublin. It was thirty minutes past the witching hour, but Dublin was still alive. They travelled by rented SUV, packed to the brim with soldiers so much so that some of them were piled into the cargo space. They drove an hour out of the city limits, to what seemed to be the middle of a field with a large rock in the center.

"Ok, tell the plan to me again," Lorcan said from the passenger seat. He couldn't drive, so Roxx was in the driver's seat and she was smooshed between Enya and a Fae soldier who she hadn't known but smelled like pine needles. She now knew his name was Hemlock, and he enjoyed this new internet thing, especially cat videos. Azar had found him incredibly endearing. She kind of wanted to keep him, but she was at capacity. She thought Bast might go insane if she tried to add anyone else to their happy little harem.

"We go into the Faery circle together. I will change into the traditional slave garb, Hemlock and Enya will change into the Seelie uniform. Roxx will just try and be as invisible as possible. Once in the Unseelie *sidhe*, Roxx, Hemlock, Enya and I will head to the portal that will send us through to the Seelie *sidhe*. We will be inconspicuous, covering Roxx's back as much as possible. I will pretend to be a slave, and Enya and Hemlock will be soldiers. If we are separated, we are to try and find our way back to the portal, then out of the portal and back to the standing stones. If one of us is captured, the rest are to get out with the great weapon if possible. If we can't get the weapon without getting caught, we are to head back to the portal and we'll try again with a different plan. Did I forget anything?"

"Keep your head down and avoid Finlay. He knows what you look like, and he will not hesitate to execute you on the spot. Why did I agree to bring you on a dangerous mission again?"

"Because it was my idea and I made you?" Azar asked, which was probably true. She'd put her foot down, and used her Council sway to invite herself along. She would never ask her people to put themselves in danger that she was unwilling to undertake herself. Or something like that. That's how her speech went anyway.

Nodding, Lorcan opened the car door and climbed out of the SUV. Walking to a tree with a hole in it, Lorcan reached in and pulled out a package. In it were several uniforms, of both the Seelie and Unseelie fashion. The Seelie uniform was white with a deep red cross down the side. The Unseelie uniform was black, with a gold dragon running across the breast. It was actually quite beautiful.

He handed her the slave outfit. It was a gossamer dress, finer than silk, in a champagne color that belted beneath her breasts with a thick gold cord.

"You need to be completely naked under that dress. Slaves are there for the pleasure of the Seelie Court. They will know you are an imposter straight away if they see you in human underwear."

Azar screwed up her nose but put on the dress anyway.

It was like wearing cotton candy. It was so soft it felt like it would dissolve in the rain. And it left nothing, and she meant nothing, to the imagination. The deep pink of her nipples was clearly visible beneath the sheer fabric. It gathered at the front, pleating down the center, so that she had a little modesty. She had no doubt that every curve of her ass was visible though.

She wasn't allowed shoes, so she tiptoed carefully around the front of the car. Hemlock let out a low whistle between his teeth, and Lorcan scowled.

Enya elbowed him in the ribs. "I'm pretty sure there's a rule about ogling demigods, so roll your tongue back in." Hemlock, bless his little heart, flushed as bright red as Enya's hair.

"Let's go." He gave Enya and Hemlock each a hard look. "Do not forget who Azar is. Her life is more important that your own."

They both nodded, and began to silently creep toward the center stone of the ancient circle. Azar felt extremely uncomfortable with Lorcan's parting comment, but she wasn't in a position to veto him. He was their commander, their Prince, and his word was gospel. She just had to hope that it never came to that. They all stood around the center stone, and Lorcan laid his hand upon a slight indent in the middle.

Then the world fell away.

She squeezed her eyes shut. The sensation reminded her of an amusement park ride she'd been on once. It spun around so fast, that you were pasted to the sides and the floor moved away, so eventually you were pinned to the wall, your insides compressing, your head spinning, and nausea rising in your throat. It was like that, but a thousand times worse.

When she opened her eyes, she was in a cavern. The walls were lined with flecks of gold, so the light that poured from the portal made it look as if the cavern was alive with thousands of tiny fireflies.

"Wow." She looked over at Roxx, who was green around the gills and looking as if he was going to chuck. "Hold it together! We still have another one to go."

He took several deep breaths, and nodded. A long dark hallway led off to the left. This is where they would part ways with Lorcan and his group.

Lorcan planned on walking right into the throne room, plucking the axe right from the wall and walking back out. She had doubts about his plan, but he seemed pretty certain it could be done. Azar was tempted to let them keep Zindagi, after all, a few less Ghul in the world wouldn't be a bad thing, right? Alas, it was needed if they were to build a good defense against the Fae/Goblin army. Maybe she'd accidentally poke Lila with it later.

Lorcan's group stood guard around the portal,

waiting for them to pass through into the Seelie *sidhe*.

Azar gave into temptation and hugged Lorcan. "Be careful, okay? We need you."

Lorcan patted her back. "Likewise. In fact, we need you more. So take extra care, and run if you are threatened."

He didn't have to tell her twice; running was what she did best.

Hemlock passed through the portal first, and she followed close behind. Next came Roxx and Enya brought up the rear.

Azar prepared herself for the sucking, twisting sensation, but this time it was like walking through a waterfall. She could feel the barrier like a heavy curtain, but it was easily brushed aside.

The portal room on the Seelie side was just as magnificent as the Unseelie. It was much the same set up, but instead of gold, the walls were littered with blood red rubies. Roxx's eyes went as wide as saucers. There was a king's ransom in rubies just in this room alone. They glittered, rough and uncut, from every crevice, large teardrops of blood leaching from the stone walls.

Roxx blinked slowly as he took in the room, dazed. Azar pinched him on the arm.

"Focus. We are here for one thing only," she whispered

He nodded. "Yasmin would love this though," he whispered back, and he was probably right. His twin did have an affinity for precious stones.

Hemlock signaled that it was all clear, and then Roxx did something she didn't think was possible for a Djinn. He disappeared into the shadows between one glance and the next.

"Holy shit. Roxx, are you still here?"

"Shh. I'll be around. I'll make my way to the King's bedroom. If it's empty, I'll get in and out and meet you guys back in the hallway. If not, I'll need a distraction," he said, a disembodied voice from the darkness.

Her heart thundered in her ears. She followed along behind Enya and Hemlock with forced ease. She wanted to look attentive but unobtrusive.

Hemlock and Enya were talking in low tones that even she couldn't understand, their heads together as if they were in serious conversation. It was a way for them to partly shield their faces and Azar, who was a step behind them, without seeming too conspicuous.

They walked past several servants, who paid little attention to them as they scurried off to wherever they were headed. She held her breath as they passed some nobles, one giving her a long look that stilled way too long on her breasts.

The Fae noble didn't say anything, and continued walking, having drunk in his fill of her near naked body. What an asshole.

A group of Seelie soldiers entered the hall ahead of them, and blood began to rush in her ears. Fuck. They would definitely know that they weren't Seelie. Enya had her distinctive red hair under a helmet, but that would do little good if they got a good look at everyone's faces.

Before she could freak out, her two Fae surprised the hell out of her. They turned and pushed Azar up against a wall inside an alcove. Hemlock wedged himself between her thighs his face in her neck, and Enya held her face, her lips a mere whisper from Azar's, her head tilted. They all held their breath, as the group stilled, said something in Gaelic, chuckled and continued on.

"My apologies," Enya whispered, so close that the small puffs of her speech spread over Azar's mouth. It was extremely odd talking to someone this close.

"Worse things have happened to me than being up close and personal with two attractive Fae," she gave their worried faces a lopsided grin. "Plus it worked. All clear this way"

Hemlock looked down the hall his way. "All clear this way." He looked down at her. He was quite tall for a Fae, maybe six and a half feet or so. "I'm sorry that I'm not sorry. It has been awhile since I have been that close to a beautiful woman. And even longer since I've been pressed between two. I enjoyed every second."

Azar flushed and Enya rolled her eyes. "Let's go before you say something even stupider."

They continued down the halls and after what seemed like a hundred left hand turns, they stopped outside a set of jewel encrusted double doors. The doors were etched ash, a pictograph of the Fae conquering something big and ugly with only one eye. Precious gems made the eyes of the epic heroes, as well as the stars in a glittering night sky. The largest moonstone she'd ever seen was the moon. It was a beautiful piece of art.

The door was slightly ajar, and she peeked in. A tall blond Fae stood naked in the room, a woman dressed like Azar on her knees giving him a blowjob.

She saw a flash of Roxx's face from the back of the room. He needed a distraction.

"I'm going in. If shit goes pear-shaped, save me,

okay?" Before they could protest, she snuck into the room.

She just stood there, staring at the naked Fae man. He wasn't Finlay, of that she was certain, but he was definitely powerful. She could feel the magic radiate off him in the same way that it poured off Lorcan. He had long, long ash blond hair to his waist, and an eight pack. His arms were bulging muscles where they held the slave girl's hair. He looked like the love child of Conan the Barbarian and Fabio. But better looking than both.

But what really struck Azar was his look of wretched sadness as he gazed down at the girl's head with stunning seafoam green eyes. His face was contorted into lines of pain and loneliness. She'd never had a blowjob, but she was pretty sure that you weren't meant to feel sad during one.

She looked at a beautiful vase sitting on a pedestal. She reached out and knocked it over, and it fell to the floor with a crash.

The man's head shot up, and a mask of cruelty slid into place; all vulnerability completely chased away.

"Whoops."

"Stupid animal," he growled. "What have you done?"

Any pity she may have had for the man vanished with that one growled sentence.

"Uh, I was looking for Fin- His Royal Highness."

He pushed away the slave girl who was still happily slobbering over the man's penis like it was an everlasting gobstopper. She sat in a heap on the floor, staring up at him adoringly. Azar realized that the girl was a human.

"You are quite insolent for a slave." He strutted over to her, his naked body a symphony of hard edges and his manhood jutted out like a tree limb. He was completely unfazed by his nudity. "Why do you search for the King?"

Azar caught the brief blur of movement behind the man on the bed, and fought really hard not to look at Roxx.

"Umm, he requested that I come and, er, pleasure him." She could have slapped her own forehead at the stupidity of the comment, but attempted to keep her face neutral.

"Well, I too am a Royal. You may pleasure me instead." He was so confident that she would drop to her knees, it made her want to kick him in his avocados.

"No thanks, I'll wait." The man looked shocked.

"Excuse me?" His disbelief was comical.

"I said no thank you, your Highness."

He grabbed her face in his oversized hands and stroked a cheek with a forefinger. "I'm sure you meant yes."

She really didn't like being manhandled, but she gritted her back teeth. "I meant what I said."

The man took a large step back. "You are not in love with me?"

Now it was her turn to look shocked. "Excuse me?" Then it hit her. "Wait, you aren't Cian, the Golden Prince of the Unseelie Fae, are you?"

He was still staring, his face contorting into different pouty looks. He looked like a teen Prom Queen duck facing for the cameras. "Yes, I am. Look at me now? In love with me yet?"

"Still no. What are you doing over here on the Seelie side of the tracks?"

"Enjoying some of the finer things in life. After all, there is a war coming, and that will be all work, work, work." He grabbed her face again and kissed her hard on the lips. It wasn't a bad kiss, the guy obviously had a lot of practice.

"Now? Are you consumed with love and desire?"

She shook her head, resisting the urge to wipe her mouth with the back of her hand. "Sorry, still nothing. But I give you a ten out of ten for technique."

He put both hands on his hips and cocked his head to the side. "You seem to be immune to my glamor. I have never met anyone immune to my glamor. Even the most powerful Kings and Queens of the Fae are susceptible." He rubbed a finger along his jawline. "I don't know whether to keep you or kill you. This is quite an unusual occurrence."

She took a long, slow look down his body, then back up towards his face. He definitely had a pretty look about him, but Azar liked her men a little rougher around the edges. He had the same lithe beauty of Lorcan, but without Lorcan's aura of confident command.

"Unfortunately, neither of those options work for me." An odd, deafening clanging noise resounded through the room, and she knew it was time to leave.

She edged back toward the door.

"Unfortunately for you, I fear the alarms have made my choice for me. I just knew that you didn't belong here. Finlay would never keep anyone so spirited in his harem. You are far too old, and far too female for the Usurper King's tastes."

Cian's lip curled in disgust, and Azar didn't want to know who Finlay's type was, or what he did with them, that disgusted even an Unseelie Prince. But she was definitely going to kill the evil bastard as soon as possible, just on principle.

Cian edged toward her, casting out a hand as if web would shoot out of his palms like Spiderman. Again, nothing happened.

"Huh." She doubted the Fae prince had ever had to participate in hand to hand combat, but she wasn't willing to test his skills right now.

Thankfully, Hemlock and Enya burst through the door in a whirl of weapons. Enya whacked Cian over the head with something that looked like a jade pestle. Cian went down hard, whacking the back of his head on the marble floor.

"Hurry, he won't stay down for long," Hemlock said from the door, keeping watch.

Enya just stared down at the prone form of Cian, and fell to her knees. At first, she thought the Fae woman was injured, but then she realized that she was entranced in Cian's love juju or whatever it was. Hooking her hand under the other woman's arms, she pulled her up and away, dragging her out of the room, Hemlock in front.

As soon as they were out of Cian's presence, Enya snapped out of it.

Two Seelie guards came around the corner, and

Enya let out a yell of anger before swinging her sword like a baseball bat into one of the guard's faces, knocking him out cold.

Hemlock rolled his eyes at Enya. "Stop beating yourself up. We all know that falling under Cian's spell is involuntarily. Who knew it would still work if he was unconscious?" He smashed the head of one of the guards into the rough stone wall.

"I'm not beating myself up. I'm beating these guys up." She slammed her fist into the guard's face repeatedly.

When the guards were unmoving, she checked to see they weren't dead, mostly out of habit, then continued at a quick pace down the hall. As much as she wanted to run, she held herself back. Running would draw attention. She hoped Roxx had gotten away with the Great Weapon. She didn't know what had tripped the alarms, but she was fairly certain it wasn't him. Cian hadn't even realized there was anyone else in the room. She didn't know where all the guards had been running too, but it wasn't in their direction. Now she only had to hope that the portal room was empty too, otherwise they were going to be in a world of trouble.

As they came around the corner, she cursed.

The portal room was teeming with guards,

jostling toward the portal opening. Azar hoped to the Goddess that Roxx wasn't the focus of all those swinging blades.

Not having a better idea, they pushed their way through the back of the crowd, and Hemlock looked over the top of their heads to the portal room.

"It's Lorcan's group!"

Coming from the back of the mass, they made it a fair way into the portal room before anyone realized they didn't belong. With Azar wedged between them, Enya and Hemlock pushed through the attacking force, daggers out, slicing throats and sticking kidneys.

Lorcan's Captain of the Guard saw them coming and shouted something. The team lunged forward in a furious attack, driving back the Seelie soldiers until her group were in arms reach.

She could see no sign of Lorcan or Roxx and her heart thundered.

"Your brother is through the portal already. You must go!" He pushed Azar through the glittering barrier and the sick, whirling pressure overcame her body.

She landed with a thump in the standing stone circle, on top of another person. It must have been raining, because she landed in a puddle and it soaked straight through the gauze of her dress.

She stared at the person she landed on, and realized it was Lorcan.

"Thank God you are ok!" she whispered, getting to her feet. She reached down to help him up when she noticed the mud on her hand. But it didn't feel like mud at all. It was tacky in the rapidly cooling Irish air.

She raise her hand to her nose and sniffed. The faint coppery tang of blood.

She dropped back to her knees and her hands searched Lorcan's body in the dark.

"Fuck! Lorcan!" Her hand found flaps of flesh peeled up from his body, blood gushing out from the wounds over her fingers.

A hand grabbed the back of her dress and pulled her off Lorcan and onto her feet. She let out a scream, flailing.

"Relax, it's me. We need to move!" Hemlock's voice sounded strained, and Azar's head whipped around the standing stones. Only four of Lorcan's six guards were standing there with them. A big man, the biggest Fae she had seen to date, picked Lorcan up like a doll and ran out of the standing stones.

"We've jammed it with an amulet, but it won't last long. We are going to have to sift back to the States," Lorcan's Captain said. "Your brother has taken the SUV and will fly back on the private jet. We came across him in the portal room."

They reached the tree where Lorcan had removed the outfits earlier in the night. He removed Umedesta, a katar which looked basically like a vicious set of Wolverine claws.

"Hold this." He thrust the Great Weapon into her hands. "We must get our Prince medical attention as soon as possible. Hold on, you might feel slightly nauseous."

With that, he wrapped his arms tightly around her waist, the dagger's sharp points pressing uncomfortably into her flesh but not breaking skin.

Then they were sifting, and her body felt like it was being pulled apart and being put back together over and over again.

CHAPTER 17

*A*zar was glad that the Fae couldn't sift inside the dens. No one would see her shame.

They came to rest in the clearing near the training rings. She dropped the Great Weapon, doubled over and vomited up everything she'd eaten in the last decade. At least that's what it felt like as heaves wracked her body over and over.

No one paid her much attention. They were crowded around their fallen Prince.

She wiped her mouth with the back of her hand and stumbled over to Lorcan.

"Is he okay? What the hell happened?"

The Captain of the Guard pulled a weapon from his back holster, and her breath caught when she spied the largest axe head she'd ever seen. His face was grim and smeared with Lorcan's blood. She stood like a deer in the headlights as he raised the axe up over his head.

Instead of decapitating her like she'd briefly imagined, he held it out to her.

"Goddess, the last Great Weapon, Zindagi."

"Thank you, Captain." Her voice was strangled because there was still a huge lump in her throat.

Halona and the Doc rushed over to Lorcan, pushing through the circle of his men.

"He has one hundred lacerations over his body, two inches deep and two inches long," Enya said calmly. "He's lost a lot of blood, but he will survive."

Doc looked at Lorcan, still fully dressed although his clothes were torn to shreds. What could have done that?

"How do you know he has a hundred?"

"It is a form of Unseelie torture." She rolled up her sleeve, and there were several two-inch scars on her forearms. The fact they scarred at all meant they were done with magic, or a magic infused weapon. "If I can survive it, so can he."

Doc and Halona still took Lorcan away on a stretcher, carried by two of his men, two more

GRACE MCGINTY

walking beside them. They would stand guard over their Prince.

She stood next to the Captain. "You need to tell me what happened, Captain…?"

"Quigley, my Goddess."

Azar held in a laugh. There was no way this tall, imposing warrior was named Quigley. But he didn't look like the joking sort, so she just nodded for him to continue.

"As our Prince declared, he strode into the throne room and took Zindagi from its place above the Queen's throne. He said that any who wished to challenge him may do so, but he was leaving with the weapon. No one would stand against the Black Prince if they wanted to live. You know the strength of his ability?" She nodded. Instant necrosis wasn't something she was likely to forget. "Not even the Queen would stand directly against Prince Lorcan in a duel. However, she couldn't let him just walk out with it. So we were surrounded, and although we fought them off, we were eventually subdued. No one had stepped toward Prince Lorcan, but she had a good threat with us. He warned the Queen that if one of us was hurt, he would rain down death on all present. He could do it, and everyone in the throne room was aware.

"I believe to save face, the Queen told him that she would spare our lives, and he could walk out with the axe, for she believed she would soon get it back when they conquered the Djinn. But he had to withstand the Blooding."

Whatever 'the Blooding' was, it sounded awful.

"The Blood Prince, Oisrin, the Queen's right hand, always inflicts the Blooding. I can tell you, Goddess, he enjoys it too. He inflicts one hundred lacerations, two inches deep by two inches long with magic, each wound affecting us as mortal wounds, inhibiting our ability to heal. It is his specialty, drawing blood. Most people don't survive to fifty gashes. Only one other person has ever survived the Blooding."

"Enya," Azar said, remembering the scars that littered her arm.

Quigley nodded. "She was Prince Oisrin's intended bride. But he is a monster, and she wished to have the engagement annulled. The Queen would only permit it if she survived the Blooding. I can tell you, I have never seen anything so awful as the last ten gashes, Oisrin so enraged that he cut arteries, trying to ensure she would die. But she didn't, she was tougher than them all. Prince Lorcan stepped in as Prince Oisrin went forward after his one hundredth slice to slit her throat and ensure her death despite the Queen's decree. Prince Lorcan prevented her death by beating back his brother, and had her nursed back to health by his own personal handmaiden. She was made part of his guard upon her recovery. She is loyal to Prince Lorcan to the very core, and one of his best soldiers." There was admiration in the Captain's tone, and maybe a touch of something a little softer. Affection? Even love?

She'd already respected Enya, but her strength of will was awe-inspiring.

"So Lorcan survived one hundred gashes and the Queen just let you all leave?"

"Yes and no. She'd said that he could 'walk out' with Zindagi, so if we carried him or the axe, the agreement was forfeit. The Prince stood, coated in blood from one hundred cuts, and dragged the axe out of the throne room and through the portal before he collapsed. His last words were to retrieve you from the Seelie *sidhe*, and get you out of there. As our Prince wills it, so it shall be."

The Fae looked stoic, but there were smudges under his eyes, signs of worry on a normally smooth face.

"Why don't you go and rest? I will watch over

Lorcan, as well as his guard. It can't have been easy sifting back with me attached."

He inclined his head. "It is more tiring bringing a passenger. By your leave, Goddess."

"Please, Quigley, call me Azar."

He just inclined his head and melted into the trees.

SHE SAT NEXT to Lorcan's still form, and entwined her fingers between his. She didn't know if it would help, but it definitely couldn't do harm. Halona and Doc had stripped him down, and all his two-inch gashes gaped at her like gruesome smiles. He was still unconscious, and she couldn't help but think that his unconsciousness was a blessing.

She'd dropped off their recovered prizes to Killian, who had the other four Great Weapons hidden away somewhere in the dens with a permanent guard. She knew that using the weapons to free the original Djinn was a solid contingency plan, but she couldn't help the tremor of trepidation. It was like busting out an entire prison of psychopaths and letting them loose on the suburbs. Fear was a physical force in the air.

She stood and pressed a light kiss to Lorcan's

forehead. She had to go and debrief everyone about the mission, and then she needed a shower. She looked down and belatedly realized that she was still wearing the blood-soaked slave garb of the Fae. That explained some of the strange looks she'd garnered on her way to the infirmary.

She met Bast as she stepped out into the hall, closing the door to Lorcan's hospital room behind her with a slight click.

Thank the gods you are safe. I hate when you go on missions and I am unable to be there to watch your back.

Azar shook her head. "You were needed here. Besides, there were plenty of people to watch my back. We were successful in the mission, and that's all that matters." She couldn't think of the two Fae soldiers who hadn't returned with the group. They'd been victorious, but not without losses. She'd made a point of asking the Guard that was watching over Lorcan the names of the fallen soldiers. He'd refused to tell her. They believed that saying the name of a person who had died recently would stop their souls from moving on to the Goddess. She resisted the urge to order him to do so, as a representative of his Goddess, instead mentally naming them Fae Soldier One and Two. They went on her list of regrets, right below Becca. People whose safety had been her responsibility, and that she'd failed. She would mourn each of them, and she knew that more would be added to that list before this war had played out.

I hate seeing those shadows in your eyes, Jaanaman.

She gave him a sad smile. "I need to feel the grief. I need to feel each and every loss personally. It reminds me what I am fighting for. I have a healthy respect for Mistress Death."

He didn't say anything else, just remaining beside her, a warm comforting presence. She walked to her room like a zombie, throwing the gauzy fabric of her slave dress into the trash, setting it on fire. Bast left her to go to the debrief meeting, but she could tell he wanted to stay.

Slipping into the ensuite, she began scrubbing the blood from every inch of her skin. She watched as the water swirled pink around the shower drain and breathed in a long, shuddery breath. She could do this, she knew it. She repeated it over and over to herself, driving it into her own subconscious. There was no alternative.

There was a light knock on the door.

"Come in."

She expected Oliver, but when Donovan walked into the bathroom, she didn't know whether she should cover up or not.

"Oh, it's you."

He turned his back, giving her some privacy. "Bast thought it was best if one of us was with you right now. Oliver is out running patrols, but I can get Jack if you wish."

She could have slapped her own forehead. She understood now how her words must have sounded. But she was happy it was Donovan.

"I'm glad it's you. Bast would feel guilty, and Oliver would try and make me feel better. Jack is Jack." He wasn't out of touch with human emotions, but his blood sang to hers, and his emotions would reflect in her own, and she wasn't sure she could deal with the heavy dose of guilt that would surely come with it. "You're perfect. Besides, I've been meaning to talk to you."

Donovan cleared his throat, his shoulders tense, but he didn't turn around.

She reached out and snagged the back of his shirt, dragging him into the shower and under the hot spray of the water. He spun, the water dripping down his face as his shirt now clung to his broad shoulders.

It was time to woman up. She was the most unsure of Donovan. She wanted him, and he wanted her, of that she was certain. But would he want more? "I wanted to tell you that I spoke with Bast. And Oliver. If you want…" Jesus, what the hell was she trying to say. How did you tell someone that she got the okay from her boyfriend to make him a boyfriend as well? How freakin' ridiculous. "What Oliver suggested, it's okay with Bast. And Oliver, of course. That is, if you still want such a thing. I mean, I do, but I respect your decision either way and it won't affect our friendsh-"

His mouth found hers and he devoured her whole. At least, that's what it felt like, his hands running along her skin as he pressed her hard against the bathroom tiles.

"I've wanted this for so damn long," he growled as he pulled away and kissed his way down her neck. "Since the first time I saw you in my office, all sassy and sexy and I just wanted to bend you over my desk and fuck the sass right out of you."

"Really?" Her words were almost a squeak. "I had no idea." His words sent electric heat to her center. Damn.

"Uh huh. And then you helped me with Freya, and that's when I wanted more from you than a quick fuck. You loved her as much as I did, more than her own mother did, and I couldn't help it anymore. I didn't just want your body. I wanted your heart and that's something I thought was purely for the fucking Jann. The that damn cat gave me hope. I am Shaitan. We do not hope. We do not love."

His mouth slipped around her nipple and she moaned, pressing herself closer. He didn't speak anymore as his mouth moved from one nipple to the next. She wrapped her fingers in his hair, holding him close but giving him free rein.

He dropped to his knees in front of her, and slid his hands down her back, squeezing her ass as he kissed down her stomach.

"You should stop me," he said, looking up at her with those normally impenetrable eyes basically begging her to say yes despite his words. "Say no. You deserve better than to live on the edge of fear for the rest of your life. You deserve fun with Oliver and worship from Bast. Wonder from the Fae. I can only give you anger, pain and fear."

She wanted to tell him that she was as far from anger as a girl can get, but he was lifting her leg over his shoulder despite his words. He dropped his head low, kissing over her hip and she gripped at his chin. The look of defeat on his face when she tilted his head up broke her heart. He thought she was about to say no. She was going to fix that.

"I want you," she told him gently, imploring him

with her eyes to believe her. "The only thing you are giving me right now is pleasure, and if you stop, I might kick your ass."

He laughed and it was a fucking beautiful sound. In response, he buried his face between her thighs and she lost all reason. He was rough, his beard scraping on her thigh and his teeth nipping so she was writhing on the knife's edge of pleasure and pain.

Her orgasm hit her like a thunderbolt. Her knees turned to jelly and she fell to her knees in front of him. He didn't try and catch her, but he wrapped her in his arms and kissed her again, as they both knelt there under the thundering water.

He pulled away, and she resisted the urge to chase his lips with hers. He reached up and turned off the water. "You need to go to the debriefing."

She nuzzled against his chest. "Or you could take me to bed?"

His body shuddered and he closed his eyes. She could see the painfully hard bulge in his leather pants. She wondered how hard it was to get out of wet leather. "I could, but you need to get to work. They'll be waiting for your report," he said, sounding pained.

Azar sighed, and looked into that face she once

thought looked cruel. The fear was a steady hum that crawled along her flesh, but she could ignore it if she tried. "Why did I agree to be the Councilor again?"

He stood and pulled her from the shower. "Because you saw an injustice and you couldn't let it rest." He wrapped her in a fluffy towel. "It's one of the things I...like about you."

With that, he gave her one last peck on the lips and left.

DRESSED IN FRESH COMBAT GEAR, she strode into the War Room, and it was as busy as ever. It appeared no one was getting any sleep. Aaron and Killian were there, along with the leader of the Werehawk scouts, who was talking to Mira and Bast. Azar had insisted Ethan, the Captain of the Unbound, be there too. The guy obviously had extensive military experience, and the Unbound made up the largest force within the army. They deserved to be represented. She refused to allow them to be cannon fodder.

As if he knew he was in her thoughts, Ethan turned and bowed his head respectfully. She smiled and bowed her head in return. If they all survived this, she would have to get lessons on Councilor etiquette. Hell, maybe it was time they reassessed the stuffy social etiquette that permeated Djinn society like a plague.

Everyone else stopped what they were doing, and gave her a slow clap. She blushed to her toes, and waved it away.

"Please, that's unnecessary. If anyone should get the praise its Lorcan and his Fae, and Roxx. Roxx was amazing. I just bumbled around and tried not to die."

Aaron gave her a smile. "Well, you did that perfectly. But you deserve the accolades, Az. We stand a chance now. We have a mountable defense, even if it is a bit of a gambit."

She scoffed. A bit of a gambit was a wild under-statement. "Let's hope it goes well, and history paints me as a revolutionary rather than the silly idiot who suggested releasing monsters on humanity."

She sat down on one of the office chairs, still exhausted. Maybe she should have had a nap before she came to debrief them. Her body still hummed from Donovan's attentions.

Killian sat down opposite her. "Report."

She ran through the events of the night, and then recounted what Quigley had told her. She'd get him and Lorcan in to give their own report when they'd recovered. There was an audible intake of breath when she detailed Lorcan's punishment at the hands of his mother.

"So, now we have a complete set of Great Weapons and discovered I can see through Cian's glamor. Maybe I can see through all Fae glamor. He's the first Fae I've ever met who even tried. Maybe I'll get Jack or one of the other Fae to test the theory with me."

As if on cue, Jack walked into the room. He smiled and grabbed her hand, giving it a tight squeeze.

"Uh, Azar. The Black Prince's Fae are always glamored. If it wasn't for the fact that they dressed as if it were a renaissance faire, I'd have a hard time telling them from all the Unbound that walk around the place," Mira said, indicating the Fae soldier who walked in behind Jack.

"What?" The Fae soldier Mira indicated, the big one whose name she still didn't know, looked humanoid for sure, but you only had to take one good look at his face to know that he wasn't even remotely human. Those big Fae eyes, slightly elongated ears and delicate strength definitely set them apart as other. "What about Jack?"

Mira looked Jack over with slow appraisal, or maybe it was appreciation. "You remember when we watched that superhero movie a couple of months ago, and it had that really hot bad guy? What was his name? Tom someone? Jack is the dead spit of that guy."

Azar whirled to face the man in question. "He isn't like a pretty pearlescent green to you guys?"

Everyone shook their heads.

"Huh. That's strange." Strange was a crazy understatement, but she would take strange over life altering any day. "We should test that later." When they were alone, without ten people all staring at them.

Jack just shrugged and dropped his glamor for the room. Mira let out a tiny squeak, but Azar didn't think it was from alarm. Jack was glorious in his natural form, his face was serene and otherworldly, his skin shimmering with a muted glow that came from within. He was tall, and his body, while lithe, was strong and unmovable. He was larger than his Fae counterparts, broader across the shoulders. His large eyes sparkled with mirth at the responses from the other people in the room. It was hard to narrow down just one thing that was so compelling about Jack, but if she was pressed, she'd say that he radiated life. It flowed from him like the ebbing of the sea. The fury and the beauty.

"Well, if we are all done with the Fae party tricks, let's get back to work, shall we?" Killian asked.

She rolled her eyes in his direction and whispered to Mira, "What a slave driver, right?" Mira gave her an equally stern look. "What? Too soon?"

Killian had all the Djinn historians looking into the best way to use the Great Weapons to release the original Djinn. They were dusting off ancient tomes that had been hidden away in vaults for centuries, reading and rereading any tall tales or folk stories about the original Djinn and their sudden disappearance from the Earth.

So far, they'd discovered relatively little considering the original Djinn, and even the Great Weapons, had played such a huge part in their history. Azar had her theories of course, and most of them centered on the Fae. Even now, the Djinn ignored a valuable resource that was sleeping in the woods right outside the den door. The Great Weapons were Fae made, it was the Fae that conquered the Djinn and enslaved them the first-time round, and it would stand to reason that they would be able to fill in the gaps. Still, the Djinn historians pretended that they didn't even exist.

Well, she would remedy that, if she had to drag one of those prissy little historians out of the library, tie them up and make them listen to Jack. She'd definitely do that, after she slept for like an hour. Or maybe a month. Maybe she'd sleep through the whole war, if she were lucky.

CHAPTER 18

*K*illian entrusted her with the location of the room holding the Great Weapons, because it was also the temporary location of the Djinn library. On the off chance, and it was a very outside chance, that the Fae hadn't been only trying to steal the Great Weapons from the vault when they attacked the Adel compound, everything had been moved to the dens.

She smiled at the guard outside the door, who bowed low and murmured "Councilor", before holding the door open for her. She strode in and a huge pair of brown eyes looked up from a desk that had been placed in the center of the room, right below a large hanging light. The historian was wearing reading glasses, which was innocuous considering that Djinn had preternaturally good eyesight.

"Can I help you?" Her voice was unexpectedly sultry, although nearly everything else about her was stereotypically bookish. She had wavy brown hair, cut to her shoulders. A heart shaped face held eyes that were way too big for her face, almost Fae big.

"What's with the glasses?" Azar couldn't help but ask.

"Excuse me?" The woman looked confused, and she stood, the office chair rolling back until it hit the wall.

"Sorry, I'm Azar. I've come to take you on a research trip."

"Azar, like the Unbound Councilor?" Her face lit up like she'd just been given a shiny new toy. "Do you think you have time to sit down and tell me how it happened?"

Now it was Azar's turn to look confused. "How what happened?"

"Everything. From your birth until right now. It needs to be recorded. You've affected some of the greatest changes in Djinn recorded history. It has to be recorded," she repeated fervently.

Azar shifted from foot to foot awkwardly. "Uh, sure. Not right now, though."

"Okay, fine. Later. But you have to tell it to me okay? Not to that old bastard, Euston. He thinks just because he is the most experienced historian that he gets to do all the big histories. But I think that's bull-shit. I mean, have you ever read one of his histories? It's like reading the back of a cereal box. Boring. They just get filed away to gather dust. I like to inject some of the passion of the moment into my recounts. I mean, who said that they had to be as dry as old fruitcake? Right?"

She was looking at Azar intently, her face alight with the passion she just spoke of, and it completely transformed her. No one would think she was a mousey little historian if they just talked to her for five minutes.

"Uh, sure. My story is all yours." The historian skipped on the spot, and Azar couldn't help but smile. "But on two conditions."

She stopped her skipping and looked at Azar shrewdly.

"Number one, you have to come with me and talk to The Green Man. I promise he doesn't bite."

The woman frowned, but nodded. "What's number two?"

"You tell me your name, so I can tell Euston who gets my history if he ever asks for it."

The woman let out a laugh, an endearing sound that was short and sharp honks.

"I'm Stacia. Suck it Euston, you stodgy old fool." With that, she picked up her notepad and pen, and indicated the doorway. "Alright, let's go meet the Green Man."

Azar was surprised how easy it was to get Stacia to agree. She seemed ravenous for knowledge though. It was a wonder she hadn't sought Jack out herself.

They walked in companionable silence down the unused section of halls, and then out into the main thoroughfare, where men and women rushed around, everyone trying to keep active even though they were basically just sitting on their hands waiting for the fighting to commence.

Nevyn and Freya ran out of a tunnel and directly in front of her. Azar's hand shot out and collared the back of Freya's shirt.

"Hey, you two. What are you up to? Staying out of mischief I hope?" They looked at each other quickly, which was never a good sign.

"Of course, Az," Freya said. She noted Nevyn's carefully neutral expression. Fae couldn't lie, after all, but Freya had no such qualms. She wanted to laugh.

"This is Stacia, a historian. This is Nevyn, Rightful Heir to the Golden Throne of the Seelie Fae. And this is Freya."

Stacia looked ecstatic. "Oh my goodness. The first Unbound and the rescued Fae Prince. Right here. It's a pleasure to meet you both." She shook their hands enthusiastically.

Nevyn smiled politely. "Hello, Historian Stacia. Your heart and soul are very pure for an adult."

Stacia blinked. "Uh, thank you?"

"That's a real compliment, trust me," Azar told her, before turning to the children. "I'm going to see Jack and Lorcan, if you two would like to come?"

They skipped around with excitement, and raced ahead of them. As soon as Lorcan had awoken, he'd insisted on being moved back to the woods with his men. No one had argued.

"Do you think they'd let me scribe their stories too?"

Azar thought about it, then shrugged. "Nevyn is his own boss, you should ask him. But remember, he's older and wiser than he looks. You'd have to ask Donovan about Freya though, and he'll likely say no. Donovan isn't someone to trifle with, and he is very, very protective of his daughter."

Stacia paled a little at the mention of Donovan,

but then, most Djinn paled at the mention of the Shaitan. But she knew that deep inside that scary exterior was a man who loved his daughter and might, one day, love Azar too. She needed to see him. She needed to see them all. Maybe she could persuade them all to come over and watch a movie. Everything was always so urgent, they'd lost those special moments they needed to just be happy.

They left the dens and walked across the clearing, smiling and waving occasionally to people who were sparring in the practice ring, or jogging, or one of the multitudes of other tasks that kept an army busy enough so it didn't implode.

They strode past the tree line and up to the large campfire, ringed by large, smooth rocks that looked like polished quartz. Stacia looked around the empty campsite, her intelligent brown eyes taking in everything. However, when Lorcan dropped down from a tree, his men falling down around them like autumn leaves, the poor woman's mouth swung open and stayed there. It was a pretty impressive sight.

Azar tutted at Lorcan. "Should you be jumping out of trees like that, considering you nearly bled out on my favorite slave outfit less than forty-eight hours ago?"

He gave her one of those gleaming grins and

lifted his shirt, showing row after row of perfectly healed scars. Visible silver streaks littered his beautiful pale skin, over each well-formed ab, and down the lean V of his oblique. Stacia gave an audible swallow.

Azar gave the woman a knowing grin. "Lorcan, this is Stacia, a Djinn historian. We are looking for Jack. Actually, Lorcan may know something also. Perhaps he could fill in some of our blanks regarding the weapons?"

Lorcan shrugged. "It is doubtful that I have any information that isn't already in your written histories. The Great Weapons had been lost for centuries by the time I was born. All I know are the same urban legends as you; that each weapon is targeted to kill one race of Djinn, that they were created by Brandr, that they acted like Anadari bracelets for the original Djinn…"

"Wait, what?" Stacia interrupted. "You're saying that it's the weapons that keep them locked away?"

Now it was Lorcan's turn to look confused. "Of course, what did the Djinn think was keeping them trapped in the Inbetween?"

"We call it Hell," Azar corrected.

"Having read your version of Hell, I have to say it's a pretty true account of the Inbetween. The space between worlds is an inhospitable environment for even the strongest of creatures."

Stacia began pacing around the fire, chewing on the end of her pencil, Lorcan's men instinctively moving out of her path.

"So, if the Great Weapons were destroyed, permanently, then what? The Originals just start running around again?"

"Woah, we need to be able to put them back again," Azar argued. "The genies definitely need to go back into the bottle when we're done."

Lorcan shrugged. "That was always the general assumption. The original Djinn were put away because they were animals, like all Djinn. We were wrong, of course. We are the animals." His eyes clouded with sights long ago seen but never forgotten. She patted him on the shoulder, the tan fabric of his tunic soft as doe skin under her hands.

"We are all predators, trampling through this world without care. Neither you, nor I, is an exempt to the circle of life. In order to survive, we must be animals."

"She is right. To maintain life, there must be balance. The spider must consume the fly for the world to turn." Jack melted from the trees.

Azar rolled her eyes. "I'm nearly certain that you

stand out in the shadows waiting for the perfect moment to make a dramatic, yet poignant, entrance," she griped as her eyes ran over him like a woman who was starving.

Jack laughed heartily, and turned toward Stacia.

"I don't believe we've met?" He put out a hand for her to shake, but she just stood there a little dumb-founded. Azar nudged her with her elbow.

"Er, hi. Stacia, uh, I mean my name is Stacia." She placed her palm in his, and then looked on like a dumbfounded spectator as he turned it over, kissing the delicate skin on the back of her hand.

Azar raised her eyebrows and looked around at the bemused expressions of the group. She leaned toward Stacia.

"Does he look green to you?"

Stacia nodded slowly, her lips still parted and the tops of her cheekbones flushed pink.

"No glamor?"

Jack shook his head. "I heard you tell the Prince that she is a historian. I thought she would like a true account of my appearance."

Stacia was still nodding slowly, but Azar wasn't sure if she'd heard anything that Jack had said. "You might want to tone it down a little, otherwise the account of this moment is going to read like a weird erotic novel."

Acquiescing, Jack closed his eyes and Azar felt the tingle of magic brush against her skin, but nothing visibly changed for her. However, Stacia's eyes bugged out.

"Is your human glamor George Clooney or something?" She would have given her last dollar to see what had put that expression on Stacia's previously slack face.

Stacia seemed to shake herself out of whatever estrogen-induced trance she'd been in. "No, he looks like the love child of Steve McQueen and James Dean."

Azar waggled her eyebrows at them both. Stacia flushed bright red. "I like classic human cinema. Don't judge me. Let's get back to the purpose of the visit. Besides, there's children present."

Azar had forgotten about Nevyn and Freya, who were busy trying to scale the trees under the watchful eyes of Hemlock. Nevyn was a natural, but Freya had trouble getting more than a few feet up the tall oak trees.

Nevyn turned at his name, and scowled adorably. "I'm fifty-six."

Stacia grimaced and muttered an apology and

something that sounded like a complaint about the immortal faces of the Fae.

"We need any information you can give us on the internment of the original Djinn. Lorcan says that the Great Weapons act like Anadari bracelets, keeping the Original Fae trapped in Hell," Stacia was back to being all business.

"The Inbetween," Lorcan corrected. "Hell is a human construct."

Stacia nodded in acquiescence.

Jack stroked his chin thoughtfully, in a very human gesture. Azar briefly wondered if spending so much time with such a seething mass of humanity was starting to rub off on him.

"This is true, to a degree. But not. The Anadari bracelets are a mild replica of the Great Weapons. I met Brandr once. He was a Fae with a closed-minded sense of right and wrong; everything was very black and white. When the Djinn started to amass to defend themselves against the conquering horde of the Fae, they did so without care for man, woman or child. They came in and slaughtered whole settlements of Fae, in defense of their own land and liberty, but Brandr didn't see it like that. He saw dead Fae, and set his mind to the task of protecting his people. So he created the Great

Weapons, studying the strengths and weaknesses of each of the races and targeting them specifically. He tested it on prisoners of war, and when every single one of them died, he gave the weapons to the Royals, who carved a bloody swath through the opposing army. When they reached one of the Original Djinn, who were bigger, more powerful elementals, the Royal Prince, I can't remember which one, stabbed Balraka with it, expecting him to die. Unfortunately, Balraka was momentarily stunned by the weapon. Within two minutes, he was on his feet, bathing the field with the Prince's blood." He paused, probably for dramatic effect. Azar was beginning to notice that Jack was a bit of a showman when he wanted to be. She shifted a little closer to him, until their arms touched. The overwhelming sense of rightness soon followed, and she held back a sigh. Jack looked down at her, his large eyes soft. He lifted a hand, as if to touch her, but dropped it.

Jack cleared his throat and continued. "Even as the Fae were mourning their fallen Prince, Brandr was tinkering with his weapons. But the original Djinn could not be put down like dogs. Their immortality was different to that of the Fae, something more primal, more akin to my own immortality, I think. So, he partnered with the Fae's best

GRACE MCGINTY

sorceress, the former Unseelie Queen herself, to
come up with a ritual to bind the weapons to the
original Djinn, keeping them permanently paralyzed
in the Inbetween. They didn't plan for the Djinn to
create their own rituals to release the Djinn, like
your fire pledge, but they are only temporary fixes
anyway. The ritual temporarily short circuits the
original binding, but the older magic soon over-
comes the newer ritual and the Original Djinn is
forced back into their prison. There is only one way
to release all six originals at once."

It sounded like every living thing in the forest
stilled in that moment.

"To put them away, they used the blood of six
Djinn innocents in the ritual. But to bring them
back, you have to sheathe all six weapons in the flesh
of an innocent immortal Fae."

"What?" Stacia paled.

"What?" Azar echoed.

"I'll do it," Nevyn said, jumping down from the
tree. "Don't you see? That's why I'm here, why the
Goddess put me here."

Azar made a grab for Nevyn and pulled him
roughly to her side, in case someone suddenly
decided to lunge for him.

"No damn way! Nuh-uh, no! You can't and we can't."

She only had to take a look at the somber faces around her to see that they may not have a choice. But she wouldn't let it happen.

CHAPTER 19

*W*hen the Fae finally attacked, all Azar could feel at first was relief. Quickly followed by nerves and then a surge of fear-fueled adrenaline.

Scouts had them setting up camps in a U-shape around the den, at least two thousand of them, about fifty miles away.

Too many for the Allied army's numbers to combat hand to hand, and they had nothing useable against them except cold iron swords and a passionate desire to remain free. They'd booby trapped the surrounding forest, but the Fae were hardier than anything a few spiked sticks in a hole could hurt. They could only hope to slow them down, maybe thin their numbers temporarily.

At the pace the Fae army were traveling, which was extraordinarily fast, they had about an hour before the first sword was drawn. She stood nervously in front of her regiment of Unbound. She didn't know what to do or say. If this were a movie, she'd give them a stirring soliloquy about honor and freedom, maybe channel some Mel Gibson in *Braveheart*, but she wasn't that kind of person. She was no one's leader. But they were all staring at her with scared, expectant eyes so she had to give them something.

"Look, I don't know what's going to happen out there, and quite frankly I am scared shitless. But someone once said that courage wasn't the absence of fear, it was carrying on despite it. Or something like that. I was never a very good student. But the chances are, someone you know is going to die. Perhaps the guy next to you. Perhaps we'll all make it through by some kind of miracle. What I want you to know is that what we are fighting for is worth more than my life, or yours. We are fighting for the freedom of our future, so our children won't grow up as slaves. That, I think, is more important than any one life. But I promise you that I won't do anything that will get you killed, at least not on purpose."

They all just stared at her. *Well, William Wallace I am not*, she thought. "Plus, we'll be attached to the Black Prince's guard, and they are skilled immortal fighters. We'll be good."

Now they looked a little more at ease; she could hardly blame them. She was a novice, despite her suddenly impressive skills with a sword, and the Black Guard were fierce, seasoned warriors.

Everyone was equipped with cold iron swords that had been shipped in under the cover of darkness a few days ago. They had been training with them for days, as they were weighted differently to steel swords. Hell, few of their army had never held a sword, but they were more reliable than bullets around the Fae, who still fought in the old way, with sword and shield.

But they had practiced, and they would do the best they could. No one could ask for more than that.

"Oh, and don't accidentally stab the good guys with your sword," she added as an afterthought.

"Listen to your Captain," Hemlock said as he walked in, kitted out for war. He bristled with blades like a porcupine.

"Ugh, don't call me Captain," she hissed at him.

She looked at her Unbound force. "Seriously, don't call me Captain!"

Soon after, Lorcan strode in, resplendent in his war regalia.

"Him you can call Captain," Azar said, walking over to Lorcan. "Are they ready for us in the War Room?"

Lorcan grunted and turned on his heel. She knew that the coming battle was bothering him. How could it not be? Killing off your own kind was hard, she knew. Killing off your family was even harder, even if they were genocidal maniacs. So she just gave him his space.

The War Room was emptier than she'd ever seen it. Just five people were in there; Killian, Aaron, Mira, Ethan and Tao. She and Lorcan made seven. Each of them would head a battalion, though hers was pretty much just honorary given they were to be interspersed amongst Lorcan's Black Guard.

"...we'll come in from the East, Ethan will guard our flank. I think they will try and surround us, and try to push us back into the dens. We have to prevent that at all costs. I don't want this fight to take place too close to the dens, but I don't want to take the fight to them either, spreading out our forces over such a large area would mean losing our defenses."

Killian didn't look stressed; he looked calm and in control. It was reassuring.

"Azar, you and Lorcan will take the West. There is a large force coming in from that side, so be prepared. Trust your instincts, and that of the Black Prince. Keep some of your men in reserve incase the battle is prolonged." He turned and met the eyes of every person in the room. "We will be victorious, but I want you to know that it is an honor to fight beside you all. I'll see you at the end of the battle."

Azar hugged Aaron and Mira. She shook hands with Ethan and Tao.

"Be safe," Killian murmured and she kissed his cheek. "You too. No more funerals for this family any time soon, okay. If you see Cy and Darius, you tell them the same thing, okay?" Killian just gave her a smile that might have actually been a grimace. There was a good chance that half their family could be wiped out in this battle.

Lorcan escorted her from the room.

She'd kissed Bast goodbye that morning, as the scouts had all been working around the clock to ensure that they had accurate information at all times. At first, they'd tried to call back using cellphones, but the large concentration of preternatural energy was messing with the signal, so they had to do it the old-fashioned way. But she wished he could be with her. He was her partner, and she felt safer with him at her side.

She walked out into the courtyard with the unusually quiet Lorcan, and found that Quigley, err Lorcan's Second in Command, had rallied all her troops into rank and file. From the back, where she couldn't see the fear in their eyes, they looked like an almost formidable force.

The rest of the courtyard was filled with other such groupings, half-shifted Weres pacing like they were caged, barely reining in their desire to hunt. The Adel were dressed in their simple black combat gear that was equipped with some kind of super Kevlar, as were the Unbound. Dressed the same, it was hard to tell the full-blooded Djinn from the Unbound. She was dressed in that same gear, plus her sword sheath complete with Basatine, and a grenade or two tucked in her cargo pocket, just in case.

Something brushed against her legs, making her start. Oliver, in his jaguar form, let out an amused huff.

"Aren't you supposed to be with the other Weres guarding Aaron's flank?"

Werejaguar Oliver let out an annoyed yowl, and nudged at Azar's flank.

He says he's not sworn to Aaron, he's sworn to you. It is not Aaron that he loves, it is you, Bast said next to her ear. Bast's voice was tinged with something she couldn't quite put her finger on, but she didn't think it was jealousy.

Azar threw her hands in the air in exasperation.

"Aren't you meant to be running the scouts? Instead of doing your jobs, you're both going to get all up in my personal space, and what? Babysit me?"

My place is at your side, as is Oliver's. You are my heart; I would not go into battle anywhere but with you.

Secretly, she was relieved. She needed him here.

She wasn't sure what she did to deserve such loyalty from these two. After all, in the short time she'd known them, she'd led them from one drama to another, but they'd stood at her side through every trial. They weren't with her because of the ratios of her blood, like her new Unbound brethren. Nor were they with her because they believed her to be the incarnation of some god, like Lorcan and his guard.

No, these two loved her despite the fear and uncertainty in which she'd always found herself. Her eyes misted, and she sucked in a choppy breath.

Oliver let out a pained noise and rubbed his face all over her hips and belly, the closest thing her could give her to a hug without knocking her down. Bast gave her butterfly kisses over her cheek.

She straightened her shoulders and rubbed her eyes with her sleeve.

"Thanks guys. Now let's get this shit over with. I need a beer, a pizza and to spend three whole days in my pajamas watching Spanish soap operas." She looked around for Donovan, but she couldn't see him. Her heart hurt. She wanted to say goodbye, to tell him to remain safe, but he could be anywhere in the multitude of tunnels in the den. She'd looked for him this morning, but they seemed to never be in the same place at the same time. When this was all over, she was going to crawl into his lap and make love to him for days.

She cast a look at Oliver, and felt Bast's reassuring presence around her shoulders. Maybe they'd make Oliver's cabin a love shack for real.

Sighing, she nodded at Lorcan, and he whistled and made a swirly motion in the air.

"Let's move out!"

They left the marshaling area with enough contained energy to power a small third world country for a year. She was positioned roughly in the center of their ranks, Bast and Oliver bracketing her side, Hemlock guarding her rear, as well as the mass of Unbound that made up their ranks. There were three rows of the Prince's Black Guard in front of her.

Enya was scouting the enemy's position and she'd appeared out of thin air at Lorcan's side, whispered something, and then disappeared again into the shadows.

They jogged along at a slow pace, well slow for supernaturals, in the general direction of the reported Fae encampments.

After about an hour, Lorcan slipped back to Azar.

"Enya says that there is a small Fae force three miles north. Given the number, it is probably just one of my brothers' personal guards." She'd seen Lorcan's guard fight, and she hoped that he'd picked all the decent soldiers, and his brothers got all the uncoordinated leftovers.

Hemlock began organizing the Unbound, the Black Guard finding their formation without as much as a word. They spread the Unbound on the periphery.

"Engage two on one if you can. Do not come between to Fae combatants. It's a good way to lose a limb," Hemlock quietly counseled the nervous looking Unbound fighters.

And between one breath and the next, the enemy force was upon them. The Black Guard closed ranks a little tighter around her.

"Brother," said Cian, Golden Prince of the Unseelie Fae, "Mother told me you were batting for the other team, but I refused to believe her. You, who were always spouting off about the oppressive nature of the caste system, coming into this battle on the side of the oppressor? Impossible. But yet here you stand with your merry band of offal," Cian laughed. He was surrounded by the Golden Guard, who were all females and all had the same feral, battle-crazed eyes. Azar was just glad to see Cian fully clothed.

"We were not oppressed by the Tuatha De Danann, Cian. We were contained by it, and rightfully so. And you know why I fought against the caste system. It was that system that forced you to stay in the Unseelie Court, under the tender ministrations of our mother. I would have spared you that if I could. I would spare my worst enemy that."

Azar noticed that not even Lorcan looked directly at Cian, so he didn't see the pain and regret in Cian's eyes, the same loneliness that she'd seen the night they'd broken into the *Sidhes*.

"You tried, Brother. Unfortunately, it is what it is."

"You were but a babe."

"I am an abomination. I am where I am supposed to be. Enough of this. Who is it that your loyal guard gathers around so protectively, if it isn't their beloved leader?" Cian's Golden Guard pressed forward and the soldiers around me raised their swords higher, prepared to defend.

"That's none of your business," Lorcan growled, drawing his own weapon.

Cian whistled between his teeth. "I'm intrigued. I think I shall find out, by force if I must. It must be quite a prize indeed."

"I do not wish to kill you," Lorcan said, and she heard the edges of grief. He obviously felt something for this sad, twisted man, although he'd assured her many times that he no longer had any loyalty to the Fae outside his own guard.

She would spare him this pain if she could.

"It's okay, Lorcan. Let me through. The Golden Prince and I have already met." When she pushed up to Lorcan's side, Cian's eyebrows rose comically high on his stupidly attractive forehead.

"It's my favorite Seelie slave girl," he exclaimed.

She looked him dead in the eye. "It's nice to see you again, Cian. With pants on, no less."

Cian boomed out a laugh. "Are you really glad to see me fully clothed? Not even a little disappointed?"

She chuckled despite herself. "Okay, maybe a little. All that gold really washes you out."

His smile was truly joyous. "What are you that you can look me in the eye and say these things to me so cavalierly?"

"Unimpressed?" she countered. It must be horrible to go through life without ever truly being looked in the eye.

"My, but you are refreshing. Perhaps I should have kept you after all."

"Unfortunately, I'm not up for possession."

In an instant, he was in front of her, amidst the Black Guard, his hand in her hair in a firm, but not cruel, grasp. "I promise you would enjoy it."

Both sides surged forward, and Lorcan's sword was at his brother's neck.

"Let her go," Lorcan growled, but she waved him away. She had it under control.

"Like I told you last time, you aren't my type." She maintained eye contact. "For one, I don't like being manhandled." She lifted her knee, and drove it into his groin. He buckled over, laughing. Why did everyone she kicked in the testicles seem to find it so incredibly amusing? "Secondly, while I'm flattered, I'm taken."

In fact, the angry force of nature that was Bast was whipping himself up into a small tornado at her treatment, sending the Golden guard into a frenzy. Oliver was now in front of her, pacing back and forth, his lips pulled back baring deadly jaguar teeth. This was beginning to escalate. If she didn't end this soon, it was going to end in unnecessary bloodshed no matter what she said.

"If you are done with your posturing, you should call off your harpies before my boyfriend causes a category six hurricane."

Cian gave a command she didn't understand, and his guard all fell back behind their Prince in near perfect synchronicity.

"Did he just tell them to heel in Gaelic?" Azar whispered, and Lorcan shook his head, but didn't elaborate. Oh well, she would ask again later. Probably better to be serene or beatific or whatever else she was supposed to be as a demi-goddess.

"Look," she addressed both of the princes in front of her. "This doesn't have to end in brother killing brother, Fae killing Fae. In fact, I'd like to get through this day with as few deaths on my conscience as possible. Lorcan obviously cares for you, and that tells me that there is something in you worth saving. So, I am giving you the opportunity to leave, unaccosted and unpursued," as she spoke, she shifted to her Ifrit form until the last words came through flaming lips. "Because I can promise you this; at the end of today, there will not be an enemy left alive on this battlefield."

"A Djinn? No, that's not all you are, I think. However, as much as my guard and I would rather be in the *Sidhes*, in bed." He made it sound like they'd all be in bed together. "If I leave now, and you aren't as victorious as you believe, my punishment for desertion will be far worse than anything your tiny brain could even fathom."

Lorcan growled then, low and almost Were like. "We will not lose. Go, little brother. I did not pry mother's fingers from your throat at birth only to have you die here. Go!"

Cian seemed to consider it, worrying his lower lip in an almost human gesture that did not fit with his otherworldly looks.

"I will go. But I am betting my life, and the life of my guard, on your skills, so I must know who you are." His eyes ran over her face critically, as if he was cataloguing every tiny bump, bruise and scar.

Azar drew in a deep breath. Her spiel was long. "I am Azar, Councilor for the Unbound, member of the Ifrit, human, and Tuatha Dé Danann races. I am Danu's chosen one."

Cian blinked slowly. And then again.

"Well. Quite the mongrel, aren't you? We'll go. But I hope to see you both soon." The 'alive' was insinuated.

I will go after them, to ensure they keep their word, Bast whispered to her.

Then, just as they appeared, they vanished between one breath and the next. She wished Bast luck trying to keep up with their disappearing act.

She couldn't help but smile. "One battle down, body count zero. That's a success in anyone's book, I think."

Lorcan was just watching the horizon and gave her a non-committal hum.

He looked back at their group. "Let's move," he barked, and everyone fell back into their ranks, and she was hustled back into her sequestered position in the middle.

She looked over her shoulder at Hemlock.

"So, Cian's Golden Guard. Are they all under his

enchantment? Are they all devoted to him because they have to stare at him all day?"

Hemlock nodded. "Yes. But it is a small consolation that most of them don't realize their love for him is unnatural. There's some anecdotal evidence that the effect of his power wears off after several decades, but by that time you are well and truly tied to the Prince. Besides, most would stay because it keeps them out of reach of the Blood Prince, and that is a fate far worse."

Her eyes shifted to Enya's arms, where she was giving a report to Lorcan at the front. One hundred perfect scars. She was on the fence about Cian's ability, but she knew unequivocally that it was better than that. She caught Lorcan's attention and he fell back.

"Do you think that I have just let an enemy go so they can circle back and kill us later? Or will Cian actually leave?"

Lorcan huffed out a sigh. "I would thank you for your compassion, but with Cian, it is often difficult to predict. His dual natures are often at war. He collects those battered Amazons he calls a guard from the slave quarters and low caste Fae, saving them from lives of degradation. He never picks from esteemed warrior clans, instead choosing to nurture the malnourished waifs back to health. But then he subjugates them, taking their free will, as if he needs an ulterior motive for his kindness. Most would probably fight for him without the compulsion of his abilities, but then, the Unseelie Court is no place for trust." He sighed, eyes constantly scanning the trees. "He may stay away, he may not. I can only hope-"

An unearthly scream echoed across the forest, making her jump in her own skin.

"What the hell was that?"

"Goblins," Hemlock answered as Lorcan moved back to the front and she followed.

Enya ran out of the trees.

"The Goblin King has arrived. I'd hoped he'd forgotten." There was a definite grimness to her voice.

Goblins. Azar had never met one in her travels, as she'd never spent much time in the eastern European mountains, where they gathered in secular clans. But she'd heard they were big, grotesque and a little bit dumb. She was about to find out if all those things were true.

A falcon flew down and landed on Lorcan's shoulder, squawked several times, and then took off with a graceful flap of its wings.

"Did you catch that?" she asked Hemlock, but it was Bast, who answered.

He said that the goblins didn't send as many troops as promised, and the King only sent his fifth best general. He didn't make a personal appearance himself. I couldn't pick up Cian's trail either.

Only his fifth best general and a small army. "We can do this without raising the Originals?" The stomach-churning hope was almost unbearable.

No, Jaanaman. There are still over six thousand of them.

Azar deflated. "Fuckballs! If that's a small contingent, how big is their entire army? No, don't tell me, I don't want to know. We are so fucking screwed." Hysterical desolation was beginning to creep into her outwardly confident demeanor. Several of the Unbound gave her the side eye, and she took a deep breath. She didn't want to freak them out. After all, they could only hear one side of this conversation.

Hemlock, however, had caught the general idea. "Not necessarily. The goblins rely purely on numbers. They swarm the enemy like ants. But they aren't particularly skilled fighters. They are almost exclusively farmers and sheep herders. The Were outclass them as fighters. If we can break up their ranks, they will be easy pickings." They'd be child's play to a Fae warrior then.

The Goblin mass let out another ear-piercing battle cry. Azar tripped and stumbled at the inhuman sound of it, but Oliver butted her back into position. She reached down and ran a hand through his thick fur.

"There is a skirmish that way," Lorcan said, pointing through a stand of ancient pines. "We will provide support. Gird yourselves."

In a normal situation, she would have laughed at anyone who used the word gird in conversation. Right now though, she was too busy keeping up as their troops began running faster than any human Olympian, but still be comically slow for the Fae and Weres.

They burst through the tree line into a small clearing, and Azar got her first look at a goblin. Bile rose in her throat. They were grotesque. An insipid green, they were roughly humanoid with large, oozing lumps on the flesh that was exposed by the rough linen rags they wore. From what she could see, every member of goblin society fought in the goblin army; men, women and children. Although there wasn't a lot of difference physically between the first two from the waist up, she could spot the difference as their, err, junk swung around between lumpy thighs, ineffectually hidden by leather loin cloths.

Azar could see a tiny goblin child, no bigger than Freya, standing in the middle of the fighting, holding a short sword and crying. It turned her stomach.

Oliver let out a disgusted growl when he spotted the child too.

"What kind of race sends their young into battle?" Azar wondered.

It was Hemlock who answered again. He was her walking encyclopedia slash guard today, apparently.

"The Goblin King sends entire clans to fight, any person able to stand and hold a sword. Often women will fight with babes strapped to their backs if there is no one left to care for them. Any goblin or clan who refuses to fight is executed. Whole villages would burn in retaliation. But do not be fooled. Even the young have been trained to kill for survival. They may not be very good, but they can run you through and will not hesitate to do so."

"That's barbaric." She couldn't keep her disgust out of her voice.

"In war, you do what you have to do, and ask Danu for forgiveness about it later." It was his barely veiled way of saying that he would kill the goblin child just as if she were an adult. She was going to throw-up.

But the momentum of battle prevented any further conversation, as swords were drawn and battle lines surged together. She drew Basatine and let the sentient knowledge take control of her arm and lift itself into a perfect defensive position. It felt eager, as if it had tasted goblin blood before.

"No children," she told the sword, and only felt slightly deranged.

Azar quickly took stock of the battle. The goblins seemed to have cornered Ethan's squad, who were mostly Unbound and Were, and while they were holding their own, they were outnumbered and slowly being pushed back.

She let the adrenaline of battle overcome her as she swirled through the oozing mass of goblins. She cut down two, four, and then ten goblins before she lost count. The sword must have listened, because it would shy away from the younger members of the goblin army.

She was splattered with pus and guts, but eventually she found herself in front of the crying goblin girl, who was still standing in the same spot clutching her sword to her chest like a life buoy.

Azar leaned down a little, always aware of her

surroundings. "It's okay," she cooed in a gentle voice amidst the violence. "Why don't you go and hide until this is all over?" The little girl blinked big, black eyes, then turned towards the woods and began picking her way to their cover.

Azar turned back to the melee of battle. She heard the tiny, high pitched battle cry too late and had only half turned to see the goblin girl's dull sword inches from her face. Azar froze, Basatine hanging useless by her side.

Then Hemlock was there, slicing the child's sword arm from her body.

Azar gaped, watching the limb writhe around on the ground, oozing brown blood.

"I told you not to hesitate," Hemlock growled as he flashed back into the fray.

She just stood there, looking at the now still arm, and the little girl who had passed out from pain or blood loss. For the first time in her life, she didn't know what to do. It was against her nature to leave a child to die, even one that had just tried to kill her. So she whacked a flaming hand over the girl's still bleeding stump, stopping the flow of blood. Then she picked up the girl's sword, which was still gripped in the decapitated hand, and turned away.

Danu could curse her for her inaction later.

While she had been preoccupied with the smallest member of the enemy army, the tide of the battle had turned, and the goblins began to scatter into the trees, pursued by the Weres. She looked over her shoulder to see someone had picked up the little girl and her arm on their retreat and she felt strangely relieved.

However, there were plenty of bodies still remaining, mostly goblins but some of her allies as well. She made herself commit every one of those fallen Unbound and Were faces to memory.

You put too much on your own shoulders, Azar. She knew Bast was serious because he hardly ever called her by her name. *They knew death may come for them when they signed up. Their deaths aren't yours to lament.*

"I am their Councilor, their packmate. Every one of their deaths is mine to lament." With that, she sheathed Basatine and walked to where Lorcan stood with Ethan.

"We will wait for the pursuing Weres to return, and then our two squads will join together. I can feel a flood of power from the north-east. It is here we need to go, but we will need numbers."

Ethan nodded in agreement, and so did Azar as she slumped down on the closest rock. The hair stood up on the back of her neck every time she turned north-east, the primal part of her brain recognizing the power and prompting her to run away.

She needed to rest and process. All those epic fantasy novels she'd read didn't really let on how much your arm hurts when you are swinging around a sword for even a short period of time. Even magic imbued, partially sentient ones.

She tried not to focus on the brown sludge of goblin blood and dirt, or the unseeing eyes of the dead. Those images she'd just store in an iron chest in her mind, to sort through once this was all over. If she died before that, then it wouldn't matter.

I would spare you this if I could, the wind whispered in Bast's voice.

Oliver let out a yowl of agreement, though it was somewhat less endearing considering he was lying at her feet licking goblin blood from his huge paws.

"I know. I would spare us all this day if I could."

A triumphant chorus went up, as the Weres came barreling back through the tree line. A wolf shifted into a very naked man. "They've scattered," he informed Ethan and Lorcan, not even out of breath.

"We head north-east," Lorcan ordered, and everyone was on their feet and in their lines in seconds.

They moved swiftly and silently for a group so large. As they walked, a medic flitted through the ranks, patching up wounds, giving out water, making sure no one died on the march.

Too soon, they found themselves on a small sheltered outcropping that overlooked a valley. Given the amount of noise, both psychic and physical, they'd found their battle.

Enya appeared at Lorcan's side. "The Queen and the Imposter King are on the ridge. Seven of our squadrons are fighting a primarily Fae force, and we are severely depleted."

"What is the Queen doing?"

"From what I can see, they are just watching the battle, Sir."

Lorcan grunted, and Ethan gave a snort. The likelihood that the Queen was just here to enjoy the show and not participate was too fantastical to even hope for.

"We can't stand here and let them be slaughtered," Ethan said, and Lorcan agreed.

"Circle around to their flank, make them turn back in on themselves. I'll take care of the Queen and Finlay." Azar turned to go with the army, but Lorcan pointed one graceful finger in her direction. "You stay."

The group split up, the bulk of their little army melting into the trees, leaving only Azar, Oliver and four of the Black Guard with Lorcan.

"Shouldn't I go with them?" Azar protested.

"No. I need you with me."

"Because you don't trust anyone else with my safety." It wasn't a question but he answered anyway.

"Essentially."

Azar huffed but she didn't argue. Only an idiot would begrudge the protection of the Black Prince.

She'd like to survive today, and if that made her a selfish coward, then so be it. Oliver stuck to her side like glue, and Bast stayed too, of course. No one had suggested otherwise.

They slanted north across the rocky outcropping, staying low and deep in the cover of the tree line, towards the northern ridge of the valley.

This needed to be over now. Every time she looked down at the valley, the bodies seemed to be thicker on the ground.

"Cut the head off the snake," she assured herself quietly, but Enya still heard.

"Unfortunately, this snake is more like a hydra. But we can still give her a few less mouths to spit her poison from," Enya grumbled. Hemlock rumbled his agreement.

"Quiet," Lorcan chastised from the front, as they went to their bellies and shimmied up the backside of the ridge, out of the direct line of sight of Finlay and the Queen.

Azar desperately wanted to know what the Queen looked like. She got brief glimpses of long straight blond hair that hung like a waterfall to the ground, where it curled gently above the dirt. It was beautiful, except that it was woven with the bones and skulls of some small creatures she couldn't identify.

The Queen turned, looking directly at the spot where they lay, still splayed out on their stomachs.

"Lorcan, you've arrived!" Lustre, Queen of the Unseelie Fae, sounded like a delighted mother whose prodigal son had returned home.

Every single person was on their feet in a flash, swords drawn. Oliver let out a roar that cracked off the surrounding trees.

"Ah, Son, I am so glad you could join us. We've been waiting for you."

Lustre stood in the embrace of Finlay, and she only looked a little annoyed when the smug faced Imposter King put his hands on her breasts. By god, she was beautiful though. There were hints of Cian in her face. Perfect turquoise eyes framed with thick dark lashes, high cheekbones on a perfect heart shaped face. Her body was something that would make grown men weep with joy.

Lustre closed her eyes, her body pressed against Finlay, who was looking down at her adoringly. Then, as one, everyone in her party dropped to the ground, writhing. Instinctively, Azar dropped with them, looking for some kind of attack. Then they started screaming in pain. Bast was shouting ancient, pained Persian in her head until she had to block him out. She looked for Oliver and Lorcan. She spotted Lorcan, his head pressed between his hands.

"Lorcan! What's wrong?"

"She's stronger," he whispered. "I don't know how, but her illusions are seeping in. I can't fight them." His eyes were shifting back and forth between violet and pure liquid black. A black so deep that it made her chest hurt. She had a really bad feeling. When he stood, the grass around him shriveled and turned black. This was bad, bad, bad. So she did the first thing that popped into her head, and swung Basatine like a baseball bat at his skull. His head whipped to the side with a thud, and he was out cold.

She glanced a look at Lustre and Finlay, who seemed to assume that everyone was under Lustre's compulsion. They were watching the ensuing chaos with gleeful abandon. The entire battlefield screeched in pain, trying to tear each other apart, even the enemy troops had turned on each other until it was just one big brawl. There were no longer allegiances, just every person trapped in their own living hell, struggling to survive.

Azar made her way toward the pair of royals, playing possessed marionette, disabling but not harming those in her group. Hemlock and Enya were fighting at a speed that rivaled the swirling winds of a tornado; spinning, kicking and striking at such momentum that it was whipping up the dirt and leaves at their feet. Using their fight as cover, Azar switched forms to Ifrit, lighting Basatine up with its electric blue fire. Stepping around the fighting soldiers, she raced towards Finlay, sword raised.

Sensing her approach, Finlay's own sword came up and blocked Basatine.

"Ah, I thought that was you. How is my cousin? I'd like to give the little abomination my regards." He parried and thrust, and she flowed away. She gritted her teeth and flowed through sword forms that she didn't know. Danu bless Basatine, the bloodthirsty blade.

"Sorry," Azar grunted out. "Nevyn is a long way from here. Maybe you could send him a postcard from Hell?"

Finlay laughed. "I don't think so, Peasant." He was continually in motion, and she was struggling to keep up. "Soon, your precious Black Prince will wake up, and the Queen's illusions will bend his mind, and he will kill everyone in this forsaken valley, including you." He grunted as Basatine's blade grazed his upper arm. "Then, the Queen and I will repopulate the Fae under one court, with only the superior bloodlines."

The Queen in question stayed pressed against Finlay's back, away from the thrusts of Azar's blade. The two royals danced around in perfect unison, always pressed so close that if Azar could manage to run Finlay through, it chanced on going through both of them like a shish-kebob.

His blade glanced off her forearm, and she let out a hiss, dancing back a few steps.

"Sounds incestuous," she said between puffs. "But you're just pretty arm candy. She's the one doing all the work," she guessed. She stepped forward, swinging at him with her sword. "So, like a man. Don't do any of the work, but take all the glory."

Finlay's face scrunched in rage. "I am the only

reason she can reach the entire valley at all! Without me, she wouldn't be able to control half this army, let alone Lorcan!"

She swung high, forcing Finlay to dance backwards and give her some breathing room.

"So, you are the Fae equivalent to a booster box? Very impressive. I mean, what's the ability to turn people into black corpses next to that?" Sarcasm dripped from her panted words.

Bless his conceited little soul. She just needed to separate them. Even as they fought though, Lustre was moving with them in perfect synchronicity, although her concentration was obviously elsewhere, or she would have smacked Finlay down for being the stereotypical, psychopathic bad guy and running his mouth.

Azar feinted, and using her wings as leverage, flipped sharply to the left, causing Finlay to turn quickly, and momentarily lose contact with the Queen. Lustre looked annoyed and quickly returned her hand to the skin of Finlay's back.

"Who is this?" her voice tinkled out, so delicate and sweet, though there were edges of cruelty that even the sweetest of voices couldn't conceal.

"The Djinn harboring Nevyn of the Golden Court. An annoyance, no more."

"Well get rid of her already," Lustre snapped, her eyes closing in concentration again.

Azar had stood there dumbfounded for the entire conversation. The sun glinting off the Queen's pearlescent skin was mesmerizing in a completely unnatural way. Even more unnatural was that, at this close of a range, Azar had noticed the woman had dimples. There was something terrifying about a woman with dimples systematically torturing thousands of people at that very moment.

Finlay's sword coming down to cleave her skull snapped her out of her Queen induced daydream. She turned, but too slow, the blade missing her head but catching on her wing, slicing it from her back.

She screamed at the searing pain, but knew that it was going to be her head next if she gave into the urge to sink to her knees.

The sight of her wing, blackened and leathery, lying on the scuffed dirt, made something inside her snap. A red haze came down over her vision, her mind went blank and all she could hear was her own feral screams.

She would later hear Oliver tell people that she went primal, a Were term for when they give themselves over completely to their animal, usually living out the short remainder of their lives as rabid creatures. Eventually the primal Were would be hunted down by their own pack, too dangerous to live.

Whether she went primal or not, the Ifrit that shared her skin roared to the surface, blocking out any coherent thought.

CHAPTER 20

When she fought her way back into control of her own body, the Queen was on the ground with the pointy end of Basatine at her throat and tiny pieces of Finlay scattered around them. And she meant tiny. The only piece of him that was recognizable was one half of his skull that had been split in two and charred around the edges at some point after its decapitation.

She was going to vomit. She looked around for someone, anyone else, that was able to dismember a man like that. Although Lorcan was standing, he was well back, staring at her and the Queen with forced blankness.

Azar? Bast's voice in her head sounded scared.

"I... I'm sorry."

It's okay, Jaanaman, heart of mine. You are you again. His voice was soothing against the rawness of her emotions. He sounded relieved.

She was back in her human form, nothing but a few scratches along her naked body. It was then she noticed the blackened wing beneath the detritus of what was once Finlay.

"My wing."

It is too late, I'm afraid. We were under the Queen's illusion, and then no one could get close to you without harming you, or being harmed themselves. You were in a frenzy. Oliver said your scent changed, it was wrong; raw, like rage and old fire ashes.

Oliver let out a discontented whine.

You almost beheaded Lorcan when he came close.

"I'm sorry," she said again, not just to Lorcan, but to everyone else who was looking a little pasty around the edges. She dropped her gaze, and unfortunately that meant it landed on Lustre, who still wore a smug grin even though the tip of Basatine was cutting into her slender throat. Azar looked harder, and noticed the fine lines of strain around eyes that held a touch of fear.

The Queen laughed, but it was a forced, cruel sound.

"Look at you, showing remorse for killing your

enemies. Such a pathetic species. You really need the Fae to save you from yourselves and your weakness." A drop of blood welled in the hollow of her throat like a ruby.

"It's over. You are at the end of my sword. Obviously, we don't need you for shit, so how about you shut your pie hole."

To Azar's annoyance, she laughed again. "Over? Oh, you naïve child. While you were over there hacking Finlay to death, Oisrin and the Goblin army were sneaking into the heart of your territory and doing what Oisrin does best. I am just a distraction." It was bullshit, she was just hedging her failure. But Azar couldn't chance it.

Bast, go! If she's telling the truth, it might be time to go to plan Z.

Oisrin and the goblin army would soon swarm over the remaining forces, especially if Lorcan's Fae weren't there to even the numbers. The thought of causing Nevyn pain, or even death, made her heart ache. But if they didn't do this, they might all die.

The remaining members of Lorcan's guard sifted away also, but not before Hemlock threw her his tabard. Azar pressed Basatine even closer to Lustre's throat. "A distraction you might be, but you are about to be a dead distraction."

Lustre scoffed, her delicate face alight with mockery. "You? Who is having such a delightfully animated internal conflict of what you did to Finlay in the heat of battle? You are going to execute me in cold blood, weaponless and powerless on the ground in front of you? I doubt it. I do not fear you, Abomination. I can take the mind of any other member of your toy army, except my son." She turned her head to look at Lorcan and Azar's blade scraped across the skin of her throat, leaving a long red gash. "But unfortunately for you, in his own twisted way, he loves me. And killing me would break him, though he would still do it to protect his stupid ideals. He would have made a terrible Unseelie King. He cares too much."

"You do not know my mind, Lustre," Lorcan growled.

"Do I not? You should have killed me years ago. We both know your power exceeds mine. Yet you did not, even when you disagreed with my...practices." The way she said *practices* made Azar want to run away and hide under her blankets like a child.

"You are my mother."

"You are nothing more than a spawn to me. I would kill you in a heartbeat, weakling."

"And yet you never tried. Isn't that a sign of

something from a woman who tried to drown her third child at birth?" There was a faint longing in his voice.

Her heart broke for him. Her own time with her mother had been brief but filled with love. Looking down at the twisted beauty at her feet, she didn't think there was any chance that Lustre harbored anything resembling love in her entire body, except maybe for herself.

Her next statement confirmed it.

"No. A wise ruler knows not to go into battles she cannot win."

"Yet here we are," Azar retorted, "with you at the end of my sword."

"I haven't lost yet, Djinn peasant. Not while I still breathe."

Someone reached past Azar and grabbed Basatine from her hands, and slid its blade through Lustre's pale throat. She could not draw her eyes away from the blade as it slid from one side to the other, removing her head with ease amidst the gushing of bright, red blood.

She finally looked up, meeting Lorcan's glass-eyed gaze, though he hadn't moved from his place across the clearing.

Azar stood there stunned as Nevyn handed her back Basatine.

"She was right. Neither of you would have executed her. But her soul was as black as a starless night. There was no goodness in her." He looked at Lorcan. "She does not deserve your grief."

"Yet she will have it, because the heart knows no logic," he bowed slightly towards them both and then sifted to the edge of the outcropping. "The Queen is dead." His voice echoed off the walls of the valley, making everyone stop. "The Imposter King is dead. I am now your Unseelie King. Lay down your weapons and be spared my wrath."

It wasn't an idle threat. One by one, they lowered their weapons and knelt facing him. He bowed low toward them once. Then he walked away from the outcropping and sifted into nothingness.

Azar stared at Nevyn for a long minute. Once again, she'd taken Nevyn as the boy he appeared, rather than the soul that had spent so many years in a treacherous society.

Then she remembered Oisrin and the goblins. "What about the pledging ceremony? The Queen said that Oisrin was attacking the dens."

Nevyn nodded. "Bast returned, but too late. Oisrin and the goblins had already pushed into the dens. Jack has taken my place in the ritual. He knew that you would not forgive yourself for my pain. He is the Heart of the World, the most innocent creature on the planet. He will raise your Old Ones. But we should hurry, I can feel them shifting beneath the earth." He grabbed her arms and sifted out, Oliver's growl at being left behind rang in her ears. She was going to have to do a lot of apologizing to him later. Probably naked. Hopefully naked.

The battle raging at the mouth of the den was fierce and bloody. Goblins, slick with gore, threw themselves at their opponents with frenzied abandon despite missing limbs. Between the blood, dirt and screaming, she couldn't tell if her allies were winning or losing. A great boom rumbled beneath the ground, the earth trembling as a chasm opened mere feet away. She ran, pulling Nevyn along behind her. Fae, goblin and Were alike scrambled away from the spreading abyss, but not all were quick enough, some falling into the darkness. A deep sense of foreboding shivered down her spine, as a black claw curled over the lip of the chasm.

She fell to her knees in the dirt and wept with fear. It paralyzed every muscle in her body, except for her heart that was thundering so quickly she felt lightheaded.

Thanamen, the original Shaitan. He was the creature upon whom the Christian ideas of Satan and his demons were based.

Some of the Shaitan and Unbound with Shaitan blood were pulling their allies out of the way of the eighteen-foot primitive god. Unfortunately, the goblins weren't so lucky, lying prone on the ground like a release-day appetizer.

Someone picked her up by the back of Hemlock's borrowed tabard, grabbing Nevyn too, and dragged them into the mouth of the den. But not so fast that she didn't see one fiery wing curl out of the ground.

Balraka.

A part of her wanted to get a look at the first Ifrit, but the human part of her wanted to run away, so far and fast that she'd never see another paranormal creature again except in the mirror

She looked up and saw Donovan, his eyes shining onyx beneath a gash on his forehead.

"Thanks," she tried to smile.

He leaned forward and kissed her lips hard. "Always." Then he was running back out into the clearing and pulling allies back towards the den.

Inside the dens, the fighting was just as intense. Enemy Fae warriors fought against the Adel and Lorcan's Black Guard.

"Drive them out of the dens!" Her shout echoed down the stone tunnels. Her foot kicked something solid and she realized belatedly that it was a body, drained completely of blood, the red liquid pooled around an empty husk. She quickly averted her gaze, not wanting to chance recognizing the face of the corpse. Her cast iron chest was getting too full.

They ran down the hall, dodging skirmishes and the husks of fallen soldiers, following the trail of exsanguinated blood that flowed like a river along the stone flooring. But she knew where he was heading. She just needed to get there first.

The weapons vault that housed the Great Weapons was in the deepest part of the dens, the route there so twisted and confusing that she'd come up with a mnemonic rhyme just to remember, but Oisrin was yet to take a wrong turn, as if he knew the way. Or like he was being led. Did they have a traitor? Could he sense the weapons? Neither idea filled her with warmth.

When they reached the double doors of the weapons vault, it was to the sound of a fierce battle raging. It filled her with intense relief. It meant she wasn't too late.

She turned to Nevyn. "Find Freya. Your mission is to protect her." With Donovan out there fighting, she worried for the little girl. Nevyn gave a solemn nod and disappeared.

She pushed the door open just a crack, edging into the battle. Oisrin was fighting with a huge Ifrit she recognized as Killian. The battle was beautiful, fast and fierce, a whirl of fire and blades. Killian should have healed almost instantly from any cuts, but he was being hit with a magic imbued Fae blade, and he was healing almost humanly slow. Oisrin on the other hand was looking singed around the edges. But it was Killian who was flagging fast.

Taking a deep breath, she rushed beneath the fiery nova of Killian's wings to where she could see Jack laid out on the dais, pierced with the six Great Weapons. He seemed to be unconscious, and that worried her. This needed to be over now.

She ran at Oisrin, Basatine swinging, but like the good soldier that he was, he sensed her coming and turned, catching her blade in the ribs. She heard them crack.

Oisrin roared in rage, opening up dozens of cuts on her brother's body, and he fell to the ground, incapacitated as his body desperately tried heal.

Oisrin turned his entire attention to her.

"Die," he said in a cold voice without inflection.

"It's over. Lustre and Finlay are dead." She edged around him, staying out of his sword range.

"You lie!" He exploded toward her, his blade flashing so fast that Azar could barely see the blade let alone parry it. Basatine was doing a fairly good job of deflecting the blows, but it only had her half-mortal reflexes to work with, allowing most of Oisrin's strikes to hit their target. Blood began to pour from her body, aided by the Blood Prince's ability. She could feel the thick liquid emptying from her veins to pool at her feet.

"They send a mortal to fight me?" Oisrin laughed, thrusting a blade toward her abdomen. Basatine moved up sluggishly, but her balance was lost, and she fell, landing on the flat of her back. She was beginning to feel the chill in her bones and the room began to spin. This was it.

Basatine was still half-heartedly trying to block Oisrin's blade, but she could barely keep her head up, let alone her guard. She turned to watch Killian try to get to his feet, but he was losing blood as fast as his Djinn body could replace it. She had no such luck. She healed mortal slow in both forms.

She could no longer maintain her grip on Basatine, and he clattered to the hard stone floor. The tip of Oisrin's sword pressed against her throat.

"For my mother," he growled. She held his gaze, defiant.

And then his head exploded.

Blood, brains and bits of skull rained down over her face, getting in her mouth and eyes.

She wanted to scream but she didn't have the energy. She couldn't even lift her arm to wipe her face.

Ethan's face came into view, and if she could have sat up, she would have kissed him.

"Seriously, what is with the fucking swords? Does no one realize it's the twenty-first century. Iron bullets beat your ornamental letter openers every day of the week. Patch her up," he said to someone behind him. He leaned down and wiped the gore from her face. "Can't lose our Councilor this early in the game."

Someone rushed over, stemming her bleeding, using some kind of staple gun to stitch the larger gashes closed.

There was a flurry near the door and Oliver ran in, still in jaguar form. He sniffed her gashes, and took in the now headless Oisrin and let out a roar that was deafening inside the weapons vault. He grabbed the corpse by the arm and flung it around the room like a chew toy. It was disturbing watching the animal form of a man she loved tear apart the headless body of her enemy. Disturbing, and a little satisfying. She had issues.

Finished decimating what remained of Oisrin, he prowled toward her. He was very obviously pissed. He leaned right over her face and she couldn't help but shy away a little. She could see his disappointment in those intelligent cat eyes. He growled and shifted to human. Ruh-roh.

"What the fuck, Azar? You can't just leave me behind like that! I was meant to be watching your back. Bast is going to kill us both when he finds out." He was agitated, waving his arms around as he spoke. Unfortunately, she was still on the ground. And he was naked from his shift. All she could see from this angle was his junk waving around in the breeze.

"I'm sorry, okay? But if you want to keep yelling at me, either put some pants on or get me to my feet. I can't concentrate from this angle."

Oliver just stared at her, his grim face slowly transforming into the grinning Oliver she knew and loved. He reached down and helped her gently to her feet. He pulled her into a tight, albeit naked, hug. They were fast becoming her favorite type of hug.

"Thank god you're alive. I saw you bleeding on

the floor..." Then he did something very catlike and rubbed his cheek along hers, his stubble scraping like sandpaper, completely uncaring that he was smearing blood across her skin.

Azar rubbed soothing circles on his back. "I know. I'm fine though. But if Bast catches you hugging me naked in front of half the den, he really will kick your ass."

He grinned and released her, darting out into the hall, and returned wearing pants. She resisted the urge to pout. Now they were officially a thing, she was suddenly very fond of his need to be nude.

She stumbled toward the dais, Oliver holding her under one elbow to keep her steady. Killian was giving orders, back on his feet and with a few new scars, but really no worse for wear. She stared down at Jack on the dais, counting the weapons lodged in his flesh. Posidagi, the dagger that had almost killed Bast, was pierced through his left palm. She hated seeing that dagger embedded in another man she cared for. She wanted to tear it out of his skin and throw it into the huge chasm that had opened up in front of the den. Umedesta, the Indian style Katar that Roxx had stolen from the Finlay's bedchambers, was pierced through Jack's other hand. Drakhul, the Ifrit sword, was pierced through one thigh, pushed all the way into the stone. The curved edge of the chakram, Ibsali, pressed into the meat of his thigh, and the spear-tip of Abazhana through his left calf muscle. But all these were overshadowed by Zindagi, which was sliced through the flesh of his ass cheek, held in place by ropes secured to rings around the dais.

His normally luminescent skin was grey and pallid, and he looked dead.

She couldn't stand them being in his flesh anymore and began ripping them out. Oliver stopped her when she got to Drakhul.

"I'm not taking any chances," he said as he drew it out of Jack's thigh, moving it carefully back into its protective case.

With the removal of the last weapon, life rushed back into Jack's body and he drew in a deep breath. His eyes fluttered open.

"Are you okay?" She leaned over him, searching for signs of pain. She rested her hands on the dais, mostly to keep herself from falling flat on her face. But it meant she was very close to Jack's face.

"It's good to see you, Azar of the Ifrit. Do I take it that you have won?" His smile was weak, but reassuring.

"It's not over yet, but the Unseelie Queen, Imposter King and the Blood Prince are all dead."

Jack gave a sigh of relief. He lifted a hand and ran his knuckles over her cheek. "You are the balance." She rubbed her face against his hand, needing the rush of energy that came from his touch. "I would be yours, if you would allow it?"

Uncaring of all the eyes in the room, she leaned forward and pressed her lips to his. It was exactly how she knew it would be, life altering. She could almost hear her blood singing as she deepened the kiss, and his hands came up to wrap around her waist, his thumbs stroking the underside of her breasts.

A voice cleared. "I'm the last person to want to break up a hot lip-lock, and seriously, we should explore my voyeuristic tendencies in depth another time, but we really should be getting back out there," Oliver said, amusement coloring his words.

She helped Jack sit up, and watched the wounds that the Great Weapons had made erase as if they'd never existed. The greatest weapons on Earth, and he healed from them in an instant. *Lucky*, she thought, as one of her staples pulled at her flesh.

"You interfered. Aren't you going to get into trouble for not being impartial?"

Jack laughed. "I've never been impartial, but as for the rest, that is for Danu to decide."

She hugged him tight against her, the need to physically reassure herself too great. He wrapped his arms around her shoulders and squeezed her back, making her wince.

She sighed. "I need to get back out there. I have to make sure the Originals stay contained. Once the goblins start to flee, they might go searching for something more interesting to destroy in their anger, and we are still way too close to New York City for my liking."

Killian came over and gave her a long once over, assessing her wounds. He was wearing that haunted expression again, the one that graced his normally regal features all too often since their father's death. She didn't need him to say the words, but she knew that watching her almost die at the hands of Oisrin would be tearing him up inside. It was just the type of man he was, he wore his responsibilities like a yoke.

"You need to rest. You're wounded." He was using his authoritative Director voice, but Azar was a Councilor now, she was not so easily compelled.

"I'm fine. Stitched and patched and ready to

rock." She kept her voice steady and strong, impressing herself, but not so much Killian.

"You are in pain, you need to rest."

"I'll rest when I'm dead, Killian."

Oops, wrong choice of words, she thought, as his face hardened.

"That is what I worry about, Azar."

She squeezed his arm. "I need to finish this. I promise, once this is over, I will rest for a month."

Oliver laughed and she shot him a dirty look.

"What? We all know that there is no way you could stay out of trouble for a whole month." She scowled harder, but he pulled her from Jack's arms and wrapped her in his own. "Don't worry, Az. We love you anyway."

She flipped him the bird, but she smiled while she did it.

"Let's finish this already. It's really turning into a drag." She hefted Basatine off the ground, her sword arm feeling instantly stronger. At least her sword was feeling excited for the upcoming battle.

Killian ordered Ethan to stay and guard the weapons vault and followed her out. Jack chose to stay with the Great Weapons. "Just in case."

Oliver also followed her out, in human form.

"No jaguar?"

"No," he said curtly. Apparently he was still pissed about being left behind. She'd apologize later, maybe stroke his fur to get it all unruffled. Maybe, she'd stroke other things too. She looked over her shoulder and winked at him, and whatever he saw on her face made his own eyes hood with lust.

They ran out of the dens and into chaos. There were no longer distinct sides to the battle, there were just people running from four powerful titans. They were at least twenty feet tall, their power so strong that it was bitter on her tongue. The punch of their presence winded her, even though she'd prepared herself for it. She wanted to scream, cry, fuck or run away and never stop. Only Killian's hand on her elbow steadied her.

"Where are the other two?" Azar panicked. Had they escaped the containment area already?

A sharp keening noise erupted from the chasm where the Originals had emerged from their deep prison.

"They mustn't have made it out before you ended the ritual by removing the weapons," Killian yelled over the sounds of screams. She did a rough head-count. Ifrit, Shaitan, Marid and Sila. Balraka, Thana-men, Kuma and Tel.

Her gaze was immediately drawn to Balraka.

GRACE MCGINTY

Killian was scary in his full-blooded Ifrit form, but Balraka was the stuff of nightmares. He had a huge set of flaming bat wings, at least thirty feet in width, a face like the side of a cragged basalt cliff and hooves the size of car tires, all encased in a tight blue flame. He was terrifyingly beautiful. Her own Ifrit begged to come out, but the one wing would throw her off balance if she needed to fight.

It didn't seem to make much difference when you were hacking Finlay to pieces, a mean little voice whispered in her head. She stuffed that voice back into the box where it belonged and pushed back against her Ifrit. She'd had her fun. Azar didn't want to risk getting lost in the red haze again.

She noticed Mira and her Adel vainly trying to keep Balraka in the clearing, and out of the highly flammable forest, and the even more flammable city.

"Mira needs help." Killian looked torn, and Azar resisted the urge to huff. "Seriously, I'll be fine. I've got Oliver to watch my back. Go!"

He changed his form, and in that second, watching him wing his way toward Balraka, she noticed how much they had evolved from their Original ancestor. She wished she had more time to really appreciate and compare, and briefly wondered where her favorite historian was at this moment.

Was she fighting, or desperately trying to record this event for future generations?

They seemed to be holding their own against the combined power of four of the Originals, and honestly, that was more than she'd hoped for. The problem was that ninety percent of the field was incapacitated on the ground with fear. Thanamen, the Shaitan original, was just too strong. Every so often, a wave of fear so consuming that she had to check if she'd peed herself, swept across the clearing, dropping everyone to their knees.

"Come on. We have to go talk to a legend," she said to Oliver, already weaving her way through the fighters.

"Talk? We are in the middle of a battle with ancient horrors, and she wants to talk," he complained as he pushed through the crowd. "Which one in particular?"

"Tel. Sila."

He grumbled something she couldn't hear over the noise of battle, but raised the guns he'd appropriated from Ethan on the way out of the dens. He hadn't left the man unarmed though; Ethan had been a walking arsenal.

Unlike the rest of the Originals, who were causing as much destruction and havoc as possible,

Tel stood in one spot, her face tilted to the sky, the sun on her face.

A small number of Adel stood around her, their weapons out but not at the ready.

"What's she doing?" Azar asked the closest Adel in a low voice.

"I think she's enjoying her freedom," he whispered back.

"I can hear you just fine, you know." The booming of an annoyed Sila was not something she'd prepared for.

"You speak English," Azar was so surprised, that it just slipped out. English wasn't even thought of when the Originals went down into their hellish prison.

"Ah, it was one of our abilities long ago, to understand all languages, despite the dialect. It was what made us such powerful negotiators. Like so many other things, that ability seems to have been lost to the steady march of time."

She sounded sad. Azar had been prepared for manic, homicidal, or even just plain angry. Any of those things would have made it easy to send her back into the depths. But sadness...

"I'm Azar, of the uh... Ifrit." She didn't think she should mention the Unbound. "I..." she didn't really know what to say to a being that'd spent a thousand years in a prison that was created before time itself. She didn't think she'd take the suggestion to go back very well.

But apparently, the ancient Sila was perceptive. "You want me to get the others back into their prison. We'll go back soon enough, Weak Blood." Tel didn't seem to be insulting her, in the way she'd heard so many times. It actually seemed to be some kind of title, said with respect.

"I'm sorry. But the world can no longer handle the enormity of your powers."

Tel thought for a moment. Azar would struggle to explain this moment to Stacia, to describe the Sila Original in words. She was greater than immense, her presence making her much larger. She was too ugly to be considered beautiful, but too beautiful to be ugly. Her hair was the color of midnight, but in the sun, it shimmered like the rainbows of an oil slick.

Finally, Tel nodded. "You are right, this I know. But I find myself unwilling to slither back into my prison quite just yet, or force my brethren back, despite what logic would dictate. However, I will tamp down the effects of Thanamen's powers, purely because he hasn't gotten any less obnoxious in a million years. We were mated once, you know." She winked, and Azar gaped.

Then suddenly, as if someone had restored the oxygen, Azar could breathe easier. People who laid on the ground whimpering could now run into the forest.

"TEL!" Thanamen's thundering bellow sent shivers down her spine, but Tel just smiled. Well, at least they now knew how one of the ancient blood feuds had begun.

Azar nodded her thanks. "I'll make sure no one disturbs you until it's time."

Tel inclined her chin at Azar, then tilted her face back to the sun, breathing deep.

Azar and Oliver moved away, and she looked back at the battlefield. None of Lustre or Finlay's troops remained, although a few of Oisrin's guard still fought in small groups. But they would be taken, or they'd flash and run. She trusted Lorcan to round up those malcontents later.

The rest of the battle was basically containment. Even as she watched, the Originals were being drawn closer to the crack in the earth, inch by inch.

For the first time since Brennus and Drustan flashed into the New York compound so many months ago, she let herself breathe easy. They had won.

Even Basatine allowed her arm to hang limply at her side.

"It's over," she breathed, scared of jinxing the whole thing. But when nothing happened, she let herself feel relief. "It's over!" she shouted, and thumped Oliver on the shoulder.

Murphy's Law would tell you that these were famous last words.

Two warriors flashed in front of her, their tabards dirty and bloody. Oliver stepped in front of her, guns drawn.

As focused as she was on them, Bast's yelling surprised her. Mostly because it wasn't inside her head, but coming from her back. "No!"

She spun around in time to see Bast fall, a bright red gash across his chest, Cian at the other end of the blade. Her mind couldn't process it all. Bast, in his human form. Cian, his blade bloody. Basatine, lifted and spun lightning fast, slicing at Cian's throat. All in the blink of an eye. As the Golden Prince of the Fae fell to the ground, and she dropped Basatine in the dirt.

She was on her knees over Bast a second later.

"No. No. No. Bast, what have you done?" She

could see the necrosis of Posidagi's curse crawl up his legs, blackening them, as the long-denied magic fulfilled its deadly purpose on his corporeal form.

"You… are my… heart." Blood gurgled out of the wound in his chest, his lung perforated. She slapped a hand over the wound, trying to create a seal with her palm.

She gripped his face with the other. "Change back, damn you. Go back to smoke form!"

"…late," he whispered, his chest heaving as the necrosis encroached up his torso. Her fingers dug into his jaw, as if the sheer force of her will would keep the rot from darkening the golden planes of his face.

She touched her forehead to his and sobbed. "No, you can't leave me. Fight! Please, you can't leave me now. Not now." Tears streamed down her face, running over his cheeks.

He couldn't die. She refused to let him. Not when they'd finally won and they could be together, like a real couple, without worrying about servitude, or Fae plots, or ancient swords. They could love each other without the weight of the world crushing them.

She could distantly hear Oliver pounding his fists into flesh.

"Why?" he roared, his voice more jaguar than human.

"She was immune. I couldn't let her live if she wasn't mine…" Whatever else Cian was about to say was cut off by her enraged werejaguar ripping off the Prince's head with his bare hands.

Bast rattled out a long breath and didn't take another. His eyes closed, the putrid blackness of death streaking over his cheeks.

"Bast, don't leave me."

She laid her cheek on his and sobbed onto the cooling chest of the man she loved.

CHAPTER 21

No one approached her for hours, and she growled like a feral animal any time anyone attempted to move Bast's body. She laid her head on his blackened chest, and continued to cry.

She begged Danu, God, Allah and whoever else she thought would listen. Then she raged at those same gods.

Night fell, and she wept some more. Her tears seemed endless even though her eyes ached. She knew she should get up, get on with business, but she didn't want to. Fuck them, she'd given enough. Oliver had shifted to jaguar, prowling around them in circles, letting out pained jaguar screams into the night. But she didn't care about anyone else's pain, even Oliver's, when her own heart was shattered.

Exhaustion finally overcame her and she faded into the darkness of sleep.

Hours later, or maybe it was only minutes, the black abyss of unconsciousness morphed into the cruelest of dreams. She dreamt she was in her oasis. Bast stood smiling down at her, no longer black with necrosis, but glowing in his golden glory under the warm Persian sun.

"About time you woke, *Jaanaman*. I've been waiting for you."

"You died!" she accused, even as she plastered her body to his.

"I did. I'm sorry for hurting you."

"You didn't *hurt* me. You broke me!"

Then she cried some more. Apparently, she hadn't run out of tears in her oasis.

He stroked her hair, his big hands warm and so real on her nape. He whispered reassuring things to her in his mother tongue.

"You know I would never leave you, *Jaanaman*. But it's time for you to wake up."

Azar snuggled closer, pressing her face to warmth of his body. "No."

He laughed, his chest rumbling under her ear.

God, she'd loved his laugh. He kissed the crown of her head, and then tilted up her chin so he could press whisper-soft kisses across her face. She caught his lips and kissed him back with every ounce of feeling in her body; the pain, anger, sadness, happiness and above all, love.

"I love you, Azar Nazemi, but you have to wake up. They need you to go back."

"I don't care." And she really didn't. She'd given them her freedom, her loyalty and the life of the man she loved. She wouldn't give them this too.

He looked at her, his golden eyes serious. "I need you to go back."

Hurt filled the places in her soul that were left untouched by grief.

"But I'll lose you forever," she sounded defeated, even to her own ears.

Bast placed her away from him, so their bodies were no longer pressed together. "You are stronger than this, to go to pieces and give up the will to live over some man. That is not the strong, smart, loyal woman I fell in love with. Now, wake up!"

She slapped him. "You weren't just some random one night stand, Jackass! You are the great love of my life."

And then she kissed him. She could feel his smile

against her lips, and he lingered before pulling away again.

"Miracles exist, *Jaanaman*. Now wake up." With that, he put two hands against her chest and physically pushed her out of her oasis.

Her eyes snapped open in the darkness. The light of the dawn sun was brightening the horizon, and she lay against Oliver's warm chest, his hand stroking her hair. She closed her eyes again and let the motion soothe her. He wouldn't let anyone else close enough to touch her.

She took a deep, shuddering breath and looked up at Oliver, to thank him for being there. Only it wasn't Oliver's green eyes that looked back at her, but Bast's golden ones.

Azar bolted upright and he let her go.

"What the fuck? You died! I felt you take your last breath and your body go cold!"

"I know, you told me. But like I said, miracles happen," Bast said, his smile strained but definitely his smile.

A million options ran through her head about how he could be alive. Was he even alive, or a zombie? Or demon possessed? Were there such things as demons? Had Jack or maybe even Nevyn brought him back to her?

Jack, in that eerie way he had of appearing from nowhere and knowing what she was thinking, emerged from the darkness. "It was not me, nor was it the boy."

She turned and stared at Bast. His hands were warm and dry, not at all zombie-like. She slapped him, hard.

"You fucking asshole! This is the second time you've done this to me. Do you have any idea how fucking much it hurts every time I think you are dead? A lot. I swear, the next time you decide to fucking die, I'm going to kill you myself." And then she pulled him close and listened to the steady beat of his heart. "You're alive. Really alive."

"Thanks to you," said a voice from the darkness. A voice that spoke to her very soul, washing away her sadness. Danu had arrived.

"Yes. Now that I have used you as a vessel, it makes it easier for us to communicate."

"Can everyone see and hear you right now?"

"They can see me, but they still get the same pictographs as you used to, although they can understand your speech." Hushed whispers echoed around the clearing as Danu stepped into the light of the fire. Jack created an orb of light above her head, bathing her in a warm, celestial glow. She gave him a fond smile, and Jack grinned back like a giddy fanboy.

"Goddess." He bowed deeply before the woman.

Danu's face was more solid now, less the burning light of serenity that threatened to scar her retinas when they'd first communed. But Azar would still struggle to describe her to anyone else, as her face slowly transmuted every second, her skin getting darker until she looked Eurasian, before darkening again so she looked like a mother from the very depths of the African jungle. Her eyes would shift colors, her nose would lengthen, or widen, and her lips would plump and then thin, all in tiny increments before her eyes. The whole time Azar stared, the Goddess's face continued to change, until she looked like every woman and no woman. It was fascinating, and Azar could have watched the slow process for hours. But she couldn't wait hours for answers.

Now that she was over her shock, her brain caught onto the Goddess's original words. "I hate to contradict you, Goddess, but I would have noticed if I had the ability to bring people back from the dead. So many people have died..."

Danu stopped in front of Bast, and he tried to stand. She placed a hand on his head. "Rest."

He bowed his head and allowed himself to slump down onto his back again. But Azar couldn't sit, couldn't rest. She stood before the Goddess with too many questions.

Danu stroked her face. "He wasn't dead, at least not in the spiritual sense."

"I felt his body go cold with death. I'm sure he was dead."

Danu's gown fluttered around her legs, drawing Azar's eye almost involuntarily. It was a deep blue that warmed to purple, then pink, orange and yellow right at the hem. She realized that it was perfectly reflecting the sunrise that was happening behind the Goddess's back.

"There was still that spark in his heart, and you used the gift I gave you to help fight the disease that was trying to consume your lover's body. You fought death with life."

"What gift?" She tried to think of anything that Danu had given her. There was Jack, but he'd already said it wasn't him, and there was no other token that the Goddess had granted her.

"Use it wisely," Bast whispered, and the answer hit her like a jolt.

"When you healed Mira with your light, some of that transferred to me?"

Danu nodded, her face showing pride. That look began to heal some of the scars in Azar's heart.

"It's only a one off, I'm afraid. I used you as a conduit, and your body was filled with the healing gift. But now you have expended it, there is no more." She looked down at Bast and shook a finger. "I suggest you avoid jumping in front of anymore sharp objects."

He laughed and bowed his head again. "I promise, Goddess. I'll try to avoid dying in the future."

Any residual fear she had about Bast being a zombie vanished. She wrapped her arms around Danu's slim shoulders and hugged her.

"Thank you, thank you, thank you!"

"You are welcome, however, nothing comes without balance, Daughter of my Blood." She waved a hand and thirteen woven baskets appeared at her feet, each one filled with a tiny infant, swaddled tight in muslin cloth against the cold dawn air.

Nothing could have surprised Azar more in that moment, not even if Finlay suddenly appeared and danced an Irish jig before the firelight.

"What....?"

"Tuatha Dé Danann, born of my body and the body of one true of heart. They will replace those of my bloodline lost in this battle, and become the anchors that will ensure the Fae remain in the Isles. Hopefully, with Nevyn of my Blood and of the Seelie Fae," she looked at the boy, perched beside Freya and Donovan on a log near the fire, "and Lorcan, of the Unseelie Fae, a true believer, will allow the babes to grow to maturity before they ever need to defend themselves in such a manner. But until then, I have entrusted them into your care and the care of those whom you love and trust." Azar gaped. Her eyes kept drifting to the baskets filled with infants, like they would disappear as randomly as they appeared. Then she stared at Danu. Then back at the babies.

Danu leaned forward and stroked the cheek of the infant closest to her. "Thank Cable for his service. He has such an ability to love purely, unmarred by the events of his past. Loyalty and love come easily to him, and the other shifting natives of the earth. The babes will have stronger foundations than my previous progeny. Families to guard them." She looked grief stricken, and Azar realized she felt every single loss of her previous brethren. Danu turned, bowed low to Oliver, and then disappeared from the night in a whirl of golden magic.

Oliver looked confused, then grinned. "That was totally the woman from my dream! I can't believe I had a dirty dream about a goddess."

Azar realized that no one had really understood anything Danu had said, except perhaps Jack, who was standing in the shadows staring at the babies.

"Danu thanks you for your service. And I guess congratulations are in order, because that wasn't a dream. Dammit, Oliver. Do you have to be irresistible to every female with a pulse?"

She watched the color drain out of his face, turning a sickly green color. He looked at the moses baskets, so many of them, and blinked.

"These aren't all mine, right? Azar? They can't possibly be all mine?"

A baby stirred, and she bent down to scoop it up and placed it in Oliver's arms. His hands came up to cradle the baby automatically, and she knew in that moment that Danu had chosen well. He might be shocked, but Oliver would protect these children with ferocity.

"She is a Goddess of fertility and life, and you are a Were, prone to multiple births anyway. What do you think?" She tried to be gentle, but she was a little shocked herself. She'd just been given thirteen tiny charges, to co-parent with a Werejaguar, a Jann, a scary ass Shaitan, the last Tuatha on earth, and a bunch of wolves.

Donovan, who'd obviously been trying hard to

GRACE MCGINTY

contain his mirth, laughed loudly. "Don't worry, I'll give you paternity leave from work."

Oliver looked how Azar felt. She should explain. "They are anchors, to keep the Fae in Europe."

Nevyn stood, and behind him walked Lorcan, Hemlock and Enya.

Lorcan came and bowed before each baby, and then in front of her. "We feel the pull already, like a burn in the stomach that is only getting more painful. We must take our leave."

Lorcan looked emotionally wounded, his eyes heavy with sadness and loss. She wanted to talk to him, help him through his grief, but she didn't have time. Enya put a hand on his shoulder and nodded at Azar. A silent communication passed between them. Enya would watch Lorcan, help him if he needed it.

Azar hugged her, this strong, wounded warrior, and Enya bowed low, disappearing into the night.

She turned back to Lorcan and wrapped her hands around his biceps. "I'm sorry for your loss. Nevyn…"

"Will still be guarded with my life. He did what needed to be done; he did what I'd been unable to do for so long. He has my thanks and my respect, but I still grieve. Hemlock has volunteered to be the Captain of his new guard. He will take care of the

Seelie King and ensure he remains the boy you love."

It was hard giving up responsibility of Nevyn. She loved the strange boy who wasn't really a boy at all. Nevyn turned to her and hugged her tight, and she felt the familiar comfort of hugging another Tuatha.

"I must go to be King. You are always welcome in the Seelie *Sidhes*. Don't bring the babes though. The world of the Fae is still a treacherous one, and they are innocent and helpless. It is best they stay here, protected by you and Oliver and Bast and Donovan." He kissed her cheek.

She clutched him close. "Be safe. If you need me, I'll come. You just have to call," she whispered in his ear.

"I know." He walked off to say his goodbyes to Freya, who was crying.

Lorcan grabbed her hand and kissed it. "You know you are always welcome in the Unseelie *Sidhes*. We must go," he said, bowing low once more.

Hemlock bowed and reached to kiss her hand also. "Still the hottest slave girl I've ever seen." He winked as they flashed out of the clearing in a ripple of magic.

The magic shockwave of their departure woke up

several of the babies, and they began to cry in earnest. Then their crying woke up the other ones, until all except one were crying. The littlest one, no bigger than the length of her forearm, slept on quietly. She reached down to check it was still breathing, and just knew this motherhood thing was going to give her gray hair. The steady rise and fall of its warm little chest reassured her, and she went from basket to basket, picking up infants and handing them to people to be soothed. She gave another baby to Oliver, who held it expertly against his chest, and one to Donovan who looked at it like it was a pit viper. The one she handed to Bast calmed instantly and looked up at him with big green eyes, just like Oliver's.

When she handed a baby to Jack, he looked down at him, or maybe it was a her, with a look of such happiness, she realized that Danu had given him a gift. He'd been so lonely, without any other Tuatha Dé Danann for so long, that suddenly having thirteen kin must fill up all the empty places inside his heart. So she handed him another baby to dote on.

She noticed a wolf prowling the perimeter and recognized the sooty white coat of Aaron's wolf. She felt giddy with relief that he was okay. He let out a sharp bark of joy and shifted in a flutter of magic between one breath and the next. He came over and took the baby that was in her arms, cradling it tightly against his shoulder then pulled her into a one-armed hug. She and Aaron had been through so much together; he was the only person that had given more to this battle than she.

"I was worried about you," he growled. "You wouldn't wake up. Don't do that again." His voice was a little more wolf than human, and she nodded.

"Exhaustion. Bringing someone back from the dead is hard work. I burned myself out, I think."

He squeezed her tight again, then let her go. "Just don't do it again." He turned to Oliver. "The pack will help, you know that. You are pack, as is Azar. The infants are family."

Oliver blinked and mumbled his thanks, his gaze drawn back to the babies in his arms like a magnet.

"I will stay to help in their raising too, if you will have me. To be around so many Tuatha, even this small..." Jack ran out of words, but he was joyous.

"Of course you are staying. Azar loves you, and you are part of us whether you like it or not now," Oliver said sternly. "Besides, I have no idea what I'm doing. What do little Tuatha eat? How long should they sleep? How often? How much will they grow in a year? How will I know if something's wrong? What about their powers? Will I be dead before they even hit puberty? I mean Nevyn looks ten and he's fifty-odd!"

So that was the sound of parental panic. It echoed her own questions far too well. But she rubbed his back and placed the two sleeping babies back into their baskets. He went to pick up one of the babies that were still fussing, and she did the same. This was going to be exhausting.

"No one expects you to do this alone. It takes a village to raise a child, and luckily, we have a large village. It'll be okay, we'll find the answers and do the best we can. Danu can't ask more from us than that."

She looked down at the tiny bundle in her arms, its wide eyes midnight blue, a weird color on a baby so young. She touched the curve of its cheek and rocked it back and forth, humming the song that she dimly remembered from her childhood.

So small and perfect, she couldn't help but think what a wonderful gift they were for a new world.

For lack of anywhere else to go, they ended up back at Oliver's love shack. Going back to the dens with all the babies seemed wrong somehow. There would be party and revelry among all the different armies, and that was no place for Freya or thirteen brand new infants. However, they did completely raid the creche for things like diapers, formula, and other assorted baby stuff. Strangely enough, it was Donovan who had the most knowledge about the needs of a baby. Who knew that it would be her scary Shaitan who'd be the one who stepped into the breach? Now, they were all standing in the Love Shack, and it was still torn up from the fight with the Fae. She hadn't gone into the room where Becca died, but the pool of Donovan's blood was still in the hall.

Jack let out a disapproving noise and wiggled his nose. Well, maybe he didn't wiggle his nose, but magic should have some kind of tell, right? The blood seeped through the floorboards, completely gone as if it had never been.

Azar raised an eyebrow at him. "I drew it into the earth. Unfortunately, I can't snap my fingers and put everything else to rights like your *Mary Poppins.*" Jack making pop culture references never got any less weird.

Surprisingly, both the couch and Oliver's refrigerator box survive the fight. Freya was exhausted, and Donovan moved down the hall and placed her on the bed. The bed was almost completely untouched as well.

Oliver was already in there, straightening everything in the room, ensuring that no remnant of the past violence remained. His thoughtfulness made her want to kiss him. But that brought up another problem.

Once all the babies were down, and Freya was asleep as well, the rest of the group stood awkwardly in the living room. Azar guessed she was the elephant in this room.

"So, about that thing…"

Oliver cocked his head to the side. "What thing would that be?"

She shot him the stink eye. "The thing where I love you all forever, in exchange for you treating me like a princess."

Jack gave a small chuckle, and she turned toward him. "Feel free to chime in anytime."

Like always, it was Bast that saved her. Her beautiful, alive Bast. She stepped toward him and he wrapped his arms around her, holding her close against his chest. "It's okay, Jaanaman. We all love you, and we will figure it out slowly. For now, just enjoy the peace you have created."

"But where will you all sleep? Where will we live? What will people say?"

She wasn't actually worried about what people

would say. She'd given enough to people. She was going to enjoy this moment, this little slice of happiness they'd all carved out with blood and tears.

Oliver walked to a cupboard and pulled out a huge pile of blankets. He put them down on the couch in front of the fire.

"We will sleep here, all of us, with you. Wherever you need us. We can live here too, if you want, at least for now until we can get a bigger place. I think the, I mean our, babies would prefer the more natural surrounds?" He looked at Jack who nodded, a tiny smirk on his face like he just couldn't quite contain his happiness.

She looked at Donovan, who was looking at her with his normal intense expression. "What do you think?"

"Wherever you are. I can commute to The Onyx. Or sell it, I don't give a fuck. I just want to be where you are."

Oliver laughed, and Donovan glared at him. Oliver, as always, was completely unperturbed. "Who knew you were such a romantic, Big D?"

Bast's chest rumbled beneath her cheek, and she couldn't help her own grin. He led Azar over to the blankets that Oliver had spread on the floor, throwing down a pillow. "These are all very good questions for tomorrow, Little Fire. Tonight, sleep. We are all where we want to be."

As if to prove his point, she yawned and laid down, and they all joined her. Bast and Donovan on either side of her, Oliver close to the fire, his hand wrapped around her ankle. Jack slept on the couch, looking comically large. He was a part of them, but still apart. She would have to take it slow with her Heart of the World.

But maybe, just maybe, this would work.

*S*he stood at the back of the crowd of strangers. They were all focused on the holy man at the front of the rows of chairs, who was chanting something in a language she still didn't understand.

She twined her fingers through Bast's, and delighted in the warmth of his palms, the strength of his fingers and the roughness of his callouses. Never again would she take his touch for granted.

"Will the families come forward to pay their respects?"

She handed the fussing baby to Bast, and stood up, walking down the aisle towards Cy and Vivian at the altar. Darius hooked his arm through hers and they walked toward the happy couple, who couldn't keep the smiles from their faces. She didn't think she'd ever seen Vivian smile, but today she looked effervescent in her silk dress that flowed down her body and into a long train behind her. Actually, she'd never seen Vivian out of combat gear. It looked odd, but she was resplendent.

The two families surrounded the happy couple, holding hands, and chanting something in the old language that she couldn't understand but mimed along. Her hand was wrapped in Malee's, who was miming along with her, and Darius' larger one. It might have been her imagination, but his eyes did seem extra shiny out in the sunlight. Vivian's Sila family were all women, and they were equally as stern as Vivian.

Finally, the family part was over, and she retook her seat beside Bast. He handed her back a sleeping baby. Although they were a few months older, and significantly bigger, they still seemed so fragile to her.

"You are now forever bound to each other, by your heart's true desire. Together, you shall be one in blood and love. May you never be parted." The happy couple all but ran down the aisle, created in the solar of the family home, toward the party and the happy greetings of friends and family.

The death toll of the Fae-Djinn War had been considerable on both sides. A month of mourning commenced soon after the battle for all the men and women, Djinn, Were, Fae and Unbound alike, who'd fallen in the battle, and the attacks beforehand. Children had lost parents, the elderly had lost sons and daughters, adults had lost spouses, lovers and friends.

But on the tail of this widespread grief came the dawn of a new era, one without hate and bigotry, where cross-species friendships had been honed in the fire of battle, and tested by steel and blood.

This was never more noticeable than at Cy and Vivian's wedding reception, where Djinn, Unbound, Were and even Fae drank together. Cy had made a lot of friends during his time at the dens before the war, and many Were had come to drink to his mating, although they'd decided to skip the traditional ceremony.

Azar, as the Unbound Councilor, had led the Unbound out of the shadows, and their presence was more easily accepted now that they had fought beside full-blooded Djinn. Every Djinn was aware that without the Unbound, the war would have been lost, and the Adel were very adamant that they get the respect they deserved, to the point of beating the idea into civilian Djinn. Killian had been right; as soon as the first battle had been won, the alliances had been cemented, and they'd persevered even after the battle was over. Azar watched Killian and Ethan, the Unbound Captain, chat over drinks, equals finally.

The Fae, on the other hand, had a quick, but ultimately unsuccessful *coup-de-tat* upon the return of Lorcan and Nevyn to the *Sidhes*. A new era of Seelie and Unseelie cooperation would follow, they said. Or else.

Aaron came up, a Were teenager close behind him. The Were boy gave the baby a goofy look, making her gurgle and reach pudgy arms out to him. Azar gave the baby over happily. Aaron and the Weres had provided a steady rotation of teenagers to help with the babies, probably to scare them into safe sexual practices. Thirteen babies crying at once would have any teenager signing up for a lifetime's supply of condoms.

Not that the babies weren't an absolute blessing. They'd developed distinct personalities over the last few months, and thankfully they all looked different. Six boys and seven girls. They named the boys after trees; Birch, Aspen, Banyan, Linden, Ash and Sylvan. They named the girls after flowers; Violet, Iris,

Poppy, Lily, Dahlia, Rose and little Daisy, the smallest. Azar wasn't going to lie, she still got their names wrong, even after three months. She color coded them now.

"We've set up a crèche in the cinema room. Have fun, Az, let your hair down. The pups will be fine with us. Freya and Kayla will make sure nothing goes wrong," The teenager, Steven, told her. He was one of the constant babysitters, who actually enjoyed being around the babies, even with the crying and constant dirty diapers. Aaron had mentioned the boy was an omega, but Azar didn't really know what that meant, except that somehow his presence calmed the babies immediately. After a few nights without sleep, Azar had wanted to adopt Steven permanently.

They'd decided to move closer to the dens, just within the Sterling Forest Pack lands. Aaron had made it very, very clear to Lila, who now lorded over all the Djinn in the US, that she had no authority on Pack lands. Lila had eventually backed down to his demands, especially when wolves started to turn up at her club, on her doorstep, and Tao, in wolf form, standing over her watching her sleep.

Aaron handed Azar a glass of champagne, and she downed it in one gulp. Bast handed her another.

"It was a beautiful ceremony."

"Your turn next, perhaps?" Aaron ribbed, and gave Bast a wink. Azar rolled her eyes at them both. Bast kissed her temple. Maybe she should put a ring on it; he was far too good to her.

In the aftermath of war, it had taken a little while for Bast, Donovan, Jack and Oliver to figure out how their relationship would work. They were still working it out. But it helped that they all lived together in a big, open plan house. Freya adored living in a house filled with so much love, and took her job as older sister to the babies very seriously.

The house was filled with cots, pacifiers, fluffy toys and an endless mountain of onesies. And the diapers. None of them really had any idea what the hell they were doing, but the babies grew and were happy, despite their guardians' mistakes and lack of knowledge.

They were active, much more like Were cubs than humans or Tuatha, or so Jack said. He said it was probably another reason that Danu had chosen Oliver. The Weres developed quicker, better able to protect themselves from a young age.

Donovan came over, pulling her into his arms and kissing her in front of everyone. Who knew that it would be Donovan that would be all about the public displays of affection? She wrapped her arms around his waist.

"Can we go home yet? All this lovey hand holding crap is making my skin itch," he grumbled against her cheek.

"You're the one doing all the lovey hand holding crap right now, you know that right?" She laughed, and he growled.

"It's not the same. I fully intend to take you home, strip you out of that delightful dress and fuck you in the dirtiest way I know how," he whispered directly into her ear, making her cheeks flush.

Aaron rolled his eyes. "You guys are gross," he grumbled, sounding like the boy she had once known, and not the most powerful Alpha in North America.

That was the other reason they lived on Pack lands. The Weres weren't even remotely fussed by the idea of her having four mates, but the Djinn on the other hand were having a tougher time letting go of the old prejudices about interracial breeding within the Djinn, let alone interspecies relationships. They'd get there eventually, even if she had to smash a few heads before it sunk in. Starting with Lila.

Aaron handed her one more champagne. "Here

comes Oliver. I'm out. He paws at you like you are made of catnip whenever he's within ten feet of you."

Azar laughed. He wasn't wrong. Oliver twirled her out of Donovan's arms and into his own, dipping her backwards and kissing the curve of her shoulder. "You look so fucking hot today," he murmured appreciatively. "Did Big D tell you what we are going to do with you when we get home?"

"Don't call me Big D," Donovan growled. "And no one invited you, Cat."

He was only teasing. She flushed, remember just how much Oliver and Donovan liked to share. Bast still liked their alone time, and she was taking it slow and easy with Jack, but these two threatened to consume her anytime they had her alone.

The newlyweds came out then, and everyone cheered. Azar kissed their cheeks, her smile so wide it threatened to crack her face in half.

"I'm so happy for you both."

Cy squeezed her tight in a hug. "If it wasn't for you, we never would have gotten together."

She laughed, and elbowed Oliver. "See? My so-called inability to stay out of trouble can have great consequences. It's not all near-death experiences and citywide destruction."

The couple moved on to the next group of

people, and she drifted around the room, chatting and having a good time. This is what she had worked so hard for, this unity was worth all the blood, and the sacrifice, and the nightmares she sometimes still had.

She may have had too many champagnes, and there may have been some dancing on a table, but Azar had never been so happy.

AFTERWORD

Thank you for reading. I hope you enjoyed your time with Azar and the Djinn!

I love hearing from readers, so you can find me at any of these places below:

Facebook Author Page: https://www.facebook.com/GraceMcGintyAuthor/

Instagram: @gracemcgintyauthor

Website: www.gracemcginty.com

Twitter: @McgintyGrace

Email: gracemcgintyauthor@gmail.com

Join my socials to keep up with new releases, exclusive content and enter giveaways.

And now for the battle cry of all indie authors. If you liked this book, or any book, leave a review, or recommend it to a friend, or write the Amazon link on the wall of a bathroom stall.

Anything helps, and it keeps indie writers creating the stories you love so much.